D1622623

BADLANDS

IN MEMORY OF
ALBERT MINHINNICK

BADLANDS

robert minhinnick

seren

Seren is the book imprint of
Poetry Wales Press Ltd
Wyndham Street, Bridgend
Glamorgan, Wales

© Robert Minhinnick, 1996

A record for this book is avalable at the
British Library Cataloguing in Publication Office

ISBN 1-85411-157-4

*The publisher acknowledges the financial assistance of the
Arts Council of Wales*

Cover: detail of an Albertan badlands cliffside,
near the town of Cambria

Printed in Plantin by
WBC Book Manufacturers, Bridgend

CONTENTS

Acknowledgements

The author wishes to thank the Arts Council of Wales, the British Council, and the Saskatoon Library Service, Canada, for grants which assisted the writing of sections of *Badlands*.

A version of 'Ryan's Republika' appeared in *Planet*.

Letters from Illyria

1

I expect you're wondering by now what I'm doing. I mean, what I'm really doing. But that can wait. First I'll tell you about the Iveco, its white fist of a face, the sophisticated tint to the glass. It has a power of which I'm wary. Actually, I'm scared stiff of the Iveco, if only when driving it. Yet one thing is comforting. Other drivers are similarly respectful. Car drivers that is. Dark men in dark glasses keep their Fiats a meaningful distance away. Jewelled women in BMWs are forever aloof. And the boys on the scooters? Forget them. They are like midges over the canals, part of the tapestry of butterfly wings singeing on our radiator grille. But it's still scary, up there in the cab, the needle of the tachometer pricking away, the two other drivers asleep over their paperbacks or the Michelin, and the autoroute unrolling before us, strange and pristine, untouched by the blizzard of traffic.

Watch it, I murmur to fellow motorists. A nudge here, a centimetre there, and you're history. Don't mess with an Iveco. We're last year's model with 200,000Ks on the clock already. Can't you feel it panting behind you, its yellow diesel breath?

Watch it, I murmur to myself. I need to relax. So I count something. There are three hundred miles of oleander blossom in the central reservation, all the way from Turin to Bari. In Ecuador there is an oleander shrub with such a strong narcotic in its perfume that anyone who falls asleep under its flowers never wakes up. An enchanted tree from a medieval fairytale. I see immediately its restful shade, the buds like babies' fingers, the cushions of starry moss between its roots. Lie down, it seems to say. Lay down your weary tune. And Christ, I have to snap awake, take one hand gingerly from the steering wheel, slippery with sweat, and rub my eyes.

I switch on the radio. Europe's airwaves are muzzed by American elevator music, the tapes they play at lingerie counters. These straight roads are the worst. Autostrada 17, all the way south. I've touched 120 kmh but that was overtaking, and I'm not happy doing that. The carriageways are too narrow. I find myself jammed between the oleander with its rockeries of drinks cans and styrofoam cups, and the coachwork of some Mercedes truck, a genie of black smoke in my wing-mirror, and the other driver's unshaven face, a yard away.

That's the trouble with overtaking in this country. Eye contact with the HGV mercenaries. No matter how grease-stained my own hands, or whether there are diesel blisters on my clothes, the other drivers see right through me. Not that I ever stare back. I merely shift the sour bolus of gum to the other cheek and put my right foot further down to inch beyond the telepathic stranger in the Daf alongside. Sometimes it works. But sometimes the Iveco lacks that last derisive spurt of power, the crucial guts to bludgeon past. Then I am left twinned with the unblinking pilot of forty tonnes of disposable nappies or 111 triethylene.

I ponder why all such drivers are clearly psychotic, their profiles straight from the pages of some medical school textbook. Is that a qualification they require to ferry heavy goods across Europe? Occasionally I can glimpse into their cabs. Some of them are little palaces. Rosaries, ikons, photos of the children, bunches of plastic flowers, photos of mum, cushions, magazine racks, tape libraries. It would be more touching if the owners did not resemble waxworks of the Yorkshire Ripper, as they change down when the inclines start to bite. I imagine them at the pull-ins, sitting alone, straightening their framed image of the Madonna, polishing the wagon front's chrome knuckles to an expressionless sheen.

Then there are the others who forgo order. Their cabins are squalid bachelor flats with three weeks' worth of tissue paper and chocolate wrappings pushed down in front of the windscreen. These are the ones who in the UK have their nicknames constructed in permanent letters, like the maker's logo, over the radiators. Usually it is something canine. Leader of the Pack. Wolfman. Moondog. They also have women in the cabs, on hands and knees, looking behind them in sunbleached cartoon ecstasy.

Yet what I want to know is, why don't any of those drivers, the religious maniacs or the chocolate eaters, why don't they ever need to watch the road? It's as if they never give the autostrada a thought as they take in the Iveco's spartanly-appointed cockpit, the incomprehensible address of the hire-yard where it belongs, and where I am beginning to wish I had left it. They stare straight in with burned-out eyes, so close I can see the chain of the crucifix or the pale weal on the wrist where they've used a sweatband. Eat my dust, I want to say, masking the panic that seems to loiter around this vehicle whenever I am in charge. But then, as always, the miracle happens and we stagger ahead, one yard, then five. And soon I am indicating right and the Ostrogoth in the Scania behind is giving that comradely blink of the headlights that says, yeah, come on home, I've opened the gate.

2

Not that we're big. I don't want to give that impression. I mean huge. But at nine tons we are way over what my licence allows, and if we are not quite an integral piece of global freight traffic, we are still big enough. In fact, we are too big, if you're still with me. That road over the viaduct, for instance, before we arrived at Mont Blanc. That was where I nearly lost it. The trick is not to look down, but the bends are so sudden that I found myself staring into a green and black chasm where the highway should have been. One thousand feet below I saw the white staves of a waterfall and the red leggo of village roofs. There were crows and magpies slugging it out where the road should have been. Christ, there were clouds, real clouds, and the milky gauze of mist, and then nothing, nothing at all where the road should have been.

I'm not a real driver, you see. You might be beginning to appreciate that already. At least, I'm not a driver in the marrow. Not in the arse, which is where people really drive. And not in my blood either, which emphatically does not start to sing when I climb into the cabin, turn the ignition so that the orange diesel light comes on, and disengage the delicate handbrake. In fact, when I climb into the cab I feel my white cells start to swarm, to overrun their red buddies. It's usually a rout. And those phagocytes – or are they leucocytes? I can never remember my 'O' level biology – the white ones anyway, start manufacturing themselves as if there is no tomorrow.

But viaducts are not the only problem. Tunnels are worse, especially the Italian ones here on Autostrada 17. These tunnels have names. The Italians are obviously proud of the way they have blasted through miles of rock, and so the tunnels have their own nomenclature. But what is disconcerting is that after the first hundred yards of each tunnel you discover that there are no lights. That they are utterly dark. But disconcerting is the wrong word. People are disconcerted if they receive tea after ordering coffee. Terrifying is a better word. Because in the tunnels, the light simply ceases. As if there had been a power cut. And then inevitably I find myself roaring ahead without being able to see a hand in front of my face. Or the rear-end of some family-carrying Peugeot a yard beyond my bumper. So what I do next is to turn on the headlights. Scrabbling in the sudden subterranean Italian midnight I hit the radio button, the windscreen washers, the heater and a whole column of switches for which I have not determined a use. And suddenly my own many-mysteried dash is illuminated like the hi-fi at home. I don't understand how that works either, but I have never thought it might kill me.

And then, after an age of hair-crawling and sweat-prickling, after a fortuitous twist of one of the column-stalks or a lucky strike against a previously hidden control, there is illumination ahead, fifty yards of my own white beams, unadjusted for foreign parts, and now innocently blinding drivers in the oncoming lane. And white is right. White is the colour of claustrophobia, the mummy-bandages that paralyse the arms, cling-film the heart. White is the colour of the rabbit-hole I have fallen down, until I switch to dipped, discover the carriageway ahead free of tricycles and invalid cars, and emerge into the waterblue afternoon, somewhere in the hundred mile long beach metropolis of Italy's Adriatic coast.

3

I think it's time you became a little curious. So if you have not asked yourself the question yet, I will ask it for you. What's in the back?

Now the trouble is, that's a difficult question. Perhaps it will be easier to open the impressive padlock on the rear roll-up door and take a look. But then you might think the correct question was, what's not in the back? Whatever, this will be good for me too. You see, I don't know exactly what's in the back. I didn't load this thing. I didn't write out the inventory. It's obvious that we're full, that we are two tons overweight, and that going uphill is harder work than it should be. Also, we are using too much diesel. Much too much. It's fine until the needle on the fuel gauge reaches half. But after that it seems to evaporate. Vanishes like dew. The Iveco's a thirsty horse and I think we are whipping it too hard. But we can't unload. We are not there yet.

So what have we got? Here is a crate and it's all whisky. But we are not humping whisky. These bottles are presents for old friends, gifts for strangers. No, we're not humping whisky. This cardboard box is packed with smaller boxes. All of them are full of sweets, the cheap, plasticky kind that turns tongues red. It's a curious feeling, driving a thousand miles and jousting with road-trains and artics, with nine tons of blackcurrant Chewitts stacked behind. What's next? Tinned food, rice pudding, and pails of technicolour pie-fillings, lots of it. Somebody thought it would be useful and who are we to argue? Now there are desks, school-desks, with names carved by compass points, rock groups in black indelibles: The Byrds; Captain Beefheart; Quicksilver Messenger Service. What a giveaway. Nineteen sixty-seven's teenage graffiti, more familiar than last week, last night. There are chairs for the desks, a sink with a box of taps, two lavatory bowls but no cisterns, all of them cheapest Twyfords. Pity we are not packing real class, Finch's or Empire with chunky brass fittings and crimson veins mottling the enamel like a drinker's face. But that is what's good about exporting old stuff. It has a life of its own, a history of associations. I think the phrase is 'refulgent with identity'. But the new Twyfords tackle is too small. It is bleached too clean and belongs in a redbrick crescent called Lapwing Close or Hazelmere, built on a hayfield behind what was the local pub, the bathrooms done out in plastic shower-rings and tiles with a beads-of-steam pattern.

Further in is a case of sheet music, whilst an organ or some sort of keyboard is tied to the sidebars. That's the heaviest thing packed. But there is also a plough, similarly roped, a sheath of rust over its blade. There are quivers of rake handles, pick-heads, ancient mattocks. A crate of soap and boxes of toilet paper. There are carefully packaged cartons of medicines, a hospital incubator, a case that says 'other way up', three type-writers, and various collections of shoes held together by elastic bands. We are only half way in but the rest is obvious. Flour, sugar, lentils in industrial-use sacks the size of body-bags. Pails of margarine, the dimpled necks of Lucozade bottles and another hundredweight of Chewitts. Raspberry ones.

That I think is better for all of us. A varied cargo, and nothing imminently perishable. I feel happier knowing; it gives me some kind of purpose. Black coffee for the soul. Mind you, there has been no trouble. Dover and Calais port officials, all the little men I peered down on in their motorway toll-booths, the army at the border and the traffic police on the autostrada randomly waving over foreign campers and vast haulage jobs: none of them have been bothered. But it costs a fortune to drive this route. We've collected a stack of payage tickets. And in case there are bureaucratic delays, we have the Caritas sign to place in the windscreen. Our phial of rosewater for the plague year.

4

I watch him. He is watching her. She is my co-driver, my friend. His post-office van is parked one hundred yards away. He has abandoned it because she walked too slowly, looking at the bowls of prawns on the pavement, the box of whitebait like a cutlery drawer, the snout of a small shark buried in ice. The market is filling up. Women cut sweet chestnuts out of their shells and lay them on cloths. Disconsolate men rearrange displays of plastic toys. Mauve and brown fungi sit like trophies on the cobbles. She examines them as you might gaze at pictures in a gallery: with respect, almost fearful of missing something: the reason for their isolation perhaps. But eyes are hungry things. Never satisfied, they are always tormented by appetite. Like my eyes now, narrowed, carefully taking in the street, already feeling the glare at 10am. Or her eyes, remote behind sunglasses like a blindfold round her face. Or his, deep set, twin hostages to something he never thought to meet, not here, not now. The post office van he was driving when he saw her, that he slowed to an impossible crawl behind her in the streets and finally the square, is parked by a bakery under the statue, under the colossus who created this town, who guarded it from others who would take it away. It is a monstrous thing, the statue, tall as a church, its marble dusty, white as mothballs, the guardian's chin jutting towards the sun, his robe frozen in ridges like sweet chestnut bark. The protector who sees everything.

So they make their way through the market, past the men with their boxes of plastic warriors, heroes who perform great deeds, who guard the universe, past the mushrooms big as hubcaps, past the bazaar itself. It is 10am and the town is alive. This is the best time for the market, but there are hours yet before we embark, and I have slowed down, right down, slowed like a viper on a rock, lidless in my cafe awning, hunched over a fiery eyelet of liquor, preparing to rejoin the tournament, feeling the electricity in my skin. After all, I am only doing my job. In this country we must look after each other. So I sit and learn to discriminate between the shadows and the colours, between the blue of his uniform, a little greased, and her pale shirt. It is laughable really. But scary. It makes me nervous, this electricity I feel when I really concentrate on what's around. It's as if I can hear them with my eyes. And when I close my eyes I can still see them. There in the market, very close together now.

5

I've been to some places, she told me. Impossible places. India is a million of them. South America. Wales. And this is the worst. The whole country is a kindergarten where men are encouraged to run amok. Buying a ticket, for instance. When you're buying a ticket they look at you and their faces say I'm looking at you in a certain way, and you know that, you know that I'm looking at you in a certain way, so you should feel pleased. Chosen. I don't look at every woman like that, but this special gift I bestow on you. The gift of my eyes. The amused corners of my mouth. That's what they are saying to you when you're buying a ticket or asking directions to the ferry port. It's their right and they are asserting it.

But don't they understand what they look like? I've had better come-ons from a Great Dane. Men are so sad. That's the real tragedy of the world. The irreducible sadness of men. If only they understood. Take that one in the kiosk who wouldn't give me the tickets. Ever seen a bullock that's pushed its head through a barbed wire fence? Slaughter-house eyes. Tongue like a boot sole. Most places you get a few like that but not every one. Every one. All of the poor cretins here stare like that at you. Handing you a ticket, waiting at the bar for an espresso. And then some of them have to speak. Perhaps I could cope with the staring, the looking. But never the speaking. One hundred thousand years of language and what do they say, shuffling up behind you like some huge badly wrapped parcel. What do they say? You're very pretty. That's what they say. Pretty. What can you do with it? Flowers are pretty. Sometimes those little furry covers you put over toilet seats are too. Pretty.

Normally I whisper something obscene. It's always better if it's in the dialect because they won't be expecting that. They know you're foreign. And whispering is important. It's dirtier. But mostly I give them a wave and walk away, a wave on their way to the abattoir. Because that's where they're going, all of them, the dogs, the cattle, the ones like muppets with candle-wicks up their nostrils. I should feel sorry for them, I suppose, but what the hell. Men are so sad.

6

I am the advance party. The others must stay with the Iveco for two more days because of the ferry strike. It is my job to make the crossing and establish contact.

Waving goodbye, I don't know whether to be pleased or fearful about leaving the truck and its cargo behind. The cabin was my tiny office. My books are still there. My language.

There are three queues for the hydrofoil. One is for Italian soldiers, savagely barbered teenagers, who must hold on to each other like pensioners on a windy street, such is the weight of their kit. One is for Albanian passport holders only. The third comprises Italian civilians and other nationalities. For some reason we are all tense, alert for line-jumpers or the next level of port bureaucracy. I've become in my brief time here a fond connoisseur of harbour administration at Bari. It has a geological profundity. Several times I believed I had penetrated to its ultimate stratum, only to discover underneath, a Silurian layer of confusion, an Ordovician deposit of delay.

Not that I mind too much. At least I am on dry land. Sea crossings have never agreed with me. The last one was, I think, a journey from Boulogne, when I and a few other veterans of a coach expedition across Picardy, had threatened a striking French ferry crew with violence if they did not hurry up and get us off the dock. It's hard to credit now, but it felt at the time that the Hundred Years War had never finished. Or perhaps the last one was the return from Ilfracombe across the Bristol Channel. The weather had been mild when we embarked. Women had worn summer dresses, children caught the spindrift high on the bow. But there is a treacherous wind called the *cadno* that blows around the promontory of our town. It brings about an unforeseeable whitening of the waters, a chilling of the air. Our geriatric barque, the *Waverley*, advertised as the last pleasure cruiser on the British coast, began to roll and dip. Trays of glasses slid from tables. I watched my daughter's face turn the colour of the underside of a sycamore leaf. A grandmother in Sunday coat rolled like a skittle out of the bar. And now here I am, poised at the low entrance to the hydrofoil. Somebody takes away my passport and I am nudged into a cinema, in which a film, something called King Ralph, has already started.

Our crossing is estimated to last four hours, and the water, at least around Bari, is suitably unfoxed. There is a very modest bar and a whole row of seats to myself. So much for the paranoia of the queue. If there is a cloud ahead, it hangs over Durres, our port of destination. It incorporates the knowledge that I have not been able to obtain Albanian currency or US dollars. Or maps. Or addresses of those good people whom I should be meeting. But that is hours away. I settle down to watch a B flick about a failed Las Vegas nightclub singer who discovers that he is heir to the English throne. The whole gallimaufry of royals and senior aristos has been wiped out by an electrical fault. Goodbye to a glittering zoo of nunks and nerdettes, rich and still asking, intelligence on a dimmer switch. At least Hollywood had got something right. Now King Ralph in baseball cap and football number called the shots at the opening of parliament. Around me, Albanian workers shovel popcorn, the troops share artillery shell-sized bottles of coke, as technicolour England, bizarre as a rainforest, propels our modest jet into darkness and a stiffening wind.

Thirty minutes later the Italian army is on its knees in the toilet. A stewardess moves carefully between the aisles offering packages to children. Tall men are curled tight as fossils into their cinema seats. Outside the black waves disintegrate against our black windows, the black spray making white noise on the perspex. King Ralph has gone home to Twenty Nine Palms, taking with him the gratitude of Britain and a cockney wife. Something rolls under my seat, something like a deflating beach ball. I kick the object into the open. So that was what the stewardess was doing. Interestingly, and of possible cultural significance, Italian sickbags are made of transparent plastic. The contents of this one are a mild orange, variegated with crimson. Spaghetti pomodoro, I decide. At least the culprit had the decency to tie up the ends before launching his dinner at the deck. We are already overdue, and as I look round note that a good half of us have the wrung-out, wide-eyed demeanour of convalescence. Half the remainder keep the sacks clamped to their mouths like oxygen masks. If the delay continues perhaps the survivors might organise a softball tournament.

7

Someone will come for you, they said. And at least it is dry. But it is also dark. An hour after docking in Durres my passport is returned, and I hand over eight thousand lire for a postage stamp-sized visa in unintelligible purple script.

An hour after docking I am the last off the hydrofoil, and step with the nonchalance of the condemned into 10pm Albania. Ahead is a white light on a gantry. It seems only to illuminate itself, a white core of moonlight throbbing above a tower, leaving everything black. It is the light you meet walking on to a stage. You expect to see the auditorium below, the faces, the empty seats. Yet there is only the whiteness of that single ray, a white shadow that paralyses and eventually comforts. There is nothing visible. The world has vanished. All that exists is the scorching ophthalmoscope that searches within you. What it discovers is something you do not wish to know.

At the centre of the light where it reaches the ground is a woman dressed in silver rags. Her arm is outstretched, palm open, her skin the unsubstance of insect wings. This is the universal gesture I know from television screens. Mute and beseeching. Behind it lies the impersonality of despair. But Albania is not a hungry country. There is malnutrition here but it is not endemic. And until five years ago, beggars were unknown. It is people like myself who have created beggars. The woman stares through her yard of grey hair, the colour of my grandmother's on the rare occasions I saw it down: white, but tinged smoker's yellow, the pride of her girlhood in a breathtaking sulphurous fan.

Somehow this woman has crept into the port. Beside her is a stooped youth, shoulders like doorknobs. I look at his face and cannot see a future. He is her son and is dying upright. Ahead there are soldiers at the gate and beyond them a silent crowd. Now comes the choice. Advance through the gate and I am in. There will be no return to the hydrofoil. But there are no hotels in Durres, there is nowhere to lodge. The road consists of mud and tussocks, whilst outside the gate is the iron kerb of the railway track, and a huge, unlit loco uncoupled from its carriages. Someone will come for you, they said, but in the crowd is no identifiable face, no paper held aloft, no sign, only disentombed strangers lit from the gantry, all dressed in bone-coloured moonlight and waiting for something I have not brought. The army wants to know whether I am coming. An officer gestures this way, you come this way, come over the line and then you are in, you are really in, you are one of us. I cross the line.

8

We vow some things will be unforgettable. And then we forget them. Birth for example. We do not retain a single memory of that insanitary expulsion. Schoolyard bullying, the commerce of love, the sheer intolerability of a six hour train journey I once suffered, with only the sustenance of a single piece of chocolate money proffered by a woman whose case I carried. But Skanderbeg Square at midnight will be different – an atom of plutonium that will remain in the mind forever.

Only here, on the fourteenth floor, is this view possible. The Hotel Tirana is the city's first and last skyscraper, the lonely vantage point for this panorama. Skanderbeg Square is empty, its winter beach of marble radiant under sodium. Not a blade of grass or human footstep has ever been known there. The monolith was created by a vanished civilization, an altar for an abandoned god. Ganymede might look like this, or Callisto, impassive beneath the electric turmoil of their atmospheres. Not a leaf blows across the square, not a bus-ticket. Under the statuary the blackness begins, the trigonometry of shadow. And I know that in five minutes I will moonwalk across that totalitarian expanse, full of the ravenous exhaustion of the traveller used to getting his own way. I know that, not trusting the lift, I will tiptoe down thirty flights of stairs, minding the loose carpets, the missing stair-rods, cross the hotel bar and drawing room where a single smoker sits with a magazine. I will push through the double doors and slip down the steps where the children sleep, squashed together like balls of paper. And then I will begin my journey across Skanderbeg Square, tiny and alien when watched from the fourteenth floor, an intruder purposeful in his lack of purpose.

For five unforgettable, forgotten minutes I am the only inhabitant of Tirana. Here at midnight in its uninhabitable heart, I forget where I come from and why I have arrived. Identity, suddenly, is less than an echo. People without names once filled this place, people without graves. Identity for them was a chocolate wrapping tossed aside, a document deleted from the software. I listen closely and there is not the merest hint of their protest, their dialogue with creation, only my own steps coming towards me from the other side of the city. Now here is the centre of their world. A shadow extends like the hand of a great clock, and I am infinitesimally small. In Skanderbeg Square I have entered the dream of a dictator, explored the architecture of his monomania. This is his memorial, where time is paralysed until I can make myself move, and the shadow hand, black and trembling, registers life at 2 a.m. Under my foot the shell of a peanut detonates like a pistolcrack. But from the fourteenth floor no-one is visible.

9

Two miles beyond the city is a graveyard. The remains of Christians, Muslims, Jews and Chinese workers killed in the building of the country's factories, lie in well-tended ranks. At the gate of the cemetery children play amongst the ruined pillboxes exposed like grey crania in the soil. A woman outside a hovel stirs a skillet. The only sounds are the voices of gravediggers, teasing a local youth, pretending to scold him. The boy is a giant with a baby's mind. He gibbers at them, cowers under marble as they pass the time with this new, mildly diverting plaything. Round-eyed as a lemur, ungainly as a fledgling toppled from the nest, he rolls on the ground, hands clasped over his ears.

Some graves bear weathered photographs of the deceased. Others are anonymous green tumuli. And here is one, modest, mid rank, with an inscription obscured by dead leaves in two jam-jars of rainwater. Parting the fronds I read the name: Enver Hoxha. Overhead passes the plume of the Tirana power station. The smoke emerges from the chimney in an enormous black helix, so luxuriant it resembles a velvet sleeve thrust towards the sky. But the stain fades, the particles disperse over the country-side, and the air smells of home, years ago: the grate's hollow clinker, the pailfuls of ash that were scattered outside on the paths.

And now here I crouch at a dictator's grave, tidying the orange fishbones of a fern, the seedheads of poppies as big and hard as walnuts. Ordinary people come here to make these offerings, small posies for the man who abolished God. For the man who made paranoia the Illyrian religion. But Hoxha has not always lain here. After his death he was buried beneath an ornate sarcophagus, the mausoleum of the premier citizen. Yet the remnants of his dynasty had no stomach for autocratic rule. Hoxha's family retired from power and in the subsequent violent demonstrations the dictator's remains were looted from the grave and his memorial smashed. So now he lies with the drivers of buses and the diggers of irrigation ditches. The spore of the power station floats around us and the young man yelps like a vixen. Some monuments are impossible to destroy.

10

I have discovered the essence of Illyria, the oil in its machine. It is called raki, a spirit distilled from grain or potatoes or anything else people can get hold of. It is drunk by almost every member of the population, Catholic and Muslim. More of an anaesthetic than an elixir of rebellion, raki is concocted in hovels and jerry-built flats, in barns and behind barrack walls, in communal courtyards and rudimentary kitchens all over the country. Sometimes as clear as schnapps, as pale green as Somerset farm cider, or as viscous as lighter fuel, it comes as it comes, but always in measures so generous that soon the tongue is thickening, the toes grateful for their amputation, the imagination warmed and slowed, and the whole of consciousness entranced by the strange benificence of life, the ruinous miracles of the twentieth century.

In the homes I visit it is the token of welcome, presented in a variety of wine and water bottles. The beggar children in Durres and Tirana, emerging from a night spent under a railway carriage or the outside steps of former official buildings, crave its potency. Raki kills pain and masks hunger. It is medicine for the cold, balm for a thrashing. In raki exist the chemicals of laughter, the proteins of hope. It builds illusions so real that people weep at the opportunity to inhabit them. And raki is dependable. Its genie of consolation will always return to the bottle until the next time. Hoxha knew that. He understood the politics of raki and that what he demanded of his people was impossible to deliver without its influence. Life was unbearable until you got shitfaced. Rat-arsed. When a son betrayed a father to the secret police, when a whole family was arrested because one member had listened to a World Service broadcast, raki became counsellor and confidant. Those who disdained its influence were seen as fools. Did they not know that this was how things worked? The gaoler and the prisoner, the informer and the informed upon, drank from the same flask. For first there is solace in the endless toasting of the raw spirit. And then there is forgiveness. The ritual does not matter. Secret nips or great public draughts perform the same service. Raki retrieves order from chaos. Ultimately it makes sense.

Here in my coat in the cabin of the Iveco is a litre of the stuff. Clear as daylight, it is apparently a distillation of exceptional purity. Good hooch to impress drinking friends at home. We are parked in the rainbowed mud of the marketplace. Pigs root in the filth, a butcher lays out a collection of rancid joints going the way that meat must go, a lustreless grey veined with emerald. The flesh lies there like geological specimens, cool and sinister. The gouts of blood are black as meteor iron.

"Piccolo," she says, and thrusts the baby at me. "Piccolo."

This is a gypsy girl of ten or twelve, her shock of hair concealing a face sunburned with dirt. Her companion is a boy of about fourteen, one arm amputated at the elbow. The stump is tied with bandages darkened with secretions. On his leg is a sore as large as an oyster.

"Piccolo," she says again, using Italian because it is better than her English, showing me the infant trussed in its cocoon. In my pocket is a yellow quince, picked today. It is bigger than the biggest pear but the fruit is mealy. I offer the girl the quince, and in a moment she has hidden it in her skirt, and nudged her friend towards a group of men sharing abstemiously a litre of homebrew. She speaks Albanian now, but her eyes, huge and dark, are multilingual. Already she craves the fierce heat of the liquor, understands its taste of ashes.

11

For two nights we have been billeted in a convent in the town of Lac. The nuns are modest and friendly, speaking together eight European languages. In brown and white robes, they resemble a flock of redwings come south in a bitter winter, misplaced but sturdy, determined to survive.

I make them a present of soap but perhaps this is a mistake. The convent is thoroughly clean, despite building work and the constant traffic of novices. Also, there is a real bathroom, with a plumbing system of sorts. This is much more than people in rural areas possess, where a toilet is usually a hole in the mountainside. Compared with the majority, conditions for the sisters are benevolent. Others might have needed that soap, aromatic loaves of white Boots cold cream, not tested on animals. Hard currency. And now it has vanished somewhere into the cloister where I cannot follow.

In fact, life is good all round for us at the convent. We eat well and trust the hygiene. Yet the day still begins with an eye-watering measure of raki, important, so one of the sisters says, for purposes of disinfectant. As brutal as chlorine, raki sterilizes all bacterial conspiracies and shortens the lives of pathogens. There are gallons of the spirit here, much to the taste of the three monks who inhabit one wing of the convent, and who greet the morning's macaroni soup with a series of emphatic toasts. I find the monks peculiar. One possesses a car and returned the first evening from Tirana cursing the thieves who smashed its window and stole a radio cassette. Another, a very old man, spends most of his time on the telephone. And when he is not speaking on the telephone he is loitering in the vicinity of the receiver in case it should ring. For the convent is prosperous. A telephone that works is an unheard of luxury for most Albanians.

Yet the monks are drawn and miserable, preoccupied with banalities, angrily swishing the cords of their habits. They complain in Greek and Serbian about the brutalities of Lac.

"As useless as a monk," is a phrase I maliciously coin, passing the cell of the youngest, seeing him sprawled on his couch watching television. (As far as I understand it, there is one Albanian channel which offers news and programmes of national folk music, although it is also possible to pick up Greek transmissions).

"As useless as a monk," I say to myself of this bored thirty year old. Neither his brain nor his cock does anybody any good. The brother lies on his sofa, toying with a catechism, face cramped with the loss of his Motorola.

What can monks do, I ask myself, but grow surly with prayer, stiff-kneed from attempts at atonement. Monks did not ask to be born. Nor did they dream it would come to this, pacing a floor, knotting and unknotting the strings of their rosaries. The men of the convent are out of sorts, suspicious as hares. Perhaps theirs is a sickness that even raki cannot ward off.

What brings relief is that for a while we are able to cheer them. Out of the Iveco, secured by twenty yards of rope, we drag the heavy electric organ, a gift from the congregation of the Catholic church in my home town for the sisters of Lac. And for the brothers too. For the work they are doing for the sick and hungry in central Albania. Willing helpers slide the keyboard down two planks to the ground, and soon it is inside the convent, plugged into the generator.

Of Japanese origin, the organ is that type of instrument that can play the part of a whole orchestra or a single toy piano. It offers drum machine backing, brass accompaniment, and banks of strings that Mantovani could only have dreamed of. It makes creepy sci-fi twitterings and salacious rhumba thrusts. Press one key for Stockhausen, another for Bach. A waltz is concluded with the last echo from 'Day in the Life'. There is birdsong and a wave machine, police sirens and a trembling octave of human breath. Switch it all off and start again and it even becomes an organ, reedy and mission-like. We gather round as one of the sisters attempts the chording of an English hymn, but immediately changes tempo. "You shake my nerves and you rattle my brain," is what she sings, but decides not to finish the couplet, and soon we are exploring less boisterous tonality.

Thirty minutes later the performance is over and the instrument locked and covered with a dust-sheet. In the shadows it resembles a large headstone a mason has abandoned. There is not a murmur in the building. Nuns go to bed early. The brothers walk the corridors, swishing their cords.

12

Rubik's river is clouded greenish blue. It winds through a broad plain, between acres of undulating gravel, away from the town. Out of the mountains it pours in a steep torrent, each wave a keel racing through foam. But at Rubik the waters become reptilian. The cascade grows snake-sluggish, suddenly wearied by the burden of copper salts that ooze from the smelting plant above this valley community.

Rubik's children are hungry but there are no river fish displayed on the stones in front of the tiny shops and sweet kiosks. None of the men bother to cast a net or a line into the waters. But they talk about the river, the furry blue-grey sediment on its pebbles like the coating on a tongue, the ulcers on the fish, the deformed fry and aborted eggs, the decline of the populations and the gradual extinction of species until only the hardiest remain, lean, eccentric, then insane, the survivors of the river that swim through the toxic milt of the outfall pipes, finding sustenance amidst the blossoming copper.

For madness is no secret in Albania. It is manifested everywhere. There are mad children at the gates of the ports, mad women whooping and whispering around market stalls, mad men who approach at night in the streets of Tirana and offer their imaginations like smeared picture books. There are dogs that cry in the pre-dawn hours, insistent as the tape recorded voices of the mullahs calling the faithful to prayer across Skanderbeg Square: dogs which travel in packs through the city's darkness.

And the fish in the river at Rubik, with their strange teeth and broken wings, their skeletons become deltas of poisons, they are mad also, and are untroubled by the fishermen, who respect their singularity and are frightened by the metamorphoses that are taking places within the long stillwaters of the river, the swift currents.

With Agim, our guide, we follow the river through its floodplain until we reach a chemical works. This has been shut for over a year, but there remains a group of watchmen in a cabin at the entrance. They do not want us to enter, but the strangeness of our English, the bludgeons of the words are too much for them. They shrug, light more cigarettes, complain incomprehensibly, and we walk past.

It is so easy to do that in Albania. To get our own way. To pretend we are important and that our English is an irrefutable password to where we wish to go. And if that does not work, we wave a dollar. American money is world money and is even more articulate than world language. Everybody retreats eventually because everybody is bewildered. There are no rules any more and suddenly the country is full of strangers making unheard of sounds. There are men with television cameras, women with telephones, travellers who come to look at the river, the foaming orifices of the factory where one hundred people worked and where one thousand people were paid, and who shake their heads as if they knew better. Such strangers are either fools or saints. They are entranced by the everyday, astonished at what has always existed. They bring flour and pencils and bags of clothes, construct window frames and glaze doors. Either they have laid waste their own countries or made them perfect. And what they demand, they receive. There are no instructions on what do do with these visitors. The chemical plant is out of bounds to everybody. But here they are with their Marlboros and greenbacks, pushing through the gates as nonchalantly as if they worked the afternoon shift, and were carrying only the bread and yoghurt their wives had provided. Here they come with their good shoes and faces that crumple so easily into shock. Here they are with their weird curiosity. Had they never known corruption before? They are as pale as a child discovering its parents furrowing the bed. The air grows prickly with their opinions.

So the watchmen shrug to each other as the explorers enter the yard. They might as well try stopping the river with its tree trunks and pagodas of smoke. After all, in this country now there is no telling, no telling at all.

13

There are two sounds. The first is the drone of a generator, almost inaudible, a harmonium's bass pedal. The second is caused by a child scrambling to the top of a hillock of coal. The subsequent slow avalanche rustles like a congregation rising from its knees. We follow Agim through the eviscerated plant, passing vats where contents have solidified to a chemical concrete, pipe mouths bearded by stalactites.

"Do you think they'd put up with this in Buckinghamshah?"

The words are as clear as if spoken this moment. But they are not uttered in Albania. I am standing in the yard of a school called Cap Coch on a hillside in the Cynon Valley. Not many primary schools are named after highwaymen and murderers. I have yet to discover the Dr Crippen Church of England Comprehensive or the Peter Sutcliffe Finishing School for Girls. But Cap Coch is special. From the playground I gaze into the glacial gouge of the Cynon and see Dante's Inferno. That is its local name. Some people also call it the Furney, others the Works. But however christened, the Phurnacite Smokeless Fuel Plant is unmissable. Forty seven chimneys, each with an unruly orange curl of flame, and all at it full pelt this morning. Here is the place where the more noxious constituents of coal – sulphur, chlorine, dinosaur turds – are extracted before it is burnt elsewhere. So the Smokeless Fuel Plant smokes. It smokes like Bonfire Night and the Blitz. It smokes like the best efforts of an army of mad allotmenteers. It smokes like China smokes, and like the Rhondda and the mills of Pennsylvania smoked. It smokes like a bus queue and the waiting room of a Social Security office. It smokes like a Prague tram and a café of Greek lorry drivers. It smokes like the lane behind my house, full of

navy-blue schoolgirls with lipstick and big hair. It smokes like
Chernobyl, like an ocean invisible in fog. Like bronchitis. It
smokes like my family used to smoke, the ceilings turning yellow
above their waving arms. It smokes like bereavement and the
popular bank at Ninian Park. It smokes like a staffroom wants
to smoke, it smokes like the four minute warning. But most of
all it smokes like Albania.

The valley floor is paved with burning coals. Something is in
my mouth, a raspberry seed starting to nag. The taste of a knife.
I rub my eyes because of the mistiness of it all. Children fall like
skylarks to the concrete yard.

"Or Herts, Berks or sodding Surrey for that matter," adds my
companion, a young Welsh teacher with the classic young
Welsh teacher's appearance: that of an Iberian scrum-half with
a hangover, the beer already blowing up the inner-tube inside
him, pushing the belly out, thickening the neck; a disgruntled
participant in the Friday evening Tesco checkout frenzy, the
weekly shop and two kids together in one of the outsize trolleys,
the list his wife wrote crumpled amongst the twenties, thinking
of tomorrow night at the Blaengwawr Inn, the Sunday quizzes
where he can feel his pissed-off politics getting their last
expression.

"Don't know," I say, but add, for fairness sake, that
Heathrow Airport was built next to Windsor Castle. He leaves
me alone after this and goes over to where some children are
fighting, two red haired boys with cropped heads. He grips them
like ferrets, tosses them apart. All I can do is look into the fur-
nace, the grey and yellow vortices of Abercwmboi. It is like the
hold of a whaling-ship down there. Smoke has its own seasons
and this is spring. In fact, smoke has its own language. It is
called Ringelmann's Shades, which categorises everything from
the finest mist to furcoat-thick effluvia. Ringelmann would have
been impressed with the Furney. It is doing him proud.

"The problem is work," spits the returned ferret master. "Or
jobs. Because there's a difference. We do anything for jobs

around here. Make ping pong balls. Plastic budgies so little Joey doesn't get lonely. We'd make bombs if they let us. Napalm. Anti-personnel devices. It's sad what jobs do to you. It's tragic. Those people down in the works, they're bloody Shakespearian. They're heroes. It's killing them and they know it, look at the trees. Lungs are like leaves. Those people are immense. Because of the way we are now the only thing worse than having a job is not having a job. Something's gone wrong."

We follow Agim over slag and clinker, between boulders of rock salt and fallen metal drums. Around us the smoke is coiled tighter than a winter viper, awaiting its release. The chimneys are trained like howitzers on the front line. Agim lights another cigarette.

"Chinese," he grins, gesturing to the stacks. "Chairman Mao's gifts to the people of Albania. And especially to Chairman Hoxha. They're trying to start them up again, but it takes too long to generate enough power." He kicks at a bucket and releases its contents which have the milky constituency of pine sap.

"I bet," he laughs, pointing his cigarette at us like a piece of chalk, "I bet you've never seen anywhere like this."

14

We take our boxes of books into the school. There is a set of *Encyclopaedia Britannica*, a Collins-Spurrel Welsh dictionary and a miscellany of other titles including *The Observer's Guide to British Birds* and *Make Your Own Wine*.

These shrapnel bombs of British languages are intended for the three hundred pupils for whom books are rarities, despite the fact that over one thousand new texts are published in Albania every year.

The school is drab but no uglier than the flat-roofed, hastily constructed comprehensives that went up in Britain in the sixties and which now exist in states of desultory repair, their outlying archipelagos of portakabins surrounded by seas of mud and takeaway food cartons.

One difference, however, is that large domestic pigs, the mongrels of Rubik, and more familiar here than stray cats, quarter the playground until they are sent squealing to the road by a volley of stones or some over-enthusiastic recreation.

Another is that there is no glass in Rubik's school windows. The reachable panes were deliberately smashed during a period of unrest in 1991, when people attacked all manifestations of state authority. Their rebellion exhausted itself, but the windows have remained broken, there being no glass to replace them.

What the town also missed was the practical common sense on how to devise alternative shelter from the wind and rain. Debilitated by institutionalisation, that's what the aid workers say, the career Catholics, the English mistresses doing their end-of-term good deed. Aid and the environment offer a new type of imperialism. Have conscience, will travel.

A woman teacher marvels at the gifts we bring. The rules that govern subject and predicate, an account of international rugby in 1971 and a set of thirty year old economic textbooks are held up and examined like medicine bottles. Albania claims that three-quarters of its people are literate: the same proportion that stays on in school after age eleven. Certainly the classes in this high school are bright and curious. But the draughts sweep in through the shattered windows, the walls are bare as bus-shelters and there are only three toilets for the pupils.

Behind the school the mountain is red and denuded. The forests that for hundreds of years were nurtured on its slopes have recently been cut for firewood. Now the unprotected soil is washed by heavy rain into the streets of the town. Sometimes the ochre mud slides closer to the apartment blocks like snow off a roof, a topographical shift that might be a lorry rumbling by, a muffled cry from the house next door. People say the mountain never made such whisperings in the past. Only the owls screamed, or the vixens on heat in the darkness. Now at night there are groans; the movement of boulders is like the creaking of bedsprings. It is as if there were miners beneath the hill, long shifts of secret labour. But everybody knows there are no miners. Everybody knows that the mountain is unhappy.

"And what is this?" asks the teacher, holding up a heavy volume.

It is *Larousse Gastronomique*, one million words on food, wine and cooking. Everything from absinthe to zucchini in a tome as thick as the deepest deep-pan pizza ever made.

"Domestic science," I say, putting down another crate. "We'll have to try a recipe."

15

I want to tell you about Agim. He is the most important man in Albania. He speaks English. He takes us where we want to go. He shows us things we had never thought about. And he is cheap. We get him for a dollar a day. One hundred cents. Or, to be precise, that is what he receives. The agency that employs him demands a little more.

Short, slight, chain-smoker in black jeans and black shirt, Agim is our talisman. If we need petrol he knows where to find it, even if he has to queue all night or buy it in wine bottles at the side of the road. He speaks to the army and the police for us, shows pieces of paper to officials. He understands who appreciates a few bucks under the desk. Agim is a dark man, deeply tanned, his humour dry as sloes. He tells us he is a Muslim but I am not sure what that means. It doesn't stop him drinking. A connoisseur of raki in all its forms, he is even polite regarding the medicinal brandy I had packed. There are a few things he is open about. He used to be a teacher, for instance, in the agricultural college near Tirana. It was a decent job. Decent jobs were unusual under Hoxha. They were privileges, sinecures, gifts. It is difficult to think of Agim as one of the state's privileged elite, but perhaps it is best not to enquire too deeply. Survival is survival. And Agim has survived.

He leans now against the convent wall, holding in the smoke, releasing it reluctantly in thin tendrils. He must, I think, be the same colour on the inside, so deeply does he suck the Camels, the Marlboros, the Greek high tars he always has to hand. One fact is clear today. He is not going to help us unload the pieces of cargo promised to the nuns, who are taking off sacks of flour, boxes of margarine. Agim simply smokes and watches the food coming out of the Iveco. The expression on his face is uninterpretable.

The next day at Rubik he adopts the same pose. We drive the remainder of the goods to what is known as the Magazine. This is a large shed filled with the bounty of earlier missions. Everything but the drugs and the incubator are unloaded here. The keys to the Magazine are kept by Catholics. All the materials stored have been donated by people from my town, most of them Catholic. There are nuns, monks, Franciscan friars helping to stack the boxes and bags. A group of youths look on from a distance. One of them wears a sweatshirt with the motto of my school. They have the faces of children, startled out of sullenness, seen in photographs of the Depression, or on street corners at home, waiting their turn as the bottle of piss-pale cider goes round.

These things are for everyone, I tell Agim. No-one cares about the religion of the people who will benefit from our expedition. He smiles at me the tired smile usually reserved for a troublesome pet animal. His nose leaks smoke. Do you think we have come to help only half the population, I ask, presenting my credentials as a non-Catholic, non-worshipper, non-believer, good all purpose non-religious type. I'd like to believe I was sceptical about everything, but I cannot quite commit myself to it.

"How much Albanian do you speak?" he asks.

The real answer is three words. Yes, no and the equivalent of cheers. Not bad, I think. A vocabulary like that might take a man a long way. Before I answer, Agim is talking again.

"It is good that sometimes you don't understand what the people say. Look around here. Family takes care of family. Muslim gives to Muslim, Catholic to Catholic. It's okay as long as there's not too much benefit for one side. And sometimes now," he shrugs, taking a long draw, "sometimes that happens."

A man pushes past, dusty with flour. The taps are coming out of the Iveco, the toilet bowls held over the heads of two laughing helpers. A sumo-sized carboy of cooking oil is wrestled to the front of the lorry.

Now, at the moment of delivery of goods saved and collected carefully by people two thousand miles away, there should be satisfaction. This is what Oxfam, Christian Aid and Band Aid are all about. Here comes nourishment. Here comes succour. Here are the powerful strangers in their dark glasses and expensive shoes. Here are angels treading the dirt, handing out lollipops, ignoring the grumbling pigs, the emaciated dogs. This is what all the Italian tunnels were for, the icicle of sweat in my arse. This is what I dreamed about, peering into the fine rain at Macon, labouring on the gradient as the angry convoy of Citroens built up behind. This is what friends waved goodbye for, one dark morning in another country. And where the smile should be I see only Agim and his quizzical aureole of smoke.

"Perhaps we should have filled the truck with cancer sticks. You would have given us medals."

Lightening, Agim condescends to examine for the first time the rapidly emptying hold of the Iveco.

"Of course," I say, "it was originally filled with illegal immigrants from Cardiff, crazed after a week fed only on raki and Welsh cakes. They were looking for a better quality of life in Albania."

Agim, master of the sardonic lip twitch and eye flicker, breathes out a long plume.

34

16

Trade not Aid, the slogans say. There's Geldof, GATT, the World Bank, the International Monetary Fund and the Caritas sticker on the windscreen of the Iveco. All of them suggest urgent and successful surgical operations in which the patient dies. But perhaps the patient has always been a corpse.

I'm hunched down, low as I can get, in the bar of the Hotel Tirana. The room is a badly upholstered sauna of smoke. Around me men in suits peer into thimbles of coffee, exchange spreadsheets, speak English. American English. European English. There are businessmen from Chicago, a United Nations delegation from Geneva. They smell of aerosoled hair gel, their cuffs so neat they might have come straight off the laser printer. One of them fetches a message from the hotel fax. A fax in Tirana. For some reason I want to protest.

Gradually I sink lower into the burst armchair, an Albanian newspaper over my chest, and watch the women. The women also wear suits, blue, dark blue, navy, like the uniforms of air hostesses. They sit with the spreadsheets and murmur in English, their legs anonymous, their jewellery muted, their hair pulled back so tight their faces have the clean, startled look of children settling down to an examination. Carefully made over, their skin gleams like fax paper. The men loll, the women sit. The men speak, the women listen. The men drink and the women watch them knock back the coffee's liquid graphite, toy with brandy in stained glass. Amongst the ashtrays on the table they have placed the laptops, three gold screens, each the size of a page, offering the statistics of profit and loss, the formulae of aid, trade and charity. These blue women, these perfumed men are the reception committee. They are welcoming back a country to a particular way of life, a process of thought. Prodigal Illyria has come home and there is rejoicing in the software, in the galaxies of microchips where money is twenty-four hour sunlight. This is the period of restoration. Of meeting old friends and discovering new allies. One of the men, his hair permed tight and shining as a bowl of blackberries, peels a banknote from a wad of dollars.

For a moment his riches are visible to all, crisp as a volume of poetry. No-one here deals in leks, the filthy, ragged local currency with its pictures of fiery chimneys and grave-robbed dictators. Leks are for the street outside, where they are now buying cloven pomegranates and Evian water bottles filled with brakefluid. Leks are for people with nowhere to wash their hands after a shit. Leks create an endless relay of disease. Leks are for losers.

And in the afternoon light, a limousine is making its way through Skanderbeg Square. There are army outriders on motorbikes clearing the traffic, parting the crowds. The crowds come to the square each day to look, to listen, to ask what is happening. To pass on the infection of leks. On the bonnet of the limousine flies a Canadian flag. In the rear seat is a man wearing dark glasses. He is reading a small gold screen.

17

The locomotive moves through a field of cabbages. So slowly it might be possible for the passengers, shuttered inside the grey, corrugated carriages, to step off the train, stretch their legs, and unhurriedly catch up.

Nothing wrong with that, say I, remembering the Iveco on the oil-stained pull-in on the A13 south of Ancona. A yard away the ceaseless volley of cars had fractured our words, poisoned our throats. They punched past like the missiles of a nailgun. Around us lay the debris of other interrupted journeys. Hubcaps, the big plastic type, like samurai armour. Oil filters with telephone dial mouths. A windscreen wiper with its rubber vane torn loose.

Only by waiting in places like that can I understand speed. The brutality of it. The ignorance. Nought to sixty in five seconds. Four and a half seconds. Nowhere to nowhere in four and a half seconds. The purity of it. Four seconds. The drivers knifed past, the road ahead an equation, a philosophy. I flinched in their slipstream as tornados ripped the grass. Their dust invaded the body's mouths, their nitrous oxide spun a cocoon. Speed is blue. Dark blue. In my mind's spectrometer, all the Alfa Romeos were blue, all the Volkswagens. And all were a vanishing indigo that reappeared again as the next vehicle crashed out of the horizon on the right into the horizon on the left. Only by waiting in places like that might I understand speed. And anyone who would understand speed has to be entirely motionless.

The train takes its time. It moves alongside us like a Sunday afternoon. We are stationary, engine ticking over, before a long river-bridge. It is wide enough to allow traffic to pass in one direction only at a time. Coming towards us, growing bigger, stranger, is what was once a lorry. Finally it crosses the last section of bridge and wheezes past. No plates, diesel exhaust a smear of Indian ink, shocks like armchair springs. Its cargo is people, who cling to each other, the hinge-drop sides, the roof of the cab. Women in local Muslim dress; children with schoolbooks; men with what men carry – lump-hammers, reels of barbed wire, sauce bottles of sump-oil. The driver bangs the horn of his lorry-become-bus and now it is our turn to cross the viaduct over the cushions of grey and orange gravel, the waters where nothing lives.

When Hoxha died there were no private vehicles in Albania. Now, less than ten years later, it seems that every clapped out, uninsurable jalopy in Europe has found its way here, motors that make Trabants look like miracles of lean burn technology. Outside Tirana and off the main highway to the port, roads are unlit and unmade. Drivers must share them with shepherds and renegade pigs, donkeys and farm carts. To those of us addicted to speed and comforting yellow swamps of streetlight, the roads of Illyria are medieval places. However slowly we drive, we drive too quickly. However carefully we comply with our own code of safety, we are still the guilty party when a glassy tyred taxi overtakes on a bend, or a jeep crammed with olive uniformed farmboys posing as soldiers rattles up behind and locks on, bumper to bumper, for two miles. What are needed here are traffic lights, the green eye the lover's look of approval, the amber that belongs to whoever seizes it first. What are needed here are giveway signs. After that, people might even take driving tests. After that, Albania can start to catch up.

18

We are parked on a rise looking west. In a field beside the road the national bird of Illyria investigates the carcass of a sheep.

The national bird is the hooded crow. I call it the national bird because it appears everywhere we travel, unmistakeable frosted shoulders, blue beak pointed like an ice pick. At home hooded crows are rare. They might be glimpsed across a field of stones in Preseli or diving with gulls at Hell's Mouth. Here they are familiar but never mundane, and always ten yards away, perched on walls or branches, patient, attentive. Sometimes I think they are listening to us. Sometimes I think they are following, strangers seeking strangers, outcasts who understand that we too do not belong. Like a bird out of a legend, the hooded crow confronts us now, talons in the fleece, mandril glinting.

From this breast we can see the Adriatic in a notch of the bay. So small is it, so inconsequential, it resembles a twist of silver paper, a sweet wrapping tossed aside. We stand amongst pillboxes become barns, chicken coops, mildewed trysting houses. A few birch trees, bark almost as thin and delicate as rose petals, have pushed through the brick-strewn soil. The inevitable children, shyly eager for lollipops and the last of our sweets, circle round. Albania is a place of youth. It has the highest birthrate in Europe. So children are the country's waste product. In a society without refuse tips, because nothing, until now, was thrown away, children are its unrecyclable rubbish. They are also, like the hooded crow, its scavengers.

These two with us at the back of the Iveco, sucking red Chewitts, these are lucky. They have homes. The beds have ticks, the mattresses fleas and the ceilings are graffitied with the heiroglyphs of damp and daylight, but they provide shelter. The boys stare up at us, dribbling scarlet juice, sweet papers in the dust. One is called Elvis. The other is Clinton. They are the first Albanians ever to bear those names.

19

Illyria is the rediscovered country. So it is curious to think that I have been here before. Or almost. Fifty of us had put out in a low-in-the-water wooden cruiser from the north coast of Kerkira. Pink UK passport holders, lean Italians, knuckled and necklaced with gold, Swedes whose hair was bleached white as autumn's vines of bryony. We had sailed north-west while Captain Gregory, multilingual pirate, sophisticated exploiter-explorer of the serrated coasts of southern Europe, lectured us on smuggling, wildlife, the birthplace of Prince Philip, subsidies for Grecian olive oil.

Gregory was a big man, the type that effortlessly takes charge of things, and we were happy for that to happen, looking into the white seamist of ouzo that clouded our tumblers. But to star-board, growing slowly clearer through the heat haze, was another shoreline. There were hillsides of a surprising height, bare of trees, houses, everything but the usual shrivelled carpet of thyme and curry plant. And down on the plain, drenched in August's caustic balm, was a city.

Captain Gregory did not tell us the city's name. But Albania was really called "Republika e Shqiperise," he said. Soon he would be conducting parties of tourists to that area of the coast we could see. The climate was good, the beaches were empty, the locals had no work. It was perfect.

"Albanians are funny people," Gregory had said, pouring himself a skipper's draught of wine. "They like to be unhappy. Complaining is their national sport."

A few of the Italians snorted. In Italy, if you wish to insult someone, you call them an Albanian.

"But," said the captain, "it's never as bad as they think. Take that Enver Hoxha. He was a great guerrilla leader. He helped defeat the Italians who thought they could treat the Albanians like shit. Like Abyssinians." Gregory laughed and an Italian turned up his transistor.

"But say what you want, he made the country. He gave it a shape, he gave the people somewhere to grow food.'"

I thought then of the island we had left. Walking west away from its neon shoreline of theme-bars and dawn discos, we had found the villages where every garden was filled with grapes and figs, where each grove was festooned with the black webs of olive nets. There was a proverb there. Plant a matchstick and it will flame. I drained the ouzo, hurting my eyes as I strained to see over the violet Ionian swell the city without a name that shivered in the heat.

Arriving home I sought maps and histories, any available literature about Republika e Shqiperise. Byron had been there. He had travelled over the mountains and stayed with the warrior clans, taking part in the dance of the eagles that soon the captain's passengers would be paying to watch. Byron had worn the costumes, learned the words. But then, he would. I dug out the momentous renunciation of world politics that Enver Hoxha had made at Albania's Eighth Workers Party Congress, held in the early eighties. This condemned "US imperialism, Soviet-socialist imperialism, Chinese and Yugoslav revisionism, Eurocommunism, social democracy, non-alignment and European detente."

"Christ," breathed a friend to whom I showed this manifesto. "They hated everyone. It's brilliant. The pure of the pure. You know, sometimes paranoia makes the only sense. It gives you a charge like clean cocaine. The only thing better is jealousy, the heroin, you might say, of the emotions. But this is lunar."

20

If children and hooded crows are abundant here, so is the military, sullen and dark green as ivy spread over the country.

Nearly two per cent of the Albanian population are soldiers, half of them conscripts. I ask Agim whether this is hard on the economy. Three million, two hundred thousand people and forty two thousand troops. Agim delves deeply into his vocabulary of shrugs.

"What else should they be? There's no work for these boys so they must hang around with walkie-talkies looking important."

"What do they do?"

"Guard things." Agim sculpts smoke. "Crossroads, the port, bigshot foreign visitors. Us. There's a lot of them up in the north, for obvious reasons, and on the border with Greece. Sometimes they're a nuisance, sometimes they leave us alone. But ask anyone. We have always had many soldiers."

Perhaps it is the guns I find unnerving. Despite coming from a country where arms manufacture and military bases provide employment, I'm a nervous virgin as far as guns are concerned. Never fired one. Never held one. Never, after the age of ten, thought about them. But here there is no pretence. Guns are not secrets in Albania but simply part of the culture, along with raki, religion, street markets. Even one of our guides carries a gun, a gaunt man in a faded blue suit, the pistol butt visible in his waist band. I wonder what it would take for him to brandish it. To fire. Would he shoot to frighten, or would he truly aim to harm? And what would happen if he killed someone? Would we be arrested or could we walk away, inconvenienced aid-workers under the banner of Caritas, temporarily prevented from performing our duties of love and renewal.

The answers are already blurred, and sometimes as the Iveco plunges through the dusk on unmarked roads, meeting cars without headlamps, brushing past old men on donkeys, braking as human shapes disassociate themselves from the darkness and step, as if hypnotised, into the corridor of our lights, the questions return like a fever. Who would know and who would care? A bundle of clothes in the ditch and in the morning our cargo miles distant, the bumper unmarked, and only a small indentation, hardly noticeable, in the radiator grille with its butterfly wings and explosions of insect blood.

On the main road out of Tirana a soldier signals us to stop, looks at our papers and waves us on. All is accomplished without a change of expression. In Skanderbeg Square a sudden huddle of troops plants an evergreen shrubbery in our path. Behind the church at Rubik, perched over the valley on a soda-white pinnacle, a platoon of teenagers dries socks on an outcrop of limestone.

Yet as if there was not enough of the Albanian military around, the Italian army is now in evidence. Ashamed of its behaviour in 1991, when it confined thousands of refugees to a football stadium in Brindisi, beat them, starved them, and forced them home, Italy now sends its own conscripts to work on Albanian projects. But these are useful men. They even repair the hydraulics of the Iveco when we break down in Durres. A fawn-skinned Neapolitan sucks air and fluid from the clutch cylinder. He smiles, spits out the burning residue, salutes, and is soon indistinguishable again amongst a knot of figures in acid green camouflage.

21

The Hassanis live on the side of a hill one mile from the nearest road. Behind the hill is the quarry where various Hassani men have worked for generations. Close by is the Chinese-built cement plant which fills the air with smoke and white stonedust, a ruined and ruinous fortress of technology now run on skeleton shifts. The Hassanis have a cow, a vegetable garden, a tree of yellow quinces. The fruits hang like lanterns in the dusk. We are the Hassanis' guests of honour.

The three of us, the drivers, the deliverers, the three ambassadors who have motored a thousand miles and crossed two seas because once, long ago, it seemed a good idea, in fact a bit of a joke, to bring flour and sugar and medicine here, take our places at the table. Each receives a tall glass of cowslip-coloured yoghurt, an Illyrian delicacy, effervescent with salmonella. Or that is what our paranoia proclaims. There is also cooked meat on the bone, an expensive rarity, thick wodges of a batter pudding, and a litre of homebrewed raki in a green Jamesons bottle.

In anyone's terms, this is a banquet, and almost matches the evening reception I blundered into in Tirana, where army officers in full regalia mixed with what looked like Greek Orthodox churchmen in green and violet robes: where the flower of Albanian politics assembled for some inscrutable ritual. Slowly it dawned on the guests that someone in their throng was wearing lorry driver's jeans and shoes encrusted with the mud of the capital's back streets. Out I went, feeling satisfyingly native.

We are here to honour Welsh-Albanian relations and soon are into double figures of maudlin toasts. One of the Hassanis is a remarkable linguist who learned his pedagogue's English listening at night to the BBC World Service. He is now training at British hospitals to become a doctor. At home we had used him as a searchlight into Albanian society. Many of the people we meet here have been alerted to us through his influence. But now it is Elida Hassani who dominates. Who welcomes, explains, translates, admonishes. We are completely in the hands of this slight twenty-one year old with wry eyes and 1960's idea of a Hollywood hairstyle.

Elida is watchful, abstemious, hard as nails. She treats raki and its moods with disdain, sipping bottled water. She has never been out of the country but is no national sentimentalist. For her the past is a garret of broken furniture, about as useful as the pillboxes and concealed tank-emplacements that ring this small-holding. What gleams is the future, like the dials of the secret transistor. The only prize.

Already she is building a home for herself on the hill next to her parents' house. Her university course should secure a job. There might also be a man. But Muslim men expect too much. Even Hoxha could not destroy everything. Yet for now Elida is content. In a country where bakers, doctors, teachers all earn one dollar per day, and what was once a furtive black-market has become the main local economy, it is tempting to escape. But the rooftree of Elida's house has today been carried by four labourers up this green hill. The cement works will continue to infiltrate the lungs of local people, but poverty is also pollution. Elida will remain, teach her children English, and watch colour television. She will walk the mile to the road and squeeze into ramshackle buses sickly with diesel, brake-linings worn down to the rivets. She will stay and she will flourish.

Behind her head, a Manchester United scarf and coloured picture of the team is displayed on the wall. Her mother, at sixty as wrinkled as a ninety year old, is both proud and obsequious at the table. Outside in the twilight a quince falls to the ground.

22

A girl thrusts a yellow loaf, long as my arm, through the bakery window. Another girl adds it to the pyramid of loaves she is balancing like firewood, and sets off down the alley.

The bakery smell permeates our clothes. I think it must form haloes over our dusty hair. The bakery smell wafts into the street outside where pigs root for corn husks and cigarette ends and the children play with mud. The bakery smell is today one of the wonderful smells of the world. So we make our respectful tour of the most important place in Rubik.

Bread means something in Albania. It is the standard currency, a source of national pride, uncertainty and preoccupation. Albanians make good bread. Here in the bakery where generational layers of flour and grease cover every surface, and the mouth of the oven seems a plausible entrance to the underworld, they make the best bread in Albania. The loaves are like people. Each is unique. A woman passes by, cradling hers like an infant. It will have to last her a week, that big, irregular, sawdust-coloured loaf, its crust a darker orange, knobbly as oak bark, the heel of the bread making a pleasingly hollow sound where she taps it, the base ingrained with tiny heiroglyphs of dirt from the oven bricks.

But bread is expensive. One loaf costs half a day's wages. Crumbs are important, as are the burnt deposits on the metal trays, given to children to scrape clean. Slivers of scorched pastry, traces of dough, are all worth the hunting. They have a meaning here.

Food itself has a meaning here like nowhere else I have stayed. Most meals are brief and desperate. Preparing them requires the ingredients of ingenuity and courage. On our last night on the other side we visited a restaurant in the town of the stone colossus. We were the only diners present. To begin, a waiter brought us the local delicacy: toasted olives glistening like sweetbreads. We spread it in a bitter purple jam, our lips suddenly dark, our tongues mauve as the gills of orchids. This was the ritual of the house, and as supplicants who had crossed the threshold, we were eager to indulge in the ceremonies of the region.

But here there exists a different colour of civilisation. In the hotel our meals are cold and melancholy. In the appartments at Lac and on the floor space of Rubik, they are guilty affairs. We wonder who owns the rice we nudge with our knives, looking away from the children, the pinched mothers who always eat elsewhere, who excuse themselves politely and squat outside with their hunger: who have triumphed over hunger by the mortification of the appetite. Food is different in Illyria. But our expectations remain the same.

As if of right, we take the warm loaf the baker offers us and bear it away like a trophy. In the street we break pieces, golden morsels of crust, the snowy flesh of bread. Soon the great hot stone is shattered in our hands. Old women stare after us as if we had blasphemed.

23

Agim stalls the car for the fifth time and swears silently. He is having trouble with the automatic gears. This is an afternoon expedition he has organised around the capital. On an avenue off Skanderbeg Square he points to a dark, robust, middle-aged man.

"Enver Hoxha's son." Agim's voice momentarily adopts the conspiratorial whisper of the past.

At once my eyes are greedy. I search the pedestrian's expression for evidence of a malign history, suggest to myself that the cut of his clothes betrays the hauteur of the deposed first family.

The man moves easily amidst fruit sellers and office workers enjoying the sunshine. These are mingled with the seemingly lost and bewildered who always frequent the square. At one of the new hamburger stalls, 'All Day and All of the Night' by the Kinks is played at full volume, its chords of sexual drama disappearing into engine stutter. On a patch of grass a family of gypsies in costumes gorgeous as jockeys' silks is singing for leks. Hoxha passes anonymously. Either nobody notices or there is nothing left to care about.

Agim drives further and stops at an attractive villa.

"Enver Hoxha's palace," he says triumphantly, as if here in bricks and mortar was all the proof necessary to pass judgement on decades of psychotic dictatorship. To try to understand Agim, I imagine the building as a temple dedicated to the debauchery of power. But all I see is a stockbroker waving good-bye to his wife who is about to leave in the second car for an afternoon's quango-sitting. There are no demons in the benevolent October light. The afternoon is as comfortable as the scuffed red leather of our borrowed Mercedes, in which Agim, unpractised driver, is scorching the transmission. The car is filled by that smell made by a braking train. Obviously the villa is occupied. There are soldiers in the garden.

"Who lives there now?"

"Someone in government." He grimaces. "You know a few years ago they arrested Naxhmija Hoxha, the dictator's widow, on corruption charges. I suppose it was a precaution in case people started getting nostalgic about the good old days when we were the only country in the world."

The Mercedes judders like a tram. I sink deeper into the ox-blood upholstery. It occurs to me that I must look important in a car like this. A visiting bureaucrat, some media type. In Albania every car is a statement. But a Mercedes is a declaration. Outside, the scrawny children give chase, thinking they can catch us in our uncertain progress. There are people now who are staring at me while no-one gives Hoxha a glance.

"Probably the crimes were nothing outrageous. A gold bar under the mattress, some fur coats paid for from the schools budget. That sort of thing."

Agim seems uncomfortable. "It's always the same, isn't it?" he adds finally. "Power. It makes men thin and women fat. Counting their medals, counting their dresses, always afraid to let go. That Imelda Marcos with her shoes. The jewels on the floor of the Rumanian torture chambers. And there's the rest of us with nothing to hold on to. Nothing at all."

He looks at me with an eye like a robin's, then drives off without checking the road.

24

The Iveco is an empty room. There is nothing left but a box of spares and the scurf of flour dust. The last items on board, the medicines and incubator, were unloaded yesterday at the hospital. The doctors were busy and seemed preoccupied. They hardly said anything to us. Sometimes they must get sick of having to look grateful. Gratitude is an exhausting business.

We sailed last night after agonies of paperwork. In the twilight a young woman cried and our armed guardian in his powder-blue suit waved with his left hand. The glowing butt of Agim's cigarette drew a symbol or wrote a word. I craned into the darkness but he did not repeat it.

And now I sit once more beneath the colossus, the stone protector of this town. My jacket smells of Agim's smoke, the markets of mud and snuffling farrow. I hold a sleeve to my face and breathe in the Republika. Soon it will start all over again. The tunnel driving, the Fiat racing, the games of chicken on the autostrada. How perverse it feels to be taking nothing home, our cargo of emptiness the proof of a mission accomplished.

Under my nails are half-moons of Illyria. My shoes are filmed with the filth of the port. There is nothing else to show as I sit for an hour and the town comes alive. As I watch him. As he watches her. Doing my job again. Keeping an eye. A man trudges past with a pannier of crabs on his back. The scooter riders shoot like pinballs through the cobbled lanes. In the churches are marble ikons, pink as chaffinches, and huge canvasses of tarry oils that seem to absorb the gloom. People are hurrying but the town is as it always was. Saints, travellers, gangsters walk beneath the twin trunks of the statue's legs and are forgotten. We have given it all away. There is nothing left. As poor as an Albanian I sit beneath the awning, the medallion in my glass suddenly black as obsidian in the sunlight.

At home the church halls are filling with the clothes we do not want, the blunt tools, the typewriters, the fifties lavatory pans. People are generous these days. They are always amazed at the quantity of things they own. The things. All that stuff they do not really need. That they never really used. It seems there is no end to the help we can offer. No end at all.

The Jukebox in Uranium City

I divide the mail into two heaps. Junk and junk. There is a gambling expedition to Deadwood City, a bulletin from the Psychic Readers Network, a free newspaper to all city employees telling us it's been a difficult year but the next twelve months are promising. If we pull together. If we make the effort. Making the effort, the newspaper says, means our future will be better than our past.

I consider this over the Sumatran, drawn from a perc that maintains a steady lukewarm regime throughout the day, sighing occasionally, occasionally increasing the sigh to a grumble. A future that is better than the past. Only a politician could write that. Only a politician could be so convinced of the exact moment when the platitudinous becomes the vacuous. When meaning finally disappears like the last guttering of marsh gas.

It is not that politicians in this country are liars. This country is like most countries. A jigsaw whose pieces don't fit. But it is the politicians' determination that we should feel good about ourselves that irritates. Slick-haired persuaders who look like holograms of themselves, they perform with the certainty of Christian pop singers, promising us a future as if it was a hotel room they were sure had been properly cleaned before the next occupation. I prefer the past. The past is the settlement at Ffynnon Pwll, the darkling canvases in Italian churches, the third movement of the Eroica. Beat that, future. It's not that these politicos lie. I don't think they have the brass gizzards to lie. It's that truth evaporates around them. That nimbus of static about those people. That fuzz. It's not their cologne or their hairspray. It's not raindrops on the microphones, the hiss of rewinding videotape. It is the truth evaporating. Listen. You can hear its slowly disappearing sibilance.

I turn on the radio that is rarely off. Shostakovich encodes a symphony with dissent. A provincial government wishes to turn an iceberg into vodka. Galician fishermen are arrested for catching turbot and are insulted by persons with Irish accents. No-one has heard of Galicia, that unsung Celtic realm. No-one has heard of turbot. But they are the last fish on the Grand Banks, on the Nose and Tail. The Galician nets are of such fine mesh they would snare mosquitoes. The baby turbot are no bigger than sweet chestnut leaves. After they have become Tokyo pizza or New York sushi the sea will be empty, a mall at evening with the drawbridges up. First it was the bison. Their bones like a wrecker's yard on a Texan plain. Then the passenger pigeon. When the pigeons flew over the prairie the sky filled with strange weather, an indigo dust before the dustbowl. In the natural history museums their feathers turn to ashes, their eyes are shirt-buttons.

And now the cod are only a dream. The shoals that pulsed like nebulae under the oceans are a guilty memory here. This country's people wear their guilt as a badge of nationhood. Guilt proves something; like little boys comparing scars. And now here are the turbot, a species plucked from fathomless anonymity, dissected by radio, a last tribe holding out. How do you cook it? asks the presenter. The expert tells how. What does it taste like? Passenger pigeon, I want to say. Buffalo jerky. And then Shostakovich is back, his symphony scored in invisible ink, the violins whispering in eerie assonance, a sound that refuses extinction, the casual vanishings.

Down at the Greyhound station I meet Mars. He is sucking like a walrus on his plastic inhaler and greets me with a fierce asthmatic shrug.

"Thought you'd given up cocaine."

"Fuck you and this climate. Air's so dry there's nothing to dampen the dust."

Mars is not his real name but it's what everyone uses. Because his last name is Barlow and because he has been known to put away a five-pack of those chocolate bars. Mars Barlow is a sugar junkie and weighs two hundred and eighty pounds. He is a big man with small lungs, a sweetly paranoiac Leo of large ecstasies, titanic glooms. Big but rarely warlike. Now he exchanges the inhaler for a goldleafed cigar. Mars is getting his fix in the departure lounge because there is no smoking on the bus.

"Hear the fucking news?"

"About the fish?"

"Fuck the fish. No. The Second Airborne, the paratroopers. The government's disbanding it."

"Well they were torturing..."

Somebody nudges me from behind and we move closer towards the silver corrugations of the Greyhound's luggage compartment. A man using a pike to arrange cases and knapsacks in this deck of the bus squints up at Mars.

"You John Candy?"

Mars examines the bubbling tip of his cigar, but before he can speak the luggage packer corrects himself.

"Nope, he's dead, so yah can't be. Can yah?"

The morning is blue through the smoked glass. We glide past Robin's Donuts and a Mennonite church. There is some snow left, the backbones of drifts, a dusting over the khaki grass in front yards, hidden five months. I glimpse the rear of a mall, a space without feature or use. From the parking lot of Julian's Ribs a Cree child scowls up at the wall of the bus. The grey billow to the right is the breath of the power-plant, feeding the city cell by cell, block by block. Near Thirty Third Street we cross railway tracks and a parcel of land unwrapped and abandoned. Anonymity rolls like a fog behind us, ahead. Mars is plugged into Glenn Gould, Jimi Hendrix or Bach's partitas, the cassette cartridges scattered on the seat beside him. His opened lumberjacket reveals a teeshirt splashed with a Nietzschean text. But Mars is a churchgoer. For the ritual, he says. For the mystery. In a city of straight roads and no hills the mystery is important. It's what keeps him going. That and his library, a basement shrine. That and his trusty inhaler. That and the odd forty burnished ounces of Bushmills.

Mars has brought two books. One is a substantial Heidegger. The other a paperback *X Files*. Stories about flesh-eating microbes, autopsies on inhabitants of other worlds crash-landed in the desert, superviruses that can wipe out cities like a neutron bomb. All based on fact, he says. Like it's happening now, man, it's here. Although he is a churchgoer, I know that Mars has stolen both books. He has told me about his expeditions to the secondhand bookshops of this city, the coffee houses with their shelves of gay poetry and twenty-first century witchcraft, the big Coles stores in the plazas with their walls of Stephen King.

According to Mars, stealing books is not theft. It is an essential distribution of knowledge and beauty. All right, stealing books is theft, but what the hell. It's an intellectual and emotional challenge. And as Heidegger or Steely Dan said, you can't buy a thrill. So there he sits with the latest strain of green monkey disease, the philosopher's stone. Like a man with a beer and a shot. Sipping one, barely holding the other to his mouth, his nose. Breathing the heavy aroma. And all the while the partita a trapped wasp inside his headset.

"Just goin to the crapper," Mars informs anyone who wants to know and lurches up the aisle. We haven't spoken to each other for an hour. I think both of us are appalled at the amount of time we have to spend together on the Greyhound. There are wars that have started and finished in shorter periods. But this is the prairie, where the hands of clocks turn at a barometrical pace. This is the prairie under its last snow, the colour of my trouser pocket.

Mars lives on the prairie because he teaches prairie children prairie literature. Mars hates the prairie almost as much as he hates prairie literature. And Mars is a man who finds comfort in hatred, its desperate sugars. Hatred burns in his eyes with a comic sugary light as he describes arts administrators, college faculties, prairie academies. Because of his hatred of local writing, Mars has created a computer literary magazine for others on the internet. He calls it *Chaff*. Or @ Mars *Chaff*,. to subscribers.

Mars urges fellow thinkers to contribute to *Chaff* the worst examples of fiction and verse published in literary magazines. The only criteria for inclusion are technical ineptitude and gross unoriginality. Ideally, submissions possess both qualifications. *Chaff* gives annual prizes, awarding the three most outstanding entries a laurel of stinkweed, a fanfare of anal trumpeting. In his basement, surrounded by plundered theology and science fiction, Mars Barlow accumulates an electronic anthology of dross. Anyone on line to the internet can contribute. Certain cruel souls have been known to offer poetry written by Mars himself. It has always been graciously included. This work is gleefully subversive. It is, he says, when he can summon the energy for the task, important work. In his basement, Mars Barlow, unencumbered by literary honours and unembarrassed by sectarian allegiances, is creating a reputation for himself. But Mars Barlow is not a popular man.

We stop at a small town. One of the yards is filled with rowan trees. A shivering flock of bohemian waxwings is stripping the fruit. The berries have hung there for six months, a vineyard in which the waxwings come to brawl. Mars gets back on with a bag of doughnuts, a Big Gulp and a newspaper. Predictably he is incensed.

"Man, it's Caligulan. We live in Caligulan times."

"Is that the name of the paper?"

"Funny guy."

"Is it the fish?"

"Fuck the fish. It's the fox. The Fox network. Aw, those cheeseheads. They only wanna show this poor American sucker's execution. Like live. Like live on prime time. Holy ejaculating Jesus."

He waves a page in front of me and stokes up on a dough-

nut. The town outside is so quiet I can hear a vee of geese over-
head, a clumsy brass ensemble, going straight north. Mars
coughs sugar, takes a draught out of the Gulp, then a slug from
a flask and gargles Irish.

"See what they wanna do is get us to pay, to pay for the priv-
ilege of watching some poor piece of white trash strapped on a
gurney and some doctor slipping him a lethal mickey and us
watching some more for the last twitch. Maybe we even get to
see when he shits his pants. Whoopee. Who's got the remote?"

I nod my encouragement. Mars is on a roll.

"Seems the star of the proceedings is some twenty year old
rapist-murderer. Jeezus, don't you just know the sort? Too
scared to feel anything, I mean anything, 'less there's Schlitz for
breakfast or china white in the grits. Sad little jerk. Just a shake
'n' bake. Should have been riding with Glanton in Blood
Meridian, not pumping gas and chasing ass around Muskogee
or whatever God-forsaken stretch of tornado country he was
wagging his jism at."

"So he should have got life?"

"Chrissakes no. I'd pull the lever myself. Got an eighteen year
old daughter, friend, so don't look to me for mercy. What I'm
asking is why does it have to be a page in the TV guide? What's
wrong with a little private ceremony no-one ever gets to hear
about?"

Mars flourishes the flask and I roll a corrosive globule of the
nectar around my teeth. It seems the giant has subsided. His
eyes are closed. Gouldian notes pass like photons in his head.
This reverie I imagine could be based as easily on Newman's
prose as the media coma which he believes has overwhelmed us.
The *X Files* is cracked open on his chest. I borrow the bottle.

We pass an alkaline slough surrounded by birches. A red hawk
lifts off from a fencepost. The lakes are numberless now and
unnamed, a powder of snow on a metre of frozen ice, the beaver
dams like broken wickiups. Last week in the wind chill it was

fifty-five below, but the teenage girls would still show their pale navels to the world, a denim jacket over a short vest, the shampoo rinse stiffening in their hair. Here is a farm where the dogwood has grown through the floor of a limousine. An old man holding a go-cup observes our cataracts of spray. For a moment the satellite bowl in his yard resembles a threshing wheel.

There is an art to riding buses. Time passes differently, despite the video monitors suspended over the seats, the toilet cubicle at the rear, the accoutrements of aeroplanes. People who ride buses now are much the same as the people who always rode buses. They are the people you don't find on aeroplanes. Native women, mottled with bruises, withdrawn. Old men in stained trousers, subversively ugly. These people know about time and how it passes. They know about bus station restaurants, the chipped tankards of coffee, the grilled cheese adorned with watery eyes of dill. They smoke and gaze at the formica. They never glance at the clock or listen to the departure announcements. They know exactly what time it is, and their destinations were fixed a long while ago.

I remember the last journey I made on a bus. The last journey before this journey. I left the house during a three day blizzard. There was an armoury of icicles under the eaves. I moshed through a bulwark of snow at the front door. There was no time to clear the driveway or the sidewalk, but the mailman would wear mukluks anyway.

I was trying to reach the town of Wales. Perhaps it was not a town anymore, but there it was on the map. Not far now, the map said, but the map lied. No bus went within one hundred miles of Wales. No train went within one hundred and twenty. When I telephoned the nearest post office they asked if I knew anyone in Wales. They could pick you up. But I knew no-one in Wales. I knew no-one in all that Dakotan snow. There is nothing, said the girl at the Grey Goose terminal. There is nothing there at all. I pointed to the map but she said no there is nothing. Do you know anyone who could take you there? But I knew no-one in Wales, and anyway, the girl said, perhaps it isn't there anymore. Places disappear you know. That's why there are no buses.

Yet I could see Wales. Each house with a flag and a dish and the snow filling the television screens. A white prairie and a white sky and no frontier between them. I could see the sign, the snow covering it like convolvulus. I could feel my hand stinging when I brushed the snow away. That night as I travelled on the journey before this journey, the Academy Awards were being transmitted live. All around the world the same audience was tuning into the Oscars. I looked out of the window and the sky was white and the prairie was white and the screen above my head was filled with interference, a glimmering of twilight where the whiteness lived. A Welsh film was being nominated for an Academy Award and a fragment of it flew around the world. I had queued in Wales to see *Silence of the Lambs*. The sky was white, the air excited with spore. The local hero played a doctor who tore out people's tongues. When we arrived back outside on the pavement after the film the sky was a negative of itself. When I looked at the people with my cinema eyes they were all negatives. I waited on the pavement for the car and was afraid for myself. There is no way out of this, I thought. There is no escape from this. The dishes on the prairie sucked the signals down, each a dark stamen, a flower filled with snow.

Outside, the blizzard was all around us but the bus drove on, stopping for no weather, merciless. The snow became so thick it hid the lights of the houses. Hannibal Lecter lived in a cage in Wales but nothing could hold him. The local hero spoke for the Welsh film at the Academy Awards but it did not win an Oscar. Hannibal Lecter escaped to wander anywhere in the world. The mass murderer found a way out as we always knew he would. We knew it like the passengers knew the time, gazing at their grilled cheese, not listening to announcements. The sky was white and the prairie was white and in every home in Wales the Academy Awards were being broadcast, and there was the fragment of the Welsh film, applauded and vanishing, and there was the local hero, applauded and vanishing, and there was Dr Hannibal Lecter applauding, the mass murderer out of his cage, moving freely anywhere in the world, on the bus that travelled through the blizzard, in the town of Wales that was not a town, travelling anywhere he chose.

The bus had become bacterially warm. It stopped at a Chicken Delight. People wanted wings. In the queue at the takeaway section of the restaurant they regarded the Academy Awards ceremony. Hungry, too scared to move, I watched through the glass. The award winners cried and thanked their mothers for always believing in them. What a marvellous world it is, they said. But this used to be a different world. I could remember it. I was haunted by it like the memory of another family, another identity. It was what I was before I became what I am now. It was where I was before I arrived at where I am now. It was a different world. Then the queue at Chicken Delight vanished. People had their wings. They settled back around me, hid under coats, sipped from styrofoam. A baby whimpered at the back of the bus. I had not known there was a baby on board. And we followed the white lines of the blizzard towards another small town.

"But it's such a perfect symbol for the whole schizo fucking country."

"Why?"

"Disbanding a regiment. No other country in the west has done it. Or would ever do it for those reasons. 'Cept France. And that was only when half the fucking Foreign Legion went stir crazy. But to destroy the paratroopers because of bad behaviour? It's bizarre. Do bears shit in the woods?"

"They were torturing people."

"Yeah, okay. The peacekeeping mission was a mistake. Like I say, paras and peacekeeping are oxymoronic. Or whatever. But we've trained the bastards to be like that. We wanted an army. They were the cutting edge."

"Well who's to blame?"

"This country, man. What else? Those boys are paratroopers and we're asking them to play patacake. What are they supposed to do? Drop behind enemy lines and give out Margaret Atwood novels?"

The doughnuts are gone. Mars is all sugared up. For a man whose breath is sometimes so short he cannot get a tune out of his inhaler, this is some performance. But carbon is his amphetamine. His beard, the buff of waxwings, marbled grey, shows a ring of crystal. Mars has also uttered the A word, an inevitable detonator.

"Aw man, this country. I was born on an island. And where I was born the pine trees went right down to the ocean. Big suckers, dripping moss. You could walk into that pine gloom and smell the trees and the ocean together. Fantastic. Like your own sweat. But can I afford to live there? It's condos and marinas for software writers and gameshow hosts. I see those reserved parking spaces and those no trespassing signs, and I think, man, I could be a serial killer. I could. I could waste those fuckers like they're wasting my island."

"Get the paras in there."

"Naw man, It's too late. This is Atwood country now. Give it twenty years and she'll have her face on the stamps and the coins. Look at me. White, British descent, male, forty-five. Do you know what that means in this country? It means end of the line. Like it's over for me, man. What's to show? Teaching kids that don't wanna be taught. Run-ins with the department. A drawer full of ten year old poetry nobody will publish because there's no grain elevators in it. No pension. Give it twenty years, no Chrissakes, ten, and I'll be sweeping up the tailings in a uranium mine. Uranium City, man. Husky shit. It's the last stop."

"You've published a lot."

"But I don't follow the play. In the arts world this country's like the Soviet Union. Our arts adminnows are just cultural apparatchiks. Meaningless meetings. Pride, mediocrity and expenses. So conform, conform. Say the right thing. An autocracy of the second rate. Third rate. Critical theory written by people who don't like literature. Gotta be PC. But people like me won't play that game. Write a novel about fist fucking and you hit the talk shows, the big grants. Tell your students to read Kafka or Lawrence and you get slapped down for inappropriate teaching methods. You know, I've seen eighteen year olds cry, cry man, because they couldn't understand King Lear. They're not challenged, man. Always thought the jukebox was gonna give them Aerosmith. So when Stravinsky comes on, like wow, there's something wrong. Jeez man. We're clearcutting the imagination. Have an army but make sure it smells nice. Yeah, there were psychos in that regiment. But wouldn't you rather have them in the barracks jerking each other off than following your wife round downtown Medicine Hat? Pretend there's equality. Call Indians First People but don't mention who's sniffing gasoline. You know what the Cree bands are doing up round Meadow Lake? Lobbying for a nuclear waste dump. *For* it, man. On their land. That so called immemorial land. And why? Jobs. Money. I'd take a city job with a contract. Mailman, garbage collector with all the retirement trimmings. You're laughing but I'd do it. My classes want to do resumés, not essays on Emily Dickinson. Least I'd have some energy left. Like for my writing."

Writing is a sore point for Mars Barlow. He is a poet who isn't poetifying. He tells me that last year's output was exactly one haiku. This year he ceremonially burned it. Mars calls his writer's block the permafrost. Unbreachable for most of the time, it yet once allowed a brief dappling of the tundra. These days the iron is in the soil the twelve months round. There are no grain elevators in the Mars Barlow universe. No mom, no pop, no family farm. So no writing that Mars thinks anyone wants. In a way he is proud of his retention. For Mars, paratroopers jump. That is what they do. Band Aid in a camouflage jacket is no part of the game.

I like to think I understand Greyhound time. I don't understand it but I like to think I might. Now there is darkness and I have not spoken for some hours. I try to remember the last thing I saw. That farmer beside his ruined farm, the fields gone to quackgrass? But perhaps that was the last journey, the journey before this. I try to remember the other passengers but am not sure now where they belong. The bruised native woman. The old man in stained trousers. Maybe they were the same journey as the journey of the thousand frozen sloughs. That journey was the journey of the dune system of drifts, their brows fuming. Another journey was a pale child who wrote in a spiral-topped notebook. Outside the Chicken Delight she had stood in the snow and taken out a cigarette. She couldn't light it so she went inside with her notebook. I had watched her through the glass. Slight; a thin jacket covered in X's and O's. She lit the cigarette and then ignored it, ordered nothing, clutched her book. About fourteen, I thought, but the cigarette disconcerted. Yet she had smoked at every stop. Once she had asked me the time which gave her away. A new traveller. Experienced travellers always feel the time. She came back on with a pattern of snowflakes disappearing from her shoulders, revealing again the X's and O's. She curled up opposite, knees under her chin, and began writing. When I glanced across I saw she had written a heading and underlined it.

She was a journey. She was the journey before this journey. I think it was on her journey that I saw the deepest snow I had seen for years. The sky was white and the prairie was white. But the blizzard had stilled itself and we had come to a small town. There was snow in the trees, on the ground, on the houses in the trees, the tiny houses hidden amongst the white skeletons of the trees. There were two abandoned petrol pumps, each topped with a mitre of snow. Behind them was a sign for the town covered by a smoking drift. I wanted to brush the snow away and could feel it stinging my hand. But the bus did not stop in the small town and all I remember is that there were no footsteps there. The snow told a secret. There were no footsteps from the houses through the snow and no footsteps returning to the houses. The snow was perfect. Perhaps to touch it would have been a misdemeanour in that town. No-one had come out of the houses and no-one had gone in. The flags hung flat in the yards. Snow rags. The dishes pointed at the sky, delicate snouts scenting. No-one came back because no-one had left. Or no-one had left because no-one had come back. The girl was writing in her spiral-topped notebook. But she was another journey. She was the last journey before this journey.

On this journey the lamps are out, the travellers sunk in the inscrutable. A baby whimpers at the back of the bus. I didn't know there was a baby on board. Mars is sprawled over the reclining seat, in his chest a songbird's snore. Outside is the night's prairie, starless it would seem, but overhead Polaris must be signalling, and the ember of Aldebaran. Half way up my window is the night's companion, the moon, waxed to the full, a beaten Bushmills gold. Around it are two aureoles of paler light, omegas of dust. In his cubicle the driver exercises his neck muscles, then sits back from the phosphorescent controls. He is almost invisible, a dark man-shape cut from the air, a ghost who guides the ghost of a wheel. And so we ride.

The Mystery Trip

1

There is no acknowledged photograph of Jack the Ripper. No-one knows what the murderer looked like. No-one that is but the landlord of The Alma. Above my head a poster announces that this is Ripper Country. A hunched figure in a cape stands in the shadows of a gaslit street. His attention is taken by a pale girl on the cobbles. Another poster extends an invitation to 'Join the Ripper Trail' and visit the sites of his or her crimes. I like the 'her'. Violence and terror must also be divided equally. Leaflet dispensers give details of authentic Whitechapel and Spitalfields, the streets and courtyards that the killer would recognise if alive today.

What the Ripper, prince or seaman, prostitute or surgeon, might also find familiar are these pinstripes who hang their mohairs and crombies on The Alma's pegs, order platters of English food, and who are soon joined by their navy-blue partners, dark-stockinged, big-shouldered, low calorie. What's discussed is this morning's E-mail, tomorrow's selling price. Today is pretty well dead, hence the relays of Youngs that go with the Yorkshires, the show of hands for custard.

"Christ knows," answer the women squashed together opposite at the round pub table, when I ask where the besuited ones work. "It's not bleedin' Spitalfields Market, though that's gone all organic carrot juice and flamin' tapas bars. Perhaps they've built a skyscraper in Grey Eagle Street."

Wherever it is, it's big. The business class continues streaming into The Alma out of a wet Thursday afternoon, and soon the red-cushioned lounge behind us, useful these days only as a restaurant, is packed. These people must be regulars, they order without even looking at the blackboard. Steak and kidney, I see them mime, sausage and mash, real pub grub. A party squeezes past demanding liver and bacon with their tray of bitter. Jack would have approved.

2

An hour later I appear from the rain, my woollen overcoat steaming, smelling of its wet dog smell, my eyebrows I notice in the glass, two threads of pearls. On the black and white stone of the entrance one hundred footprints shine before they fade, and a box of root-ginger waits to be carried in or out.

A boy with a handkerchief tied over his head hurries by. Across his shoulder is the carcass of a pig, and as he passes I can see straight into the iridescent cavern between its haunches as far as the blackness of the abdomen. If I look closer, I think, I will be able to stare through its whole body like a telescope, down through the shop and into the warehouse, from the warehouse into the cold-store, where the meat-packers in their aprons await its arrival. The pig's eyes are two dull cinders behind the boy's head. Its splintered hooves embrace him like a midnight drunk.

That's me, I want to say, as the youth runs past, that's what we used to do when there was a sty in the garden and a mottled pink Glamorgan sow with her huge ears brushing the dirt, and the pig-killing man swigging from the flagon of Rhymney ale, the one with the fat red-coated huntsman riding a firkin on the label, and all the laughter as everyone came into the garden, a party atmosphere almost, and after the fuss and the squealing they would pretend to place the youngest child inside the split belly, with all the delicacies and inedibles taken away in buckets, and they would pick me up and make-believe I was coming out of the sow, that they were rescuing me or that somehow I was being born, because that's what they had always done with the youngest child, even though I would cry and the women push the stopper with its marble back into the bottle and say that's enough then, you'll spoil his best clothes.

Someone has moved the golden knuckles of the ginger. But there is so much else to entertain, here at the entrance. Yams and the prickly sceptres of artichokes, panniers of chillis like shotgun cartridges, strings of garlic, green tomatoes, creamy tubers. But for most of this food we have no words. Another civilisation is displayed here, puzzling and aromatic. To touch might be to purchase so I do not touch, merely wander this first aisle, wondering at the food that is not food, a curious harvest. Down the galleries of the store I take my quiet speculation, searching without vocabulary for the more easily familiar.

I read the ingredients of a carboy of chutney. There are demi-johns of the sweet and the piercing racked against the wall. Jeroboams of lime pickle, methuselas of chundah paste stand above me on the shelves. Here might be the source of every dirt curry I ever ate, the 11pm dose of napalm paid for before I sat down with the southern-comforted wing-forwards and early disco casualties. Now gherkins in their bottles loom like sea-creatures, hundredweights of rice build a head-high barricade.

"Help you?" asks a girl with a caste mark on her brow, but I am off up another aisle, gone again, gone back years to the chemistry laboratory and its snivelling retorts, the nuggets of sodium angry as wasps as they fizzed about my experiment's crucible of water.

3

I don't suppose I thought about murder – or murderers – that much until I went to England. True, once my parents had driven me as a child to the notorious Pear Tree Cottage in the Vale of Glamorgan where, it was alleged, a husband had beaten his wife to death. We parked outside the now empty house and stared at its whitewashed walls, thatched roof, garden of currant bushes and waving lawn. I imagine we wanted to feel a joint horror, but the sunlight was too bright for anything more than almost instantaneously satisfied curiosity. We travelled home in silence. The only other Welsh murders occurred in Cardiff Docks and involved foreigners, and on the Gurnos Estate in Merthyr where every street was named after a flower or shrub. Usually the killings happened on a Friday night and involved riot, attempted arson and binge drinking. The local paper on Mondays invariably carried details of a "slaying in Acacia Close" or "callous assault" on Honeysuckle Avenue. It was an expected fixture, like the listing of rugby injuries or details of child abuse in local authority homes.

But real murders, the gruesome consummation of a relationship, the sociopathic or sadistic, rather than the sad conclusions to domestic or tribal violence at home, took place in England. And especially an area I knew vaguely as 'the North'. The North? I started to visit there regularly in the late 1970s, and quickly formed impressions which have not been completely obliterated by later discoveries.

The North was Arndale Centres and opencast mining. It was the vodka lake at Warrington and the smell of chicken tikka over a rainy street. The North was a visit to Hadrian's Wall in the snow and a long cold gaze into the Northumbrian desert, where the cold prickled my skin like goosegrass and icicles on the stones spurted like hypodermics tested before insertion. It was a poetry reading in Durham where I had stayed with a librarian whose home I thought was a Johnson-waxed mausoleum. Until that is, I walked into his bedroom when he was at work to discover bluetacked to the wardrobe that poster of Madonna with her skirt up in the air and her athletic bottom pursed in a wry smile. And the North was that other librarian, exiled in a dockland city, adding weekly to his cheerful archive of pornography.

I used to drive into the North through the tangle of motorways that all have the 6 in them: M6, M62, M63, M66, M600, an intimidating blue sheaf of routes between Cheshire and Leeds. I found myself on the M603 once, convinced that I would finish up in Scotland. My shirt was soaking, I had to continually wipe the steering wheel as the Roadtrains overtook in explosions of spray and airport buses and office-perk Cavaliers monopolised the fast lane. It gets like that sometimes, wanting, and wanting badly, not to be driving.

Especially not on motorways. They have their own offensive protocols. As when after an hour in a traffic jam you see those signs. Sorry for any delay. And then a little later, the Cones Hotline phone number. I rang it once when I arrived home. For the hell of it. Answer-phone of course. But why is it there? They must be selling them. England, motorway England, is coneland. But in a way cones have their charm. I have almost grown to feel comfortable with them, to accommodate them, as you might a disease. But I'm no motorway person. I used to think Adverse Camber was a service-station. (Most probably somewhere in rural Oxfordshire.) When I drive my hands leak and the vehicle begins to take control. I hit ninety and the car shakes like a dishwasher. One hundred, and I can hear the engine complain, that low, desperate chord the orchestration of the pistons cannot quite obscure. And always I think, Christ, is everybody like this? It's sheer insanity.

But then somehow, ten minutes later, the M603 was behind me and I found myself coming down a slope into Bradford, through darkened Odsall, passing the stadium that once held crowds of over one hundred thousand for rugby league games, rolling down that hill and braking slowly to a halt, opening the window and breathing it in. Chicken tikka. Or a combination of all the spices, better than night-scented stock or a sudden waft of perfume that brushes the skin like chiffon. It smelled like somewhere. Somewhere at last after the insane roads with their shredded tyres and contraflows. It was real, as they say up there. Which means, simply, great. I stepped out of the car and looked at the lights.

4

The lab was always locked but it was easy to get in through the side-door of the store-room. At break the masters were down-stairs smoking their pipes, sharing pieces of *The Times* and *Western Mail*. All the boys were out on the field shouting something urgent and indistinct.

I dared not put on the light, and without it the laboratory was a turbid green. The air smelled like an aquarium in which the water needed changing. But there was quiet. I could hear a gas-tap hissing, the one that wouldn't quite turn off. High on a shelf a filtration experiment made a tiny kissing sound. A bell-jar of sulphur, suddenly at eye level, shocked like a sunflower. This was a terrifying place but I had entered it of my own will. A hydrochloric irritation rankled in my nose, each step I made stretched huge and echoing. At the far end of the room was a small shrine. This was where the vitriol was kept, the oily brown of sulphuric acid, the attractive gin-and-tonic whiteness of nitric. I stretched to touch the neck of the first vial. It was of coarsely-dimpled glass, rough as a cat's tongue.

"Dissolve a rhinoceros this would," Mr Puw would say proudly, gesturing to his cabinet. "Or a boy."

I liked Mr Puw. We called him, with typical originality, Phew. Despite his name, he must have been the first person I immediately identified as English. His laboratory was therefore England, to which I was summoned twice a week, an intimidated immigrant. As a chemistry teacher he could bring out the mysterious, the alchemic side of the subject. He saw his classes, I think, as the apprentices to his sorcerer. Even a basic experiment, such as that to prove that oxygen encouraged combustion, could become, under his tutelage, a frankly creepy ritual. He would turn down the lights so that in the underwater gloom of the lab, the sudden budding and blossoming of flame from the heated salts appeared more dramatic.

Every lesson with Phew resembled Halloween. For an hour

and a half each week he was our priest in a curious celebratory ritual. He talked of poisons, showing us the white powder of arsenic and an ordinary brown bottle labelled 'cyanide'. Once he held up a single crystal with the antique silver tweezers he carried in his breast pocket and said that placed strategically, in the canteen gravy perhaps, it would send every boy and master into frothing agony. We were mesmerised. Explosions were also his specialty. He shattered glass and created wonderful stinks with detonations of various gases.

Outside the lab Phew was invisible. Five foot six and grey as candlewax, he wore a waistcoat, acid-mottled patent-leather shoes and a seriously-hunted expression. His wit, dry and blue as a bunsen-flame, vanished in daylight. He wasn't dangerous anymore. For him, the kryptonite worked only on his own territory.

5

If England, no matter where it is located, is another country, then rural England is more than that. It is an inheritance and a state of mind, exquisitely foreign. Above all, it is a series of place names that for me always included Stow-on-the-Wold and Bourton-on-the-Water.

These were the destinations that the mystery trips from my village and its surrounds headed for every summer. Mystery trips always went to Stow. It was traditional. You would see the pensioners and a few doubtful younger couples queueing for the coach at eight in the morning. Sometimes, it was claimed, even the driver didn't know the route till the very last minute. Fools, I thought, spending my time sticking like goose-grass to home. There they were in headscarves and plastic macs, off to their soup-of-the-day in Stow-on-the Wold, still pretending they didn't have an inkling where they were going. It was Stow, Stow, bloody Stow I wanted to shout down the aisle of unadjustable seats, a short coachtrip away, utterly predictable, immeasurably strange. How desperate do you have to get, I wondered. And then, one day, I went there too.

It was a friend's fault. He had been listening to Laurie Lee's *As I Walked Out One Midsummer Morning* broadcast daily on BBC radio, and was entranced. One evening he visited my home and claimed what a pity it was that camcorders had not been invented earlier. Then Laurie Lee, instead of writing about that woman in Spain who gave him eggs and purple wine, or those mysterious girls in the port who walked about with their hair shining like oily cables, could have filmed them for posterity. Or, he could have written his book and made a documentary, for instant effect.

I brewed a pot of the strongest coffee I had ever made and sat him down at the kitchen table. What if the wine hadn't really been purple, I asked. What if there was no wine at all?

Yeah, yeah, literary licence, he understood that. But think about Bruce Chatwin doing the songlines. And that place, Oz or Uz. And Eric Newby in the Kush. Think about it. My friend, caffeine-jagged, was still half-serious. So I thought about it. In fact I thought about it for several days. And then, without the camcorder, I went to Stow-on-the-Wold.

Or rather, I went to Adlestrop. Map-browsing one evening amongst the corners of mystery-trip England, I saw the village name in tiny letters on a green road to Warwickshire. Poet Edward Thomas had written about Adlestrop one year before his death in France in 1917. His train had halted there for a minute or two, an express train (it looked impossible now from the map) and he had described what he saw and heard. Like others, I had been disturbed by the poem, so much so that when I was nineteen I laboriously typed it into a collection of my favourite verse.

Silence, a hot day in June, flowers, birdsong. And out of it Thomas had made me feel something for which there is no vocabulary. It was not the war, or his own coming death which in other poems he seemed to anticipate. The power of the writing was that it suggested the shadow in the cells of all living things, the quiet grief that is carried in the daylight like pollen, a film of rain on a blade of grass. But nothing as obvious as that. Nothing so clumsy. Adlestrop was a place that could only exist in the mind, but there it was, a mystery trip away, made famous, if that is the word, by the man who had spent one minute of his life there, and been surprised to do so.

The first thing I noticed about Adlestrop was that it is a Neighbourhood Watch area. For consumers, paranoia is a form of Asian flu. It is a virus that either kills the host or burns itself out. The inhabitants of Adlestrop had contracted it.

My second impression was really my last. Adlestrop had been perfected. There was no tavern touting for business, no cream teas in Edward Thomas tearooms, no people, no cars. At every silent cottage a hollyhock stood sentinel. Poppies filled the banks, and there, in a wooden bus shelter, was the old Adlestrop sign from the railway station, brown and cream in that unmistakable railway font that vanished with the creation of British Rail. Edward Thomas had seen that sign. His poem was there also, on a discreet plaque. A girl passed by on a horse and spoke to me. Then there was silence and behind that the mythic sounds of rural England: a blacksmith's hammer, and a faint, insectivorous drone as if somewhere something electrical had been left on. A sign said 'To our church', and I pondered its exclusivity, sitting beneath a yew that screened the stacked rubble of broken inscriptions and angels' wings. Adlestrop had been perfected and here I was throwing my shadow over it, peering up at the window panes in the ruddy flints of the rectory, where Jane Austen had once paused with her papers.

We are all perhaps entitled to a minute in Adlestrop. Wherever it is. But there is nothing more for us there. And for many, one minute would be too long. Before leaving I tried the church door, and exclusive or not, it opened. Light from the stained glass, the colour of wine-must, cut flowers and the usual ecclesiastical damp characterise St. Mary Magdalene. Few parishes are better documented. Birth and death notices in Adlestrop for the last four hundred and fifty years are deposited there, along with 'an act for the better preventing of clandestine marriages'. Leaving my donation for the preservation of this immaculate, exhausted place, I set out for Stow.

6

The problem is wind. The invisible harvest. The stuff that blows where it will. James Kitchener Davies understood it all. As windmills have begun to sprout on hillsides, so the environmental movement has found itself engaged in civil war.

The first windfarm I visited in England was near Broughton-in-Furness. Searching for the blades of the turbines, I discovered them stilled in a wind-drouth, limp above the mounds of greened-over quarry tailings that dominate the area, the chalky tors of spoil. Looking at those enormous engines I thought them beautiful and useless.

Perhaps one day they will attract names such as ancient stone circles possess: Nine Maidens; The Brothers; Seven Virgins. Yet it was difficult to see why people hated them so deeply. A few months previously I had published a short article on the merits of wind farms. The response was hate-mail, obscene answerphone messages, and the personal appearance of someone at my office who is the only person I have met to whom the description 'apoplectic' was an understatement.

Despite the farcical nature of such reactions, I prefer to imagine what Shelley would have said about wind-farms. Or more aptly Coleridge, wet and tired, with one of the more delirious passages of 'Christabel' on his lips as he ascended a rise beyond Broughton, nearing the end of a thirty mile fell expedition, suddenly encountering the white semaphore of the windmills on the already pock-marked hill. But if we are dealing with apoplexy here, we must think of Wordsworth. After, say 1810, he had become a kind of Bernard Ingham of blank verse, in other words a suitable patron of Countryside Guardian, the most virulent of the anti-turbine lobby, and a bizarre alliance of drop-outs, urban refugees and rural Tories. Wordsworth would have killed wind-farming as he was slowly killing the sonnet. By boring people to death with it. But that's another story.

And then, after gazing at it for what seemed a slow, dreamy quarter-hour, I saw one of the Broughton turbines move. First a blade shuddered a few inches, and slowly made one rotation, like a child in a park at evening, trying one last somersault. And then they were all going, as if the wind had awoken them and there were urgent things to do. Instead of useless, they had become beautiful again. And exhilaratingly practical.

About this time I received a letter from the literary burghers of Brontëland. They were requesting money to oppose plans to build wind turbines on the moors above Heptonstall. It was an area with which I had recently become familiar, having walked it for hours, frozen-footed, face and hands turned to brass, to reach the new wind power station near Halifax. I stood directly under one of the immense pale stems. The generator and gear box sounded no louder than a tumble-drier. The windmill above me consisted of three white scythes endlessly dividing the air. Its metal was smooth as beech bark, dirty-white as classical statuary. What was there to hate?

The moorland seemed at that time completely inhospitable. Yet it was only a predictable acid outcrop of dark rushes and tarns. Ice glimmered on the moss like salt from an evaporated sea-pool. A barn at the side of the track, sullen as a menhir, was beginning, molecule by molecule, to disappear into the mist, until at last there was nothing left but my memory of it, already imperfect. Windmills would be an intrusion, but so in a way is everything else there but whinberries, the pools whose banks are the colour of dried-out tea bags, and the patient, carnivorous sundew of the hollows.

The Heptonstall letter burned in my case as I took a slip road on to the M6 at Penrith and found myself in the maw of early rush-hour traffic. The guardians of Brontë Country are the enemies of literature. They imprison the reputations of writers in museums of cliché and self-serving worthiness. They subdue, they sanitize, constantly evoking the ghosts of those who would despise them. The guardians are blind because they can see only what they desire instead of what is actually there. What they wish to protect is their own thoughtscape. Their moorlands are dead – spectral images of places that never were. The guardians ask us for money so that we might pay to glimpse their own atrophied imaginations. Their hologram England is an exclusive resort, patrolled forever by their own good taste.

These unbidden and unworthy thoughts knotted round each other as I accelerated south. I was superior because I had remembered my personal Brontë connection. Venturing into Yorkshire for the first time, I discovered that my wife's grand-mother and uncle lived in rambling quarters where once Anne Brontë had been a schoolteacher. On a steep hill overlooking Halifax, Law Hill House appeared to have changed very little in the one hundred and fifty year interval. Anne's pallid legend trembled in the candle flames lit at dusk. It flitted through the stables and urinous outbuildings. The house groaned, wearied with being. All it could accommodate now was death. On its roof, the flat sandstone slabs that the Pennine winds disturbed and threatened to pitch into the road, looked as if they belonged in a graveyard. A pump dripped a long stalactite of moss. Here was nineteenth century Yorkshire without a pressure group in sight. But Law Hill House was no hologram. I could smell it.

8

I had paused above Bradford, breathing its rich air, looking down at thousands of lights. Thinking about only one of them.

The fuzzy association between England, the North and murder, persisted. Murderers become famous in England. Creepily famous yet rockstar famous. Headlines, crowds, and all that aridity and anguish when the career ends. I almost shiver when I think about it. Take today. A man in Hartlepool must be protected from a crowd as he walks from a police-van to a magistrate's court. They say he killed a child and kept her body in a drawer until the police arrived. As he knew they would. On an ugly estate at Seahouses facing the grey staves of the ocean, he held the child's hand and walked her to his home.

The connection between England and murder continued with Peter Sutcliffe from Bradford. He had not been apprehended when I began to visit Yorkshire and discover the aromatic corners of Brontë Country. The killings he was perpetrating were part of most conversations I had during those years, whether in friends' homes, shops or pubs. We were disgusted but also excited. Life, or the losing of it by an unfortunate few, had become more interesting. Most people I spoke to knew someone who knew someone who had been followed home, accosted, looked at strangely or momentarily intimidated by someone who might have been the murderer. Their stories fascinated. They told the police about the incidents and the details were laboriously written on to index cards, to join the thousands of files that already existed. A relative joined a building society staff party and returned across a frosted parkland where a week later, another body was discovered. Male relations and friends were interviewed at their homes, like all the other men in the area.

And I toured, intermittently and questioningly, suspicious of my own motives, the scenes of the crimes. They were usually neglected inner-city districts of sooty brown-brick terraces, corner groceries and abandoned mill buildings. Bankrupt company names dominated the skyline, dobermans slouched behind razor-wire and broken glass. The future for these streets included crack-dealing, an explosion of music, canal-side marinas. Perhaps in a few years there will be a tourist trail of the murder sites. Yet at the time they seemed terrifyingly hollow, a pit of introspection. One day I navigated the one-way system in Leeds and asked to be directed to Chapeltown Road. An Irishman said I shouldn't be wanting to go there. Despite the warning, he pointed a direction.

I found a street of mansions boarded up behind a twisted for-est of elder and buddleia, yellow pizza boxes jammed between the branches. Some of the houses, boasting ornate balconies and impressive corbels, had become private residential homes for the elderly. One was an abandoned nightclub, coloured electric bulbs crunched to sugar in the imposing entrance. It was what the television calls a red light area, patrolled in the evening by child prostitutes, dressed in deliberate waif-style by their pimps. At night older women with thoroughbred legs and paste jew-ellery eyes stood under the lamps. It was a district so exhausted by its history that when I walked its streets the present seemed an illusion. Everything was in abeyance. Yet I found myself feel-ing almost happy there. Almost lightheaded, almost free. It was a ghost town and it attracted desolate souls like Sutcliffe and other less certain, slightly more or less complex men who stared into a jar of Tetley's in a corner seat, summoning the courage to go home or act the trick.

9

"What are you doing here?" a voice had asked.

I burned my hand in the chem lab once. Without thinking I picked up a test-tube I had been heating over the hottest setting of the gas. A red powder had been reduced to a dark residue as big as a hazelnut, and the test-tube replaced in its rack. The heated glass left two small white crescents of scorched skin on my forefinger and thumb. But it was the shock that hurt.

Do people spin? I don't know, but if people spin, I spun round, my worst, my only nightmare coming true.

She stood three yards away behind a bench. Her white coat was open and her red hair combed out over her shoulders. I could see for the first time there were long golden hairs amongst the red. Perhaps when redheads turned grey they first went gold. This laboratory technician was about twenty-five years old.

"Getting my pencil-case."

The lie was the obvious one but at the time it felt like a work of genius. There was nothing else to say. I had not crept in to sniff the gas taps. I had no thought of stealing the samples of diamond and platinum in their display cases. Yet I could hardly explain I was there to experience the feeling of an empty church, or even better, a department store after closing time. This was a different country. I was there to look at it. And to breathe it. I wanted to breathe in another country. I was there only to be there. Perhaps I was mad. Perhaps I was getting pervy. Perhaps I should go to England soon, the real place. After all, I was fourteen and nine months old.

She came up to me then, in her white coat. There were freckles on the bridge of her nose. Her eyes were green. I had never seen green eyes before and have rarely done so since, but I was too scared to look at them more than once. Theoretically, this woman had no power over me. She was not a member of the teaching staff and possessed no teaching qualification. The boys called her the science nun, and it was her responsibility to ensure that the operations of the various laboratories were carried out as smoothly as possible. She ordered rubber tubing and potassium chlorate from a catalogue, reminded the masters where the boxes of filter-papers were stored, counted the pipettes.

Until that moment I had never heard her speak. But I had often imagined how her voice would sound, and where she went to in her raincoat, slipping quickly down the drive through the school shrubbery at four o'clock. In our classrooms she was more than rare. She was unique. Her hair with all its brilliant combs was a minor legend. Her legs, exactly the colour of ginger, the ginger of a spice warehouse, were famous without ever being discussed. In teaching terms she held no authority but now her influence was total. This was her estate, this foreign place, and I was the trespasser with nowhere left to go. Putting down a book she started towards me. Above our heads the filtration vessel sighed.

10

Emerging from behind a wicker bath of cashews, I decide it's time for a cup of tea. There is a place across the road, and taking nothing from the wholesaler's but its anthology of aromas, I enter a small café. At the far end of the street I can see policemen. There is the sound of a drum being monotonously pounded, a treble chorus of recorders and kazoos. A distant, megaphoned voice, tinny as someone else's Walkman, is also audible.

Because of the light I seek a window seat, but the proprietor forbids it. Instead he ushers me to a table at the back of the empty dining room and I order a simple house specialty of potatoes and steamed spinach. The tea is so hot and strong it sticks to my teeth.

The drumming is louder now, the piercing fifes maintaining a siren's alarm tone. Blue-shirted constables appear and then the first figures in a long procession, talking, laughing, low-key. The leading fifty marchers hold placards at half-mast. Cocking my head I read the black and red slogans. 'Smash the BNP'. 'Racists Out'. 'No Nazi Councillors'. Down Brick Lane and all the streets of Spitalfields and Whitechapel these small tributaries are flowing towards a confluence of angry people somewhere in the East End. I ask for more hot water.

They stream past like a crowd to the big match. Perhaps a

little slower. There are even the programme and souvenir sellers in the shape of badge-encrusted members of various red and green pressure groups, offering potted manifestos, unanswerable reasons for action or anger. Badges are interesting. There was a time when they became respectable. Everyone wore a slogan on their lapel. Caring was a craze, and like any fashion, it passed. (Any day apparently, it is due to return.) But nobody told the programme-sellers. There are two of them outside the café-window, exquisite archetypes.

One, the elder, has his bicycle padlocked to the nearest lamp-post. He wears a faded jogging-suit, trousers tucked into fell-walker's socks. His hair is a bursting thistlehead, a crown of pale lint. At least he smiles as he hands out his briefing-sheets. The game is up, he knows it, but what else is there to do? A few hours on a Saturday isn't too arduous, especially with a ready-made audience.

His companion is different. He is younger, determined, and hollers like an *Echo* boy. Whatever is spelled out on the photo-copied sheets, which for all the miracles of home desktopping, is densely typed on an exhausted ribbon, is gospel. It must be. He wrote it. Life, after all, is a series of statements. His leather jacket is one, the heavy army boots, twenty-two eyelets' worth, are another.

Normally there is a girl attached to this adherent of margin-alised causes. She also makes the statement of a scuffed leather jacket, plus wrinkly black leggings tucked into socks tucked into DMs. Her hair is usually a feather-duster of henna'd braids. Often she is drawn and white; always she lacks stridency. In pubs she orders pints she never finishes and is invariably the one who must pack up the paste-table of leaflets at the end of a session. But today she is missing and I miss her. It is her devotion that humanises the *Echo* boy, and without it he is a brass-mouthed evangelist, about as loveable as Elvis Costello. Somewhere along the way there will be a career in this for him. The smudged ink of politics is already in his palms, consensus with its drug-pusher's insistence, whispering in his sleep. But now it is the hard line that counts, and his exhortations this late morning in Brick Lane ring only of certainty, a pure voice from a back street.

11

The road is a graceful atrocity through the hills. Motorway services at Tebay and Killington are its monuments, disguised in dressed stone, boasting of old fashioned welcoming. Comfort is all. Passing the Road Chef, I watched the RAF buzz the eight lanes of the highway, two Phantoms so low I could see the badges on the pilots' helmets, the teats of the missiles. The Phantom wings were the colour of Buttermere, and then they were flashing over Scotch Corner, where people, surprised like me that morning at our own side's audacity or sheer bloody-mindedness, craned their necks.

Post-modernism's uncertainties extend further than art, and involve the nature of warfare. The battlefields these days are Ponty, greater LA, some trashed Tyneside estate. So much for defence cuts, the regimental extinctions, the Red Arrows reduced to a darts team. Above Killington, a sheepdog crawled on its belly through August's brown reeds; a vee of swans started to descend, and the children clutching their bags of Doritos did not even look up after that first time as the Phantoms reappeared going north above the south-bound carriageway. Instead they hunched down in their coachseats licking sodium-crusted fingers and slotted new batteries into the Walkman.

I was returning from the Sellafield Nuclear Waste Reprocessing Plant on the Cumbrian coast, and the newly opened Thermal Oxide Reprocessing Plant at the same site. I had arrived there after staying at nearby Drigg, home of the country's largest radioactive rubbish dump. This is not featured on tourist maps, but the village is worth visiting. It is one of those rare places in England that possesses an enormous secret of the present which it is trying to conceal, and not an all too eagerly displayed oiled and cadaverous past.

Drigg is also interesting because of its railway station. The station master's office and waiting rooms are now a craft shop, and unless an engine happens to roll by it is easy to surmise that the line is closed. From my observations, two types of train go through Drigg. The first is of the rickety Sprinter class. The other comprises larger diesels pulling flasks of radioactive debris. These are not publicly timetabled, but the stranger, enjoying the flower beds at the station and the grassy plain that leads to the beach, might be lucky enough to encounter one.

Close to, in the Visitors' Centre, Sellafield resembles a modern university. It might even pass for a library, with tasteful exhibitions, cafeteria and pleasing atrium. The Visitors' Centre is a marketing phenomenon. It attracts more tourists than Dove Cottage, Furness Abbey and nearby nature reserves such as North Walney. In fact, Sellafield is the clearest example that yet exists of a modern industry fattening itself by exploiting increased leisure time and interpretive tourism. This process happens only where a way of life once flourished and has declined. In these places, museums are constructed like sarcophagi over the spruced-up ruins and collected remnants of derelict mines or factories.

But Sellafield develops the theory that we have all become tourists in our own pasts. It will have us believe that we can view images and scenarios from our future in which nuclear power saves the world from fossil-fuel addiction. It is a strategy that should ensure knighthoods, or their feminine equivalents, for the public relations boffins behind it. Fed on Schwarzenegger videos of the near future, if not their subversive Ray Bradbury originals, we flock to the show.

Sellafield is the capital city of the new tourism, determinedly ambitious in the way it seeks to demonstrate that our future is dependent on success of the plant. It is also practical in a profoundly cynical sense. In the 1980s, nuclear power had come to mean pollution and high costs. Marketing remedies were required.

The result is that Cumbrians, especially those in the coastal towns, remote from the attentions and understanding of the rest of England, bewildered by the extinctions of ship-building, and increasingly thrown back upon caravan culture, the genteel banalities of literary tourism and the grinding deference of the holiday season, find themselves in a strange alliance. With various Cree bands of Saskatchewan and the Mescalero Apaches of south-western USA they are the only people in the world who wish to see nuclear waste imported into their homelands. The first peoples of North America believe their reservations have appropriate geology for bulk waste storage. They will be paid to take the poison. The Cumbrians, meanwhile, possess a state-of-the-art reprocessing plant that can deal with all nuclear detritus. It offers employment and a future.

Pointing out the similarities with the Cree, who anyway inhabit a frozen ocean of uranium, and understand every nuance of cultural exploitation, does not ensure progress for the concerned visitor here. Because what sells this waste-importing idea to Cumbrians is the image of the Visitors' Centre with its plant life and honeyed receptionists. What sells it is the comforting sensation that once inside this edifice of smoked glass and anaesthetising carpeting, the stranger is an object of consideration. Like Disneyland or plaza shopping, it is a clingfilm experience. Nothing can go wrong. I could even see myself on the television screens in the atrium when I looked close enough, awaiting the guide.

12

Summer had been surprisingly fierce, but the weather had broken the previous night. The hunter's moon over the Bristol Channel had disappeared behind clouds the colour of the glass of the Ty Nant mineral water bottle, that implausible, before-midnight cerulean. Now rain was an incense in the air and shrink-wrapped pensioners gazed at menu-cards. I sat in one of the licenced teashops watching French teenagers come to terms with Dorset Blue Vinny and glasses of Old Speckled Hen.

"Never seen it so quiet," complained the owner.

I had heard him say the same thing to every person served, but perhaps this was an individual form of prayer. If so, he was soon answered. A party of five Americans pushed in, shook the dirt off their hiking boots and commandeered the largest table in the room. After brief calculations they made the order.

"Pot of tea for five," announced a college-lecturer type in lurid shorts.

"And a scone," added a woman.

"With cream and jam?"

"No thanks."

"With butter?"

"No."

"Without butter?"

"Please."

"One scone without butter?"

"Yes."

"One scone without anything?"

"That's right."

The only symptom of hysteria the tearoom owner displayed was to suck in both lips so that his mouth became a red money-box slot. He transferred the order to the kitchen and sitting near its door I listened for the reaction.

"Absobloodylutely unbloodybelieveable. General Motors, Microsoft and EurobloodyDisney, and they come in here and order one dry scone."

A teenager in petticoat and Doctor Martens entered five minutes later with the offensive sweetmeat on a silver plate. I looked round to check if anyone else had noticed the sudden bristling of human electricity as torpor turned to tension, but there was only the chink of dentures against china, and coaches with their engines running parked all over Oxfordshire and Gloucestershire.

Travelling out of Stow along the top of the Cotswolds I saw a crop circle. In the valley to my left stretched wheat and barley fields, and in the immense sweep of the former were patterns that might have been a deliberate configuration. Nearby, an English Heritage sign pointed down a lane to a long barrow. Such signs are dispiriting evidence of the leisure world we inhabit. They are labels that deny the unexpected; well meaning attempts to interpret the inexplicable. It is difficult enough already not to conclude that the entire Cotswolds is a theme-park patrolled by the Country Landowners Association, without the exegesis such notices attempt.

Yet I was grateful to English Heritage and its mission to explain. Without the sign, emphatic and permanent, I could not have made my spooky connection. Long barrows, new age science will have it, were constructed on sites known to be frequented by UFOs. Alternatively, aliens would identify long barrows as sources of power, of prehistoric magic, and therefore investigate. That summer England was full of crop circles. A song by The Troggs, a rotund rock group from the sixties had been disinterred and re-recorded by some slick musical Thatcherites. It had almost apologetically loitered at the top of the charts for ten weeks, so weak was the competition.

The chief Trogg, writer of the song, had vowed to use his sudden enormous windfall not on a swimming pool filled with cocaine, but a definitive study of crop circles. Aztec connections and figures used in native Australian art would all be part of the investigation. I walked down a yellow lane between the fields. The hedges were thick with the flowers of July: scabious, St. John's wort, bindweed striped like a barber's pole. Coming to a gate I found the tide of wheat breaking a yard behind, and by standing on the top bar, could see the flattened patches in the crop.

Inside the entrance, a viper lay coiled on a piece of corrugated iron, tight as a fist, the diamonds on its back like dirty teeth. It was a curious field, large but hummocked, as if the wheat had been sown over a succession of small tumuli. I climbed on to the gatepost itself. Perhaps the circles would take the form of DNA's double helix or the mathematical symbol for infinity. Willing them to ooze significance I glimpsed only rain-smashed islands, a small archipelago of destruction as if cattle had been rolling about in the grain.

Turning around I discovered a man approaching in a wheelchair. Passing slowly, he murmured hello and laboured on up the rutted path that skirted the barrow. He was a young man, his barley-coloured crew-cut skull bouncing alarmingly as he rolled across the clods. After he disappeared, I could still hear the wheelchair ticking over the flints, like gorse seeds detonating. Surprisingly soon, I saw him again, now a quarter of a mile further up the lane that ran like a gutter through the hillside, a kestrel above him and grass in its last luxuriance higher than his wheels. He was waving.

Crop circles exist only for the bored or the desperate. They are rarer than corn cockles. They have never been. Balanced on the gatepost and taller now than the tallest hollyhock in Adlestrop, I scanned the barrow that existed two thousand years before England began to create itself. My family had picnicked some time earlier on a similar eminence, before a tribe of wasps had appeared from a crevice and pursued us back to the car. The swarm stayed together, long and black, the size of a welder's glove.

Now beyond this hill, not many miles away, a team of archaeologists were cutting into another barrow. The team comprised members of the Gloucestershire police, who had erected a small marquee over the pit they had dug. They were searching for human remains, linked to those of ten women found buried in the cellar of a house in the county town. The women had no names. Nobody had missed them. Yet eventually out of the ground had come what even our remembrancers had forgotten.

Slowly I walked towards the man in the wheelchair. He was still waving. The path was narrowed to the width of one person, and the grass, creamy-bearded, alive with shield-bugs and cinnabar moths. Fifty yards away I could see now that the man was not gesturing to me but struggling with the reins of a pair of binoculars. Hearing my step he turned around.

"Need any help?" I asked.

"You'll scare it off. Get down."

"What's wrong?"

"It's a goshawk. There's a pair, I'm certain, nesting in that wood. It comes down over the fields for prey. Bloody rare."

I crouched beside the ornithlogist who tilted his lenses at the sky. They flashed black and silver, then Ty Nant blue. We sat silently, looking over the barrow with its wheat and almost-crop circles, waiting for something to appear over the trees. I had never known it so quiet.

13

The antidote to the Sellafield Visitors' Centre lies a few miles south on the Cumbrian coast. It is the seaside resort of Seascale. Entering this easily bypassed town is a curious experience. I noted the expected villas with their pleasing names – Petrel Bank, Singing Surf, Manx View – and there indeed on the far western horizon, grey and indistinct, almost like a low cloud, was the small bulk of Manaw.

Seaview House looked worth investigating, but a resolute 'no vacancies' sign sent me elsewhere. Strange, because it had appeared almost deserted. The tide was out and the beaches moderately attractive, heaped with black and orange moraines of fly-busy bladderwrack. But the only person visible for a mile along the strand was a distant figure walking a dog. This beach is still used for the testing of artillery shells which are fired out to sea, yet there was no indication that such practice was imminent.

But I could hear a voice. Wordless, melancholic. It was a cry that suggested the past, or the future. But not the present. It belonged to a scrapman, then emerging from an alley, singing his trade. Behind him came a younger man, edging a rust-tumoured transit over the pavement. The back doors were open and I could see the day's spoil. A mangle, an exhaust manifold, a plastic bag of drinks cans, some blowtorch-scarred pipework, and right at the back of the van a gearbox opened like a carcass, its jewellery aglint in the swarf and seepages from old machinery. The scrapman led the Ford away, serenading the back lanes. Slowly I made my way up the hill, past a large hotel, the only place that was offering lunch, and discovered the irrigated undulations of the golf links.

And golf seemed a brave idea considering how the course was dominated by the sudden panoramic shock of the Sellafield complex. The plant glowed silver and intestinal in the afternoon light. Here was Bradbury's space city, product of that architectural urge that must turn everything inside out, emblazon the workings of an organism across naked daylight, and proclaim the delicate musculature of the industrial machine as if it was a challenge or a boast. Sellafield filled the horizon like a thunderhead. Its silhouette magnetised the attention, spread out as it was before the mountains, before the sea, the source not of a nightmare but rather a sudden sharp taste of defeat.

It looked as a box of fireworks does, when all the contents are placed together on the kitchen table. Pinnacles, clusters of towers, a peculiar sphere. And below the plant, within the shadows of its minarets and pale, reflective stacks, the golfers pulled their carts and searched, hands vizoring their eyes, into the distance.

I walked on and discovered Seascale School, a big enough establishment that must have served several hundred pupils. Yet there was no glimpse of any young people in town. On the beach and in the streets, Seascale was abandoned, a quaint anomaly and a promise betrayed.

In this resort, despite the extensive sands and a railway with some of the finest views of any line in the kingdom, the game is up. Few parents would bring their children here to dip into rockpools or fire golfballs out of the heather. The newspaper photographs of the balding, big eyed infants on chemotherapy, sitting in bed in striped pyjamas, have done their work. Escaping the Visitors' Centre, with its soundtrack of waterfalls and photocopiers, I had discovered this ring-fenced fortress, busy with guards clutching walkie-talkies, its prismed surfaces darkening from blue to Venusian cyanic to black as the sun descended. Two worlds, each the product of genius. The English, that amazing race, have created both.

14

But Seascale nagged at me. I understood its torpor, the melancholy outcrop of villas and guestless guest-houses high above the muddy sand. I too live in a seaside resort, a place that has abandoned earlier pretensions to gentility and now suffers its schizophrenic seasons in silence.

My resort possesses a funfair, locally-owned and jealously guarded. In winter it is as quiet as an abandoned industrial park. But in summer it displays every mania of desperation. The town makes headlines for two reasons. The first is that sometimes people drown there. The other is the fair. It kills children. One year a ten year old boy died on the waterchute and the story was the first item on the British news, itself a reason for perverse satisfaction and the short half-life of pride. Within minutes of the accident local children had gleefully elaborated the death, and now it exists as part of the folklore of the fairground, as real or as surreal as the crimson eyes of the werewolves in the Ghost Train, the painted destinations glimpsed on the World Cruise.

I thought there could be nowhere like my town. I pictured its enticements, straight out of the 1950s and before: echoy pavilions, stonechat-haunted common, fifty disappointed bars, all waiting, if not abandoned, upon a windy promontory. Once or twice every year the newspapers publish profiles of the area. These come complete with photographs of disenchanted restaurateurs who are selling up and not-so-old codgers who remember a golden age. Reading the entry made about the resort in an edition of *The Rough Guide* – that indispensable travelling companion to the tight-fisted adventurer – I was sure I was right. The condemnation of the town's dining-rooms, main streets and general atmosphere filled me with approval. It was still safe. Safe from discovery. No Sunday supplement special pull-out travel-section reader would go there. No broadsheet small-ad browser would biro around its name. The rough guiders would never understand. They didn't know what to look for. They didn't know how to look. No, there was nowhere like it. And experience proved me largely correct. At least until I discovered New Brighton.

Inevitably that day I was searching for something else. I wanted to find the birthplace of Malcolm Lowry, writer of *Under the Volcano*, victim of the most bizarre lifestyle of any important English writer, and therefore an unlamented native son of The Wirral.

I had approached from the east, braving Runcorn's chemical prairies, the ammoniacal cirrus created by industrial farming and the phenol breweries of the Cheshire plain. Now, to the north, was that hammer-blunt boar's snout of land between the Dee and the Mersey. But for what appeared on the map as a nicely wedge-shaped, easily navigable area, Wirral proved puzzling. I should, I told myself, have been in open country on the west of the peninsula. Instead I was snarled in Wallasey traffic and soon afterwards passing the concrete forecourt of the Tranmere Rovers football ground.

Yet fifteen minutes later, there was nothing at all. Nothing.

The Wirral ended. So did the world. After a long movie I was left gazing at an immense dead screen. But somewhere far off a bell sounded and slowly I recognised it as the dull plangency of a marker-buoy. Gradually I deciphered where the horizon should lie between the cement-coloured sky and the cement-coloured sea. A fisherman cast out his line into the grey air and moved away from a coign of the breakwater revealing a sign. King's Parade.

The rest was easy. Moving down the Parade I was back home in the Ghost Train, riding again on the World Cruise, where the mountains are always snow-covered, Niagara permanently frozen, and the Taj Mahal in need of sand-blasting. Here was New Brighton like a lost city of innocent pleasures, where children still rode on dodgem-cars and their parents sipped scalding, well-sugared tea in over-filled cafés.

Under clouds the colour of unbattered hake, the Queen of Merseyside was having one of her better days. In the indoor arcades a hundred video screens maintained an epileptic orthodoxy as the screaming in the chamber of horrors rose and fell like the litter-strewn waves against the promenade. Everyone was dressed in jacket or coat as the August wind sniped unimpeded off the Irish Sea, and everyone wore the same expression. It was that end-of-the-season, now-or-never, let's-have-a-good-time-even-if-it-kills-us look. A kind of radiant grimness. A victory over self, circumstances and whatever else the English climate and economy had conspired to create.

The gleaming ordures from Port Sunlight still slid into the Mersey in faithful tributary. Over in Bootle the scrapyards raised rust-red monuments to obsolescence. Everywhere the air was filled with the pollen of petrochemicals, asthma-dust, the voices of children yet to realise that they are lost. But here, at least for a minute on the last day of the holiday, was happiness. Or its nearest equivalent, which is increasingly hard to come by: the unawareness of self. Then the green sea slapped the balustrades like a bather shaking sand out of a towel. The children foamed around the sign that said: Do not press buzzer. When they pressed, the Ghost Train siren sounded, over and over, echoing into the late afternoon, part of the King's Parade cabaret, or, when I thought about it, like a summoning of the people, the end of a last shift.

15

"Yoor no fookin Welshman, yoo."
I adjusted my position in front of the brass nippled beer-pulls.
"Why's that?"
"Coz yoo woont fookin sing wi us."
My friends at the bar of the Beverley had stewed themselves in Guinness and now begun a process of marination in Famous Grouse. They looked like father and son but were in fact unrelated refrigeration engineers on contract work. Ex-miners from north of Glasgow, it was the older man who spoke and on whom I depended for a translation of the other's originally slurred and now completely incomprehensible dialect.

And what I'd been getting for the last hour is the familiar sob-story of unemployment, death of careers, retraining, further unemployment, the necessity of taking jobs which embarrass or bewilder the new employee, no pension, no camaraderie, no interest, no future. I had made exactly two verbal contributions during this time. The first was an inaccurate assertion that every deep mine in Wales had now been closed. This was delivered, I have to say, as if there was some merit in the fact, and that I could take satisfaction in it. But after all, living in a culture where fame is the measuring gauge for value, we have to have something to boast about. My second remark was a pithy "Welcome to the twenty-first century", delivered to head off the worst of the maudlin, porter-spittled effusions that had been coming my way, and also as an attempt to assert my triumphant realism. It had been ignored.

The Beverley is one of those hotels that looks pricey, even a little grand on the outside, but quickly reveals an endearing combination of eccentricity and incompetence in every dealing with its guests. I had booked the last room. Strange, but everywhere I go, I always end up with the last room. It is usually conferred on me as a species of local honour, and the assumption is that I am bloody lucky to have it, piebald cigarette burns on the formica tabletop, cloudy brylcream smudges on the small mirror behind the headboard included. I imagined the last inhabitant of this topmost room smoking in bed, perhaps fanning through the glossy Guide to the Lakes which had been provided. He was a thin man, about fifty, with a good head of slick hair and yellowing eye-whites. A salesman of some kind, for something old fashioned. Trusses perhaps. I called him George. He scared me but I could not stop thinking about him. Perhaps that's why he scared me. The more I rubbed the brylcream stain the larger it became. It spread over the mirror like my own breath.

And in a way I was. Lucky, that is. I was in Whitehaven, north of Seascale, idiosyncratic and remote Whitehaven, the least known town of its size in England. Yet Whitehaven was full. Every bed and breakfast vacancy had been snapped up by refrigeration engineers. All the pubs were crammed with refrigeration engineers describing what a horrible job it was, and how they used to be stockbrokers and disc-jockeys and everything else in which the country had put its faith. Until. Until it had all disappeared. Like a freezer's exoskeleton of ice.

The two in the Beverley were now well defrosted. It was one thirty in the morning and the Scandinavian girl with the streamers of platinum hair, the one who seemed to do all the work, had been replaced by the half-cut night porter whose alsatian, tawny ribbed and dribbling lager-free alcohol from blackened gums, was slumped under the footrail. I stood at an uncomfortable angle in case I trod on the beast. Slowly the Scottish soliloquy was dying down as another voice, also thickened by recent indulgence, but one in which a higher percentage of the words had spaces between them, began to attract our attention.

"An oor problem is," the woman was saying, the obese, happy-faced woman in the sky-blue pinafore dress, "oor problem is that when we goo doon sooth, like to Liverpool say, the people theyer think we're fookin Scotch."

She was gazing straight at our little party, although there were plenty of others in the bar. In fact, customers had been entering the hotel through a back door at regular intervals since closing time had been rung in less thirsty establishments.

"An then when we goo up to fookin Scotchland, the fookin Scotch boogers think we're fookin, fookin...."

Words momentarily failed her. "Fookin cockneys," she asserted triumphantly. "Yurh. Yuh noo yuh can't fookin win if yuh coom from heerafookinboots."

With that, the oration was concluded, and the woman returned to a quieter conversation with her friend, a slight forty year old with moles. The alsatian twitched in its dream.

The younger of my companions stirred himself.

"Well. Fook. Me", he breathed, the only intelligible words I was to hear from him all night. But he paid for the next round, unsteadily peeling off the golden rasher of a fifty pound note from a wad like the payment to a ransom demand, and his companion ordered. The night-porter accepted the money without blinking.

With difficulty we went back to discussing the rewards of installing and ripping out refrigeration systems in shops, lorries and warehouses. From there we advanced to comparing degrees of urban blight and deprivation with the Scottish native heath.

"Gateshead?

"The fookers don't noo they're born."

"Barrow?"

"The Costa del fookin Sol."

"Port Talbot?"

"Fookin rollin in it."

I could tell that this was merely skirting around what had

suddenly become the main subject of the night. The older man's eyes kept flickering across the bar.

"Doo yuh think yon lassies are, uh, oop foor it?" he asked, dropping his voice to a gentle conspiratorial rasp.

"Up for what?"

He looked at me as if I hadn't answered. I could feel the dog pressed against my ankles like a suitcase on a crowded train.

"Yon lassies," he tried again. "Doo yuh think they're hoors?"

"Hoors?"

He made a supreme effort. "Yeh. Hoooors." His breath was warmer than the alsatian's.

The blonde woman in the pinafore was now gazing benevolently out at the peasoupy room. Her companion, bug-eyed, stared doubtfully at a foil-necked bottle of 9% that had materialised before her.

"They're just having a drink."

My friend was enraged. He scowled into the last smears of his whisky, then looked at the women as if they had skinned him of a week of refrigeration money.

"Yoo stoopid coont," he eventually hissed. "They're oop for it. Which is yoors?"

His partner had by now slipped off his bar stool and was holding an intermittent conversation with a cigarette packet. His change from the round had been spread out on a bar towel by the night-porter, of whom there suddenly appeared to be two identical versions. I visualised a steel-grey door covered in condensation that was already becoming ice. I thought of resting my forehead against it and the chill travelling like a healing draught into every recess of my brain.

Then I remembered the long climb to my lucky room and its brylcream-fogged mirror.

"Fook off," I said.

16

In Brick Lane the marching is over, my dessert long finished. Somewhere to the east the lines of people had converged, formed a reservoir of good humour, anger and bewilderment, listened to the megaphoned speeches, and dispersed. Even the leaflet distributors with their unarguable appeals on behalf of windmills, animal rights and the unemployed have vanished, the splinter groups of splinter groups, the bedsitter anarchists and lifestyle revolutionaries, the bored, the sensible and the purgatorially lost, gone to The Alma for further plotting, or to The Bricklayers, to be warmly insulted by the regulars. It had been only a small march. Politics has no place in the middle of the week. Politics belongs to Saturdays and the nights when the brownies aren't using the local hall. This had been a practice session.

And Brick Lane is as busy as ever. Yet differently busy. In the dusk of grocery stores and religious butchers, the lights flick on and shadows grow tall in the street. The women are arriving for the next shift in the sweat-shops two and three storeys above in the Huguenot silk warehouses. The evening is mauve and police-siren blue. At the end of one exit a shoal of taxis waits, and in the gutter lies a bouquet of tuber roses, broken like china, dropped perhaps by one of the marchers.

Taking a short cut I breast a tide of real darkness, passing a school, a glimmering brewery, an area of nothingness. A black tree grows out of a lintel. Pigeons huddle together in smashed rooms. Since the light vanished, other people have emerged. There are new voices in the terraces. Pausing to listen, it is impossible to tell if they are coming towards me, or drifting away, like gas. And I hurry on, for here is nightfall with its different odours, pungent as a laboratory, whispering like an experiment.

Silurian Weekend

'Shall we pack it in?' Geoffrey didn't want to. The black Daimlers had gone and the men with cameras and pistols had vanished from the dome of the Pavilion. But Geoffrey thought we should try another chorus. He wanted to see who else might come out and what they would do when they heard us shouting.

I thought they would do what they had done all afternoon: ignore the voices washing up and down the promenade. I was getting cold and it was getting pointless. I didn't want to look like some sad crowd-shouter without a life at home. But Geoffrey didn't care. He hollered in his little voice, cupping his mouth and his words blew away. Geoffrey hollered and nothing happened. In his flannels and tweed jacket and woollen tie he made his protest and a constable with a radio glanced over and looked away.

At least I had the book. The book of dragonflies. An hour or two earlier I had walked down to Glan Road and picked it up at the warehouse. In the quiet afternoon I had turned its pages regularly. The wardens would be amazed. The book cost forty pounds and I had gone way beyond our monthly budget to secure it. Now it would take pride of place in our library, next to the aquarium, below the high tide chart. The book of dragonflies was surprisingly slim. Yet each plate was a stained glass window. There were close ups of the wings' mosaics, the cannibal young. The pictures of dragonfly eyes looked like photographs of Saturn's moons taken by Discoverer. And then there were the names of dragonflies. They were better than ice hockey teams: Essex Emeralds; Cardiff Devils' Darning Needles. The wardens would love it.

The tide was going out behind us. To the east was an amber

light against the cliffs, bright as a wedding-ring. The Daimlers had disappeared and the Pavilion dressing-room with its pink bulbs around the mirror was empty. Tommy Cooper had made-up in that dressing-room, and The Who had complained about the space when they played here thirty years ago. Today another entertainer had used it, but now had disappeared, glided away in the limousine down cordoned-off streets. The conference was ending and the television crews had completed filming. I wanted to go home to watch television to see if what we had been doing at one o'clock happened again at six. Even Geoffrey now seemed ready to call it off. A man of seventy, he had a yoga class that evening. He picked up the bag with the thermos of raspberry tea and we walked west down the esplanade.

Policemen were unroping the avenues. I still couldn't understand where the other people had been. Ours had been the only group there the whole day. Our group in Hawaiian shirts and sunglasses and swimsuits. Only Geoffrey had dressed as he always did, while the others had come as tourists. The town was a tourist town but today we were the only tourists there. Nobody else had been present but the television crews and the bystanders who had nothing to do but watch the black cars as they arrived and departed, as the women in flowered dresses and the men with florid faces and white hair walked in and out, labelled, identified, secure.

Nobody else had been there, none of those people who wrote about freedom, none of the people who wanted to ban things. The cliffs glowed silver behind us, the ruddy men and the floral women wandered into hotel car-parks and consulted menu boards. The only ones who had been there were us, and we were walking home to see ourselves on television: a tourist in a Hawaiian shirt and a tweedy man with a flask of herbal tea. I couldn't understand it. Perhaps the television would explain. Behind us the cliff shone like a mirror. Radiance engulfed the promontory, but in an instant the tide was darker and the light had vanished.

The promontory was a dangerous place. Occasionally, late at work and getting ready to leave my office at Heritage Coast headquarters, I would look out into the darkness. At the tip of the promontory, in the rocks and fractured sections of cliff-face, the size of house roofs, that had fallen from above, the first lights would be visible. These were the yellow hurricane lanterns lit by anglers.

According to folklore it was a wonderful place for fishing. I would look at the lanterns, tiny in the blackness, fragile in the insistent westerly, turn on my headlights and begin the ascent of the opposite cliff. Miles out to the west, there would be a dull gleam on the horizon, the glow of a hidden town. But even on full beam, visibility was meagre. The shore seemed to possess a special quality of darkness. There was an impenetrability to it, as night settled as a black fog in the caverns and hanging valleys. Sometimes, walking from the office, I felt as if I could taste the darkness, a flavour intangible as snow's, or scent it like the mothballs and perfume of a wardrobe a child explored.

Yet the smell of darkness was a more private smell than that. It was a smell of my own. Darkness maintained a presence on the coast: daylight was mere empty air. The full beam revealed notices warning of dangerous cliffs and falling rocks, and if there was a high tide my lights would sweep momentarily over uncoiling waves. But the ocean was a pit I never peered within. It was there on my left as I ground in first up the valley side, eager to put guts in the ascent. It was there over the rim of the road, beneath the precipice. The ocean was the blackest part of the night, the source of the darkness. At the top of the cliff I would meet a panorama of the invisible. Black fog. And the only evidence of where the beach met the waves or the headland loomed would be the yellow lights of the anglers on the furthest tip of the peninsula, tiny and erratic behind the sea's smoke.

"What I want, you see," said the boss, blue eyes disarmingly blue, head cocked like a budgerigar, "is magic."

"Magic."

"Magic. And you know what I mean by magic?"

"Yes."

"Well what do I mean?"

"It's got to be good."

"No. It's got to be magic. People will start to read it and want to keep reading and when they've read it they'll understand."

"So keep 'em reading?"

"Keep 'em reading and when they move away it goes with them."

"What does?"

"The magic. You understand?"

"Yeah."

"Sure?"

"Course."

"So there's my effort with the facts, the dates and whatnot, but minus the magic. Keep it chronological but make sure the magic's there. Okay?"

"Okay."

"I'll be down to have a look at it by the end of the week. If I don't make it, stick a copy in the post for Monday. All right?'

"All right."

"See you soon then."

My desk looked as if I had been awarded a recycling franchise. The boss was now dislocating the gears of a landrover and driving up towards the gardens. From the window I watched him halt at the gate that blocked off the driveway from public traffic, swing it open and start up again in a stain of diesel. Five seconds later he was reversing to secure the gate behind him, business suit tucked into wellingtons and protected from the rain by one of the paramilitary anoraks the wardens wore.

Above my head the walkie-talkies winked on the recharger: a marine map showed spiders' webs of blue fathom lines. Under my feet was a thick film of dried mud. The floor was littered with lobes of the same muck, kicked off the boots of the wardens and deputy wardens and voluntary wardens. There was a hegemony of footwear here. Insiders like me wore thin-soled Clarks or moderately clean gym shoes. On his more mutinous days, Dafydd the cleaner, and most hermetic of Insiders, boasted a revolutionary pair of green plastic sandals. Outsiders sported mountaineering boots, hiking boots, Royal Marine yomping boots that buttoned to the shin. The Outsiders came in to drink tea, open letters, talk about peregrines and moonwort, recharge their radios and disappear before the boss telephoned. The boss was the Great Insider who thought of himself as the Great Outsider. The wardens hated him because of this presumption.

The wardens, after all, were ecologists. They had taken degrees in ecology in places like Southampton and Norwich. To them, what the Great Insider achieved for ecology was what Hitchcock's *Psycho* did for motel bookings. I looked around. The wardens had left their spore over and under every khaki-painted desk. The deposits made a point. The Insiders talked about the environment. The Outsiders were part of it. Or that was the perception in the office. But within the Outsiders existed another rigid caste system. The Outsider aristocracy included the wardens and the education officer. They were scientists with research years spent on slug safaris and micromoth counting. On the coast, the locations of peregrine falcon nests and colonies of moonwort provided the mystic associations of their freemasonry.

The Outsider proletariat, meanwhile, comprised hired labourers on short-term contracts. The wardens never consorted with these people unless there were walls to repair or stiles to build. The proletariat were men in their early twenties: hard nuts, dim wits, the occasional university drop-out. Only when the wardens had emptied their pint mugs of sweet tea, thrown their sandwich wrappings on the floor, and jackbooted it back into the hinterland or down to the rockpools, did the proles dare to enter the office. Their proleish rituals never varied. They dragged on rollups, opened mayonnaise jars filled with coffee-sugar mix, and rubbed up against the radiators, tapping their dented steelies against the pipes. The hard nuts had patrolled Belfast alleyways. The dim wits were driven to the office by their mothers. The drop-outs kept quiet.

Occasionally, other groups of Outsiders would arrive for work experience. These were younger men with learning difficulties and bad health. Learning difficulties meant illiterate. Bad health translated as epileptic or permanently pilled-up. Terrified of being ragged by the older boys, they would sit on the floor of the exhibition room, under the stuffed gulls. Their cigarettes would burn the window ledges but there was nowhere else to put these Outsiders until a digging detail was organised in the gardens, or a blitz made on the litter flung out of the sea.

The Insiders suffered in silence. We were outnumbered, and the Great Insider, our protector, was never there. I sat at a desk. Dafydd leaned on a mop and studied the *Financial Times*. Batgirl took telephone messages and whispered to the latest bat casualty brought in for her ministrations. The bat would cling to her jersey like an autumn leaf. She would nudge a Q-tip soaked in milk towards its unfinished face. The Insiders would look at the Outsiders and ask them to turn down the ghetto blaster. After all, the public would be coming in to peer at the aquariums. The Outsiders clung to the radiators and begged for teabags and tobacco. We all understood our roles.

I watched the boss's landrover travel the driveway to the castle walls. The castle was a flattened ruin but one tower remained. The airforce grey jeep stopped at the tower and the boss climbed out. He gestured. One of the wardens appeared, very slowly. Normally the wardens were impossible to find when the Great Insider was down from head office, but today one of them had either been slack or now acknowledged an appointment.

The two men approached the iron door of the tower. This door was rarely opened. It was a forbidding door, studded, rusting, monumentally heavy. It was a door appropriate for a ruined tower. The warden fitted a key in the padlock, released a bolt and pulled the door outwards. Both men entered the tower. I turned back to my desk.

The squalor in the office appeared greater than usual. The spilled tea, the ripped envelopes scattered under chairs constituted evidence, deliberately placed in Insider territory. The wardens were fed up. They were humiliated. And I understood, whilst delighting in, their humiliation. Two days previously we had staged our greatest fundraising event. It was Roman Day on the coast. Because it was claimed that a Roman legion had briefly occupied the Silurian fort on the promontory, the boss had decided to stage his Roman circus. There was a mead tent. There was a sandcastle-building competition. Whether the Romans had built sandcastles or not our Roman Day featured a sandcastle competition. There was a Silurian marquee filled with hairy people with fake tattoos.

The boss had tried to convince the ex-paratroopers and jail-birds among the Outsiders that they should take part. After all, they boasted proper tattoos. They were scary. They had real Silurian blood. He offered them authentic Silurian mead. But there was no deal. Instead, our Silurians decided to spend the Roman Day in deepest Siluria, sleeping off their Friday night saturnalia. Which was a pity because in their shredded denim and amphetamania, they would have given our imported Roman cohort, a troupe of jessies with little red skirts, eagles on broom-handles and plastic breastplates, considerable food for thought. It almost made me proud to be a Silurian.

The wardens, inevitably, had been opposed to the idea of a Roman Day. It was tacky. It would create litter. Raising the marquee would take hours. The Great Insider won the argument. So the wardens appeared in centurions' costumes, bristling cockscombs adorning their helmets. One of the wardens was an ex-police officer, and in an admirably ironic gesture, displayed his service medals on his chest. The wardens entertained local dignitaries in the mead tent and grindingly, imperceptibly, got pissed.

I suppose I sympathised. The evidence for Roman occupation of the Silurian fort was less than circumstantial. It was not as much as tenuous. In fact, there was no evidence whatever that even one legionary had bivouacked on the peninsula. Come to think of it, there was no evidence of the existence of a Silurian fort there either. Yet as the Great Insider said, history will absolve us. I didn't know what he meant but there was a sonority to the sentiment. History, according to the boss, was where the imagination might freely wander.

The wardens had remained tight lipped. They saw history differently. History was a theme-park where the Great Insider was setting up his stall. History was merchandise. But if history was the means by which the Great Insider could raise funds and so protect their jobs, the wardens would not protest too bitterly. They would chat to the dignitaries in the mead tent. They would numb themselves with fierce honey. They would hold their centurions' helmets under their arms and secretly yank scarlet bristles from the combs. They would nod, mouths like lemon slices, as the mayor of our Silurian borough complained about the loss of his pigeons. The pigeons were lunch-on-the-wing for the peregrines but the wardens never mentioned the peregrines. Instead they discussed wheelchair access to clifftop viewing sites and the Victorian wishing well in the gardens. Or they remained tight lipped, clutching their helmets, mouths like lemon slices, tasting their humiliation.

At least the mead was decent stuff. Our absent Silurians would have approved. But after one glass I was forbidden more. As an Insider I had been spared the fancy dress, but my role on Roman Day was one of considerable importance. The Great Insider had taken special pains to explain.

"Make sure people see them. And keep telling them to wave. And drive slowly. Once you've made one circuit pause for a minute, then start again in the opposite direction. And so on. Got that?"

"Got it."

"Sure?"

"Sure."

The good thing about my job on Roman Day was that I could drive the Land Rover. Driving the Land Rover conferred a mystique upon the Land Rover driver. It was a feeling of ruggedness, of masculinity and a kind of Silurian primitivism all combined. Driving the Land Rover was a hairy bollocky thing to do. It was like getting my own pair of warden's boots, with the brass eyelets and laces thick as baling twine. I had driven the Land Rover many times but never in front of crowds. And never in front of hundreds of Roman citizens clutching plastic thimbles of Silurian mead and paper plates heaped with Roman food. The Roman food consisted of finger-sized portions of pizza, which was as close as the Great Insider could get to legionary cuisine.

The bad thing about my job on Roman Day was that accompanying me in the Land Rover was the Emperor of Rome and the wife of the Emperor of Rome. The Emperor of Rome was a building society manager and international rugby player. We had known each other by sight in secondary school. Twenty years earlier we had regularly sat together for dinner in the school canteen, but by telepathic agreement on Roman Day we decided not to recognise each other.

Now I called him Emperor. He called me Drive. The Emperor wore a white toga made from a bedsheet, with a moneybelt about his waist. Upon his head was a narrow circlet of plastic leaves like a crematorium wreath. The Emperor's wife was also dressed in a toga, interestingly split and revealingly scallop-necked. Her blonde hair, minus the laurels, hung over her shoulders. She looked like an extra from Ben Hur. I was proud to chauffeur her. Of the Emperor I was less convinced. His face was puffy with recent bruising, obviously gained from an outing at the National Stadium or during a bad day at the building society. A tall man with an appropriately high Charlton Heston fringe, he was imperiousness without the imperial.

"'Sgood this," he said to the Empress, through a clenched

104

smile. "Round again, Drive, but a bit slower. I'm working on the wave". And he bestowed another blessing on the throng.

The warden and the Great Insider remained in the tower. The Great Insider was attempting to reveal his ecological credentials and the warden was humouring him. Within the tower down a flight of stone steps was a chamber. It was pitch black but the wardens kept a hurricane lamp and a flashlight there.

Inside the chamber lived a colony of spiders. The spiders were very rare. No other colony of their species had been discovered in this part of the country. Occasionally spider specialists and well known biologists would arrive on the coast and the wardens escort them to the tower to look at the spiders. I had once been allowed into the tower but the visit was not a success. We shone the flashlight around the chamber but there was nothing to be seen but fallen rubble and ancient webs. The spiders were in the crevices, the wardens had said. They were there but we couldn't see them.

It was cold in the dungeon beneath the tower and very quiet. I could smell the sea. The flashlight stroked patterns on the walls. We had climbed the steps, swung open the iron door and returned to the office. Now the boss was inside the tower receiving the spider treatment. He was very proud of the spiders, although he had told me he had never seen them. The spiders confirmed the special qualities of the coast. Equally important, the spiders were a bargaining tool in the Great Insider's battles for grant aid. The spiders were what the coast was all about, he claimed. The spiders were rare. The tower was old. The coast was unique.

I had never seen the spiders and the boss had never seen the spiders. In fact, I had met several people who had crouched in the chamber, shining the flashlight, who had never seen the spiders. But I believed in the spiders. They guarded my job. They were very large spiders and, according to the wardens, unusually ravenous. I wondered where their food came from but never said anything. Believing in spiders is not difficult. Having seen the darkness in which they lived, and having felt the chill of the sea-smelling dungeon, I could imagine them. Imagining spiders is not difficult. Spiders exist in the dark. Waiting. The two men were still in the tower. I turned back to my desk.

The drift of papers and pamphlets referred to the coast as it was three hundred years ago. Specifically, it concerned the wreckers. Compared to the penurious hills to the north, this had not been a poor part of the world. Despite the salt and the sand that blew over the fields, families had farmed and the castle had provided work. But there had been other ways to earn a living. That is how murder became a tradition here. At night bonfires were lit on the beaches and clifftops. Sometimes ships steered towards them. Frequently the vessels were wrecked on the promontories of rock that invaded the sea, or ran aground on the black castellations of the island that even at high tide was concealed by only a few feet of water. Whatever came ashore from the betrayed ships was useful, but any crew or passengers who gained the beaches had to be disposed of.

That was the phrase in one of the pamphlets. According to the histories, the wreckers were men who dressed as women, although both sexes took part in the wrecking. The wreckers were murderers who had become an integral part of the history of the coast. History made them dramatic and my job was to interpret that drama for visitors.

Already I could picture the wreckers in the words I would write. They were locals engaged in colourful traditions. They were the ancestors of the people who lived here today. Murderers it appeared, but quaint murderers. Beards, bonfires, bonnets. And murderers was a word I would have to dispose of. Instead I would capture the thrill as the bales of silk washed ashore, the dead sheep, still hobbled, the mysterious boxes that splintered on the rocks. It must have been exciting to be a wrecker. I could have been one, no problem. We are all wreckers at heart, after all. Build the beacon, keep it dry, watch it cackle and spit. Then wait for what its light attracts, a guttering moth-trap on the cliff.

Batgirl muttered something. She was learning Silurian. Sometimes I would hear her crooning it to one of the bats that clung to her olive breast.

"Ta," I said when the scalding orange tea arrived. It tasted microwaved. But I needed something. Inspiration would have been welcome. The deadline approached and I was entrusted with the task of discovering magic. As if. The proles had finished the cairn that would hold the display panel for the text. It was set high on the castle site, a thirty mile coastal vista to east and west. Our artists had completed the drawing that would share the panel space. Now only the words were required, a variant on the Great Insider's melodramatic one sentence paragraphs.

"Windswept and isolated," I began, "this stretch of coastline in the seventeenth century..."

"Isolated from what?" queried Dafydd. Who cared? It sounded good. By tomorrow I might have a draft to give to Fran who came in three days a week for office-work experience. Another Insider. Fran was learning to use our large electric typewriter which printed its letters from an inscribed silver golfball. It was an impressive machine but presented challenges for Fran. Chief of these was feeding the paper. Fran could never feed her letter-heads properly into the typewriter, so that her correspondence always emerged printed crookedly. But I was optimistic that by the end of her work experience contract, we would have sur-mounted the problem. She would then be able to confront the world of real employment as a straight paper golfball typewriter feeder.

"See Maggie on the news last night?" asked Dafydd, leaning his squeegy against the office aquarium. The office aquarium contained a large crab, several rocks and a piece of weed green as a shred of snooker table velvet. The fish, the shrimps and other rock pool denizens we regularly ladled into the aquarium had disappeared again. The crab held out its pincers like a knife and fork. Its eyes were cowled. Dafydd soaked his sponge in aquarium brine.

"Yeah. Both sides."

"Got to admire her for coming down here."

"Why?"

"This is Apache territory this is." Dafydd breathed on the aquarium glass, polished with his sleeve, and peered into the water. "No. More like Fort Apache. Ever see that film? *Fort Apache, The Bronx*?"

"No."

"And those secret service people with guns. See them? Crawling with Special Branch it was. Automatic rifles too, plus the video cameras and the polaroids. Must have been some kind of demo. Fran in today?"

Continental Drift

1

It was war outside. So bad they had stopped counting the bodies. I listened to artists who had turned their work into scientology, read about an English songwriter whose mind was scoured clean by lysergic acid, asleep on the fixed plastic bench at the job centre. Sir Anthony Hopkins organised a tribute for a film from his native land. He was solicitous and gentle but when I looked in his eyes he wasn't there. Travelling. That's what did it. Unravelling the world. Airport influenza. Caffeine trance. The ceaseless blind migrations.

So I flew the Friendly Skies, ate chicken that had never seen daylight, drank water that had never been rain. Rush Limbaugh, the British Council and my visa waiver told me I was right. And now below me the turkey vultures, wings like fraying doormats, drift above the wooded slopes. In the valley the Coast Starlight locomotive moans its aching, B movie moan, falls silent, then moans again, a little further north into the Bay area. There are books and medicines scattered about my chair, set amongst beds of orange poppies, the state flower. Something fallen, metallic, is mired on the skin of the swimming pool, its arms waving. Out of reach.

The blister I have developed on my right heel by jaywalking around this suburb of a suburb, has grown to resemble a long, pale cocoon within which something moves. Last night I pricked the wall of the growth and a measure of fluid, the quantity and colour of a double vodka, seeped out and soaked the bedclothes. Today the size of the eruption is slightly less astonishing, but remains impressive, a long pod shielding the raw skin beneath.

Watching replaces walking, so today I am less of a subversive. To the north are the mansions with their terraces of purple ice-plant, and a plain of estuarial salt whitening as if frost was forming there. That was yesterday's walk. I paced a long crescent around the shore to look at the egrets at the outfall, each poised on one leg as the sewage boiled up like a jacuzzi in the swamp. Out of the prozac landscape and computer weather I walked on scorching heels down to the water, said nothing to the fishermen, understanding their vigils as wordless explorations of a single mood, and moved on towards the fogbank. There in the haze across the bay were the usual tankers, an endless succession of aeroplanes, and then, almost invisible on the frontier of sight, a blue promontory on which a city sketched itself, all vertical pipework and straining towers, like some heat-blurred refinery or already dated Hollywood model of an extra-terrestrial resort.

2

There are some Californicators who want the state split in half. And they don't mean by earthquake. The problem is Los Angeles. They see it as a growing and untreatable melanoma on the country's hide.

For one thing, it takes all the water. Forget oil. In the twenty-first century, war will be fought over possession of ground-water drilling rights, river catchments, tributary diversion, sewage treatment plants. Fighter planes will strafe the clouds with silver nitrate, private security companies deploy their arsenals around reservoirs and holding tanks. LA squanders water with infantile innocence. Its golf courses are so green they might have been laid on dumping grounds for copper waste. Together, the golf courses and suburban lawns use more water than certain African countries. It's time, some northerners say, that the taps were turned off.

And it's not only water. LA is three tribes. Forget the Crips and the Bloods and all the gangsta mythology. First, LA consists of the rich, who are as phoney as a three dollar note. Then the middle classes, geekdom personified. Then the poor, a self-destroying warrior-caste, turning their everyday lives into pornography. Don't go there, urge the northerners. It's a silicon universe of pizza orders on the internet, astroturf farms, digital malice. All the industrial-strength weird scenes you ever heard of start down there. If the border was drawn at Monterey, then both Californias would make sense. As it is, we're schizoid city. Siamese twins. Division is the only therapy.

But some see it differently. California should be a nation apart, they say. After independence from the US, it would be the fifth richest country in the world. America is a dinosaur, and dinosaurs never evolved, no matter what Michael Crichton says. They died in the mud from their own stupidity and a flukey meteorite shower. Warm-blooded California needs to fly off and do its own thing.

Others view this as surfer's politics. To even think about a place called 'California' is to reveal a blond rinse of the mind. California is yesterday's concept, made redundant by computers. From now on it's a question of language, and if you are using the right software then you are speaking the right language. In the future a nation will be defined as a community of users of a particular computer programme. Geographically, such a community will be atomised. Yet culturally, it will be instantly definable, a kind of West Side Crips of the Information Superhighway. And the coolest thing is, you get to choose what you belong to. Instead of being born into somebody else's incomprehensible mindwarp. That history garbage? It's over.

3

Upstairs in the doubledecker Caltrain the opinion is that California is not the state it was. There are too many people.

And we all know what type of people we mean here, we Caltrain riders with our newspapers and cases. The population has doubled in fifteen years. Those who are alarmed at the growth and can afford the move have vanished into Oregon or New Mexico, resentful that this has become the land of someone else's opportunity.

Meanwhile, in the Museum of Modern Art, the black and white photographs of Dorothea Lange are drawing record attendances. Lange, it is considered, captured the essential dignity and desperation of Okies fleeing the dustbowl, dirt-farm refugees who had driven their children two thousand miles to queue all day for a job picking cherries.

Lange photographed real Americans and in so doing transformed their penury into a religious condition. A mother in filthy floralprint, the father holding two children, offering for sale the tyres on their car. A sturdy beggar from Texas smiling out of utter destitution, his hair matted like a rock star's. Lange's Americans cranked up their ramshackle Fords and farm wagons and found themselves on the rim of a continent. They were escaping the fields they had ploughed into oblivion, the sour breath of Wall Street. Today, Nevada Bob's Discount Golf and Karate occupies the apricot orchards they helped plant, but their place in history is assured. Outside the museum, the urban sharecroppers push trolleys loaded with recyclable cans and bottles. Others spit, cry, sing, piss and sleep. Their rags are not the honest raiments of Oklahoma, but stained by bodily functions Dorothea Lange could not show. The consensus is that Lange's subjects reveal dignity in suffering. But the druggies from the housing projects cannot know the meaning of words like that. When you walk past and refuse to give them money they tell you to fuck off. As if that changed anything. And some of them are obviously insane, whispering in a private language to themselves as they mix their cocktails of beer and brake fluid, or nibble round the crescent of yesterday's cheeseburger, drawn from a secret pyx.

People are getting tired of the homeless. Perhaps it's because they never go home. They stay on the same stretch of sidewalk all day, a polystyrene cup raised for nickels. Some are definitely alcoholics. These fall into two types. The ones with adobe-red faces and thickened voices, the legacy of endless libations behind the sheets of their parking-lot shanties. And the ones who are drained grey as old snow, the skin round their eyes delicate as moths' wings. Drinking the nuclear runoff they do, they'll never get better. So giving money might be bad for them. Save it for the eugenics labs instead. But here's a comforting thought. Perhaps in the next life they'll come back as lawyers.

Yet even their little sidewalk empires, a patchwork created by cunning and violence, are having to shrink. California's filling up. The Vietnamese have come to the Tenderloin and discovered that their landlords are dope merchants and there are pesticide-resistant rodents under the floorboards. So what? Soon their restaurants and tea-houses are open, their washing- and repair-businesses, their tiny temples. The Tenderloin possessed a certain reputation. People didn't go there at night. People didn't go there in the day. If they did they were hustled and followed. But it was cheap. And when you came from a country of children who had lost their legs in mined paddyfields and where agent orange was a constituent of mother's milk, you tended to see things differently.

It's like the Mission district. The Mexicans are there now, their music an invisible carnival, the green salsa, the red salsa on every restaurant table. In this city you can eat out every night for eleven years and still not get around all the public dining-rooms. The trouble is, every other evening you'd be ordering burritos.

Those Latinos. They're like the Chinese. Can't tell them apart and there's so many you never try. Boxers, waiters, foot-ballers, dealers, all hidden until nightfall when they can cut through the wire. Good luck to them is what you have to say. Anyone seen those Mexican villages? If you kept farm animals like that here you'd get a holiday behind bars. At least the ones we're getting are the ones with initiative. Next year we'll all be taking Spanish classes.

Such conversations simmer on the Caltrain. Outside are the pastures of garlic bulbs, the estuaries of rice in the Central Valley. Our newspapers flutter. Too many people. People. Overweight, underfed, will work for food, false memory syndrome, the Sierra Club, earthquake simulation, special offer, closing down. The software designer in ponytail and cut-off jeans alights and unchains his bicycle, rides away into a landscape pale as lemon rind. At the trackside a eucalypt is burning, its oils fizzing and molten in the grass. Someone says good riddance. Eucalypts take all the water in the soil. They're not a social tree. Too many of those and the whole system starts to crack. We move on.

4

Newspapers here are thin and quickly tossed aside. There is no edge to them and the keenest political comment is found in the cartoons, the best journalism in the music and restautrant features.

That is where the writers are today, throwing sushi dice or anticipating the arrival of the Rolling Stones' *Voodoo Lounge* tour in Oakland, grandfathers whose risk-taking these days is on the stock exchange. There is even a Stones credit card now, for people to use when they buy their Stones stuff, the voodoo sweatshirts, the jackets with that Indian goddess's tongue logo. The usual dreck.

This year there will be more essayists travelling with the Stones than groupies, more documentary makers than dealers. Somehow the group still makes the front pages, but is eclipsed by this week's story of the century. A mountain lion has eaten a jogger. Attracted apparently by her strong musk perfume, the lion followed the runner in a semi-suburban park and dragged her into undergrowth.

This is only the second death to be caused by a mountain lion in ninety years. Taking revenge, wildlife wardens tracked the animal to its lair and killed it, orphaning a cub. A fund has been established for the young animal and has so far attracted ten times more money than the fund for the jogger's two children. Which only goes to show. And what it shows, says Rush Limbaugh, who has his teeth into the story like the cougar had her claws into the jogger's arse, is social decay. Warped values. Peverted compassion. And all of them created by sentimental television environmentalism. Earth First claims, on the other hand, that it is proof that civilization has not fully alienated Americans from wild nature. Meanwhile, the perfume manufacturers are debating the marketing consequences of the killing.

People here are good at moral dilemmas. There are more moral dilemmas in this state than basketball teams. And the only people who benefit, apart from the therapists, are the teeshirt makers.

Already the slogans are parading the sidewalks. Some for the cubs, some for the kids. Nobody agrees so everybody debates. Everyone that is who can distinguish between baby cougars and young middle class whites. To some people they are all the same. Especially perhaps to the black man on the steps of the housing project I passed today. He too was wearing a teeshirt. His teeshirt said 'Fuck the World' in the biggest letters that could fit across an XXXtra large chest. At first, I thought the words were Feed the World. But that was yesterday's legend, incomprehensibe now as a foreign language.

Frank Schiavo has not yet committed himself on the mountain lion issue. I sit in his home with the newspapers thrown around, listening to one of the state's more troublesome celebrities describe the futures we might face. Terrifying or benign. Take your pick. Apparently we still have that power. Schiavo's ambition, already mostly realised, is to enjoy a high quality lifestyle and yet make no polluting impact at all on the sun-rich, wholly anonymous suburb where he lives.

While I occupy the lounge, he escorts a prospective mayor around the other rooms and garden, explaining his battles with County Hall. Frank Schiavo's battles with County Hall could be tedious. They are battles about garbage. Schiavo wants his tax bill reduced by the annual charge for garbage collection. He doesn't think it fair to make him pay the garbage charge. Because he creates no garbage. All his garden rubbish is composted and everything else recycled. If by chance he does come by something that is unreuseable he simply takes it to the college where he works and uses the collection there. A toothbrush say, worn to the nubs. A broken shoe.

Not that this happens very often. Frank Schiavo has a mission in life and that mission is not to leave his mark. He is an orderly man, profoundly retentive. Some would say inordinately so. He is also very stubborn and quietly indignant about a system that rewards waste and the wasters but penalizes the Schiavos.

But the politicians have dug in against him. To give way would create a dangerous precedent. Soon other people would seek lower taxes because they too had stopped making garbage. It was their taxes that paid for landfill sites and the vehicles that fed them. And it was their trash that created the sites. A Big Gulp's waxen chalice. The incidentals at Julian's Ribs. That was a neat, comprehensible way of working and there was no need to complicate matters. Schiavo is threatening because he wants to change things. He has learned that the most important household item is not a television or a blender. It is not a portable barbecue set, a swimming pool or even one of those electric garbage dispensers that growl like mountain lions under the sink. It is a simple, good old fashioned dustbin. Try living without one of those for a week is his advice. "It'll change your philosophy more than an earthquake".

Outside, the mayoral candidate is trying to make conversation about the compost heap built with orange peel and guinea-pig shit. Its architect has screened the site with banks of jasmine that now shivers with bees and pours out perfume like a shaken censer. In the south-facing garden he has built a brick patio that holds the sun's heat, and filled the outer-wall space not with felt or injections of chemical ooze, but one and a half tons of water contained in matt black-painted gallon oilcans. The sun, the dry air and the patio bricks helps warm the water which then acts as a central-heating system. Solar power provides all the electricity the Schiavo family need, and although they never sprinkle the lawn, their garden is as insistently green as all the other meticulously-irrigated quality-time grass in Silicon Valley.

Even Frank's car is a model of impact minimilization. Perhaps the surprising thing about Frank Schiavo's car is that one exists in the first place. But in Santa Clara county there are more automobiles than people. The smog, like a photochemical mistral, brings a common neurasthenia to the tables at Denny's, the terminals at Wells Fargo. But Frank's car is thirty years old and runs on propane. Because of the dry climate of his suburb, nothing rusts. Frank's car will outlast him unless it is stolen on orders from the oil companies or wrecked by motor manufacturers. It goes, he says, like a nun on amphetamines. Carbon dioxide or no carbon dioxide.

I don't ask Schiavo about oil or his air-conditioning. He is too busy to argue. His telephone rings incessantly, journalists call round to tour his empire. Even now the maybe-mayor is staring at the notice in the kitchen that proclaims it a junk food-free zone. Frank is no extremist. He reads the hockey results and concocts curry. All he has done is to take a principle and investigate how far he can follow it. Handing round beers from the local microbrewery, he looks what he is. A technology teacher with a talent for DIY. He never wanted to subvert the industrial-military complex. The trouble is these days, at least for anyone with a glimmer of originality, it is difficult not to. Frank Schiavo is going to court because he had the time to think about garbage. Already there are people who hate him for it.

5

Jack Kerouac is a fish-smelling alley. Kenneth Rexroth a dead-end of suppurating trash. The campaign to name streets in the city after writers succeeded, but the city had the last laugh.

On Kerouac, the kitchen boys from a Chinese café are sitting on the back-step, eating noodles and chicken feet, all talking at the same time. These are infantry in the catering war. In this country there are two types of people. Those who are eating and those who are preparing to eat. Mongolian, Lebanese and Dutch restaurants are all launching this week with banners and children in folk-costume. Regional idiosyncrasies and the desperate initiatives of poverty have been combined to form a series of national cuisines. The Irish have built an international empire bigger than the Mafia's on stout and soda-bread. Every street-corner offers an eight buck pasta stupor. It is a war of ten thousand frontiers without even considering the kitchen at home. Eating is religion now. Food is worshipped at its glass altars, and a never-ending iconography splash-paints the auto routes.

Babies are not dressed more carefully than food: gaming-wheels and football tactics not studied with more avidity. The war, inevitably, has nothing to do with hunger. Only the stupid or the insane are hungry, or the homeless, who anyway boast of it. Hunger has been banished like smallpox and the other old diseases. There are some things that should not exist and hunger is one of them. People came to this country to escape it, like a political regime, an oppressor's language. Tormented by its memory, we medicate ourselves against its return. Hungry is what we used to be before we became ourselves. None of us can go back to being hungry. Those people don't exist any more.

But in Vesuvio's there is no food. If you want lunch you bring your own. But nobody does. In Vesuvio's there are four things to do and not one of them is eat. Instead, people drink, talk, read, observe. Not necessarily in that order.

In forty years some things must have changed at Vesuvio's,

but not many. The main difference is that now it has become aware of itself, but that is unsurprising. Everyone and everywhere today is self-conscious to the roots of being. That is media pollution, inescapable as traffic exhaust. Vesuvio's knows that Ferlinghetti, Dylan Thomas and a thousand other writers have come here seeking the brown mugs of its coffee, its tumblers of scotch. That is history and cannot be undone. So there are photographs of Kerouac on the walls, pictures of North Beach poets, some shabby memorabilia of a literary age before computers, before fame, but no big deals are made of the past.

Old haiku-masters sit for hours with iced water and a Jackie Collins paperback. Young men redraft verses, having yesterday stepped off the bus from Des Moines, the plane from Houston. Such writers have no natural community, so today this will do. The regulars of five months or twenty-five years know why these others arrive and silently accommodate their hopes and bewilderment. The new writers look out of the windows at the beggars and the arroyo of washing-up water coming down Jack Kerouac. They stare at the photographers on the sidewalk who are taking pictures of them, the new writers within Vesuvio's, and who are now a part of its history. A part of Vesuvio's after only five minutes in. With the cramp of the Des Moines Greyhound still in the small of the back the new writers are already famous.

Writers can have no community but this for a moment feels like one. I think of Shelley and Raymond Carver and Bob Dylan before they were turned into theme-parks, looking up from their manuscripts and blinking at the light. Shocking themselves with words. But then writers are easily shocked. That is why they are writers. And despite the cynicism of its bartenders, Vesuvio's is as innocent in this city as any place possessing a history might remain. Open twenty hours a day, it succours delivery-men and disc-jockeys, blue skirted professional women fleeing the sexless air of Citibank.

Upstairs the writers sit, chewing nails, nursing the last centimetres of clamato. No-one needs a watch at Vesuvio's. The

119

depth of the drinks tells the time. Few glasses are emptied here because there is nowhere better to go. Which is scary but true. It is the end of the road. Outside, the hutches of young pigeons, whispering like a video game, are stacked outside the Chinese restaurant. The adult shop displays a poster that says 'for Mother's Day, check out our unique bare essentials'. Tourists, identity-free in clothes that are strange to them, cruise the racks of dildos and plastic anuses. A pillar of sunglasses, tall as a totem-pole, has been erected on the sidewalk.

The writers in their windows see all of this but make no judgement, make no sound, as around them the chess matches continue, the one minute blitzes, the crushing mathematics of the end-games, and the poker-school sends down for vanilla tea. The view from Vesuvio's is open to everyone but there are always empty seats. People have grown old here, staring through the sleeve-wiped glass, leaving their books face-up on the bar as they seek a fuller cup, an interlude in the restroom's dark mirror.

6

Sundays are different here. They are busy, early-rising days, filled with leisure opportunities. Crowds for the over-forties' mini-marathon mingle amongst lines awaiting the outdoor clam-bake. But the biggest audience has arrived for a concert in one of the squares by a group of musicians who call themselves The Young Dubliners. People in the crowd are wearing paper sham-rocks and green and white rugby scarves. There are tricolours held aloft and already at 11am a boozy euphoria.

The Young Dubliners don't necessarily come from Dublin. They are called The Young Dubliners to differentiate them-selves from everybody's favourite Irish group, the cuddly, soused but apparently still dangerous, Dubliners. They comprise the Dubliners' progeny but are clearly less cuddly, not particularly soused and nothing like half as dangerous. I don't blame them. Very few people can be any of those things at 11am on a Sunday.

What I do blame them for is their music. From the moment they start playing I know this is going to be Irish music with a capital I. This is going to be a severe case of the diddlies, with all those ineffable jigs and wauling reels that everyone knows constitute real Irish music, the inescapable fiddle and tin-whistle pixilations heard leaking out of Maggie McGuire's and O'Riordan's in this city most nights of the week. That is what I blame The Young Dubliners for, apart that is, from the shameless strip-mining of their fathers' fame.

Irish music played this way is a form of sedation for the audience, despite its usual frantic pace, and is as predictable as any drum-machine and synthesizer anthem for teenagers pumped up on ecstasy and lemonade. Irish music parodies itself because the emphasis is on the Irish and not on the music. It is as aware of itself as any rock group talking on MTV about being famous before being famous. As if fame itself was now as inevitable as Thursday or Walk-Don't-Walk.

What compounds the problem is that there is no satire in the parody, no irony in the effortless regurgitation of what The Young Dubliners think the people think they want to hear. Irish music has become so self-knowing that it is in danger of congratulating itself to death.

Diddly, diddly. There they go. The Young Dubliners. Diddlying this morning as if it was the last morning for diddlying. Ireland deserves better than that. Patrick Kavanagh, St. Kevin and The Cranberries deserve better than that. The IRA and Ian Paisley deserve better than that. But standing under a tricolour we take our methodone like the desperate patients we are.

I want to say something, but suddenly there is no room in the soliloquy of spittle and Guinness cream directed at me by a new acquaintance. He is fascinated by my ancestry, my nationality and my refusal to purchase any of the attractively priced recordings of The Young Dubliners' ferocious diddlying.

"You," says my new acquaintance. "You. Are. A. Cunt. You. From. A. Nation. Of. Cunts. No backbone. No..." His mastery of anatomical detail falters. As this man is all of six foot five, pushing his face into mine must place considerable strain on his neck muscles. His eyes are malarial yellow, but there's no mountain lion in them. His weapons are words.

"Spleen," I offer, to help out. "Or guts. We're pretty short of sinews too. And spunk is good."

"Balls."

"Or brawn. Then there's silverside. Scrag."

"Only the Irish had the nerve to rebel. Only the Irish kicked the English out while the rest of you sat around playing with yourselves."

"I..."

"Assassinate the Queen, that Eurotrash, and I'll believe you're serious. Go on, assassinate her."

"What, now?"

"Until you do that you'll just be another cunt in a nation of cunts."

Our discussion is interrupted by the arrival of my companion's girlfriend. With difficulty, she leads him away, only achieving this by proffering a whiskey bottle concealed in a brown bag. She returns in a few minutes, grinning, freckled, tipsy. Her hair swings about in bracken-red rastafarian ropes.

"I suppose that was the booze talking," I say.

"Oh no. He's always like that. Just another Boston Irish asshole. The closest he's come to the mother country is the bottom of that Jameson's bottle. He thinks armalite is a kind of glue. But I still love him. He'd never hurt a fly, not even an English one."

"Who says I'm English?"

She raises a styrofoam cup half filled with a colourless liquid. In the square the choruses are swollen by a thousand flat, uncertain voices.

"Who the fuck cares?"

7

At the poetry section of the City Lights bookstore I listen to the couple on my right.

"All these people must still be alive."

"Why?"

"Because I've never heard of them."

City Lights is a surprise. Along with the predictable quantities of refried beatnik tofu, the screams of Burroughs, the automatic writings of Ginsberg, there is a certain fastidiousness about the selection of books. City Lights doesn't feel alternative. It feels better. It also acknowledges the obvious by offering little space to literary criticism and theories of poetics. Litcrit's day has come and gone, an unmourned sepia Sunday back in the fifties. Today's liveliest writing deals with sport, music culture, the cyberverse. Of all things. Greil Marcus sketches figures of the media badlands, like the smack-pale ghost of Keith Richard, owner of the world's dirtiest electricity. I flip through investigations of angels dancing on microchips, the bureaucracy of paedophilia, an astrological chart for Romario, the new Brazilian Senhor Goal. There are atlases of cyberspace, manuals on chess ecology, the cuisine of witchcraft.

There are also the writings of Rush Limbaugh. Which is a suprise, at least in City Lights. Limbaugh is a broadcasting phenomenon, a cross between a sneering, bourbon-driven newsreader and a satellite TV-funded ex-politician. He is a chatshow supremo, a polemical disc jockey with opinions of bluebag toxicity. People love him. Not surprisingly, his audience is 50% Democrat. But then, the middle classes like nothing better than to be scandalised.

I have heard Limbaugh only once (in the media he is instantly identifiable as 'Rush'). His guest on a radio talkfest was a well known environmental activist. She explained that it was in the American interest to lobby for a moratorium on rainforest clearance. Her point was the old standby. The species of plant or insect made extinct today might have provided a cure for AIDs or the common cold tomorrow.

During the time she presented her thesis I started perspiring. Limbaugh could be sensed behind her. Fearfully poised. Like an intruder who had stolen into her appartment. The national radio audience waited for him to strike. And when it came, it was a hugely predictable lunge, more spiteful than deadly. But effective enough. Limbaugh ignored the threatened Peruvian orchids. He merely inquired of the guest whether she agreed with abortion on demand.

The woman knew it was a trap but there was no way around. She supported abortion for the usual reasons. So Limbaugh skewered her. What about all the babies sucked out and incinerated today, he asked. Couldn't one of them have grown up to discover an AIDs cure? Or save the trees?

The woman never had the chance to answer. Environmental groups have corrupted the American way of life for too long for Limbaugh to show mercy. Earth First are John Muir's bastards. A tribe of Indians living in igloos made of horseshit are holding up work on a trillion dollar nuclear dumping site. Banks have imploded because of the bills for cleaning up poisoned land, flushing their little-old-lady investors down the can.

Limbaugh spoke so quickly his guest could not reply. Another jogger had vanished. And thinking about it, I realised I loved his programme. There is about its hero a fascinating aura of menace, rarely achieved by the rotund. If he is merely a chancer then he has struck spectacular paydirt. Somewhere in Limbaugh's politics are the obscene chords of 'Street Fighting Man'. There is also James Last and a leavening of country & western wisdom.

The last item on that day's edition concerned the President's penis. What he had done with it, to whom, and when. More importantly, what it looked like and who might identify it. All through the subsequent discussions, Limbaugh's voice was ground glass and molasses. These days assassins don't have to use bullets.

8

The shape two stools down in the gloom of the East LA asks me if I mind if he smokes. Immediately I say no but ponder his politeness. His fear. This is a large, murky bar where daylight is an alien sheen. The fine afternoon outside is full of purposeful activity and the creation of wealth. The most resourceful people in the world are hurrying down sidewalks, back to their E-mail, their telephone conferences, the glossy imperatives of the fax. Vietnamese, Italian, Thai faces chew tofu-and-eggplant, knock back ampoules of organic pear juice. They carry free newspapers which detail exhibitions and lectures, the nine hundred different evening classes available here, everything from Etruscan grammar to how to use rapist repellent technology. None of them look into the black windows of the East LA, which are of gangster-glass, empurpled, veiled in soot, barriers which prove there is in life an inside and an outside with nothing much between, not even a state of mind.

Inside, a lonely minority gathers the darkness around itself and simultaneously assaults it with sodas or tumblers of bourbon. Outside, the drama continues without intermission. Even the starvelings at the street corners with their cardboard signs that say 'hungry, homeless, will work for food' play immaculate parts. But in the East LA we are dismissive of such soap opera. And desperately jealous.

Outside, the tough have already got going. So inside we compete by scaring each other. People deal drugs at the East LA. They knock each other to the floor and pitch bottles of Mexican beer into the fracas. Some choose a corner, open a book, and turn everybody paranoid. Others stare for hours through their psychosis at a cocktail glass or the green neon exit sign. There are weapons in the East LA. The barman remembers the Somalian campaign bayonet, the pistol pulled from a brown grocery bag. There are empty seats here too, that belonged to the missing-in-action, the disappeared ones. The talk includes an acronym: UHR. I try to work out what it means. UHR in an orange grove. UHR at the city dump. When I succeed I wish I hadn't tried. There is a meanness to this place. Even the television programmes are mean. The big cable job on the wall is blasting out some southern networked confrontation between a divorced couple who have been paid to relive some of the horrors they put each other through. The slivering mirrors, the stolen children. "Stupid white trash," somebody at the bar murmurs. "Do anything for a buck. Real UHR."

The next item brings together a released murderer and the parents of his victim. The predictable pandemonium is divided by adverts for funeral insurance and pet cemeteries. The screen violence becomes so wonderful that the murderer is hurried off set and interviewed in a toilet. This is intercut with images of the weeping co-stars and a bellicose studio audience. But the East LA is that type of place. It doesn't apologise. So why should anyone care whether I care if they smoke? They might blow Camel fumes into my eyes and I still wouldn't be any less co-operative. I'm that type of person. Relatively quiet. Relatively sober. Relatively scared.

The reason for the request is that smokers are an oppressed sub-culture, harried by environmental moonies, driven underground by medical special forces units on search and destroy missions. Soon there will be organisations set up to treat smokers as endangered species. I can sympathise. I come from a country of brown ceilings. My grandmother used to smell as if she had been tending a bonfire. My father could create a smoke-ring olympiad over the supper table. They were shortening my life, but so was self-abuse, Mother's Pride and a daily ration of tea so strong you might distill tar from it. Smoking wasn't considered either clever or a social misdemeanour. It wasn't considered at all. There were more people who smoked than people who drove, people who worked, people who drank.

I bought my grandmother's Woodbines in the tavern opposite our house. Slim green packets of fives, innocent as today's

condoms or asthma inhalers. I have seen pictures of that tavern
and its 'fifties' regulars, men in dark suits and ties in a spartan
room, each holding a cigarette. All look pale, slightly wasted. Yet
I know them to have been thirty and forty year olds. Still young.
Or what today we would think as young. It was a hard life.
Perhaps that was why they smoked. Smoked and never dreamed
of asking permission first.

Now in this city the guilty ones must leave their offices if they
crave a drag, though presumably not at the headquarters of
Philip Morris. The onyx forecourts of the banking houses, soft-
ware empires and airline companies contain incommunicative
groupings of three or four besuited lepers, sucking at the nipple
of nicotine, blowing sulphuric genies into the underground park-
ing. Without their cancer sticks they would look ordinary
enough. Young, middle-aged, charcoal and navy, good blind-
date material. But we need our caste systems. If we cannot
demonize HIV positives or punks, smokers will do. Because
smokers are like heavy metal fans, trainspotters, Albanians. They
are kind of stupid. Kind of nerdy. Untrustworthy. Don't marry
one. They probably kill their children.

The result is that smokers are perpetually uneasy, as if trou-
bled by intermittent toothache. And the city ordnances grow
increasingly hysterical. In the capital of this state public employ-
ees are not allowed to smoke within fifteen feet of their offices.
This means they have to cross the street to the opposite sidewalk
to light up. And the neurosis has seeped even into the East LA,
and claimed the leatherboy, the mailman with high-tar eyes, sort-
ing his letters from a bar stool, my shadowy neighbour. He
pushes a duty-free parcel of Marlboros towards me, sensing a
friend. I recoil as if he had made a pass.

9

My blisters are healed, the miraculous new skin, first fragile as rose petals, now established and less baby-like, is tough enough for a long walk. I join the fifty thousand students and twenty-two members of the Brazilian World Cup football team at Stanford.

A groundsman in clean overalls refills the humming-bird feeders. The humming-birds, motionless, ceaselessly moving, flicker against the air like a sleeper's eyelid. Lawns here are smoother than golf-greens, the apricot trees abundant, the computer-controlled sprinkler system a sibilance at the back of the mind. I move up the slope and discover the National Particle Accelerator. This is an almost Disneyesque construction, a grey serpent that runs across the turf for a mile, a stretched gunmetal intestine, ten feet high, seamless, inscrutable, the work, it must be, of some billionaire artist, the type that pulls a condom over the Empire State or takes a plaster cast of the Acropolis.

The National Accelerator is a telescope that looks inside itself. A camera that photographs the rush hour of protons and electrons as they head home. Within it move atoms and the atoms of atoms, smithereens that are monitored like migrating birds. Some are petrels and circumnavigate the globe. Others are sparrows which fly only within domestic confines. In the laboratories behind the hill the university scientists gauge the flight patterns, gaze at dials that measure the anguish of molecules as they fragment on their journeys.

In the laboratories they discover many things. That there is a speed of light and a speed of darkness. That atoms are made of triplets of particles called quarks. That in the original stages of atom-building, quarks are the smallest constituents of matter that can exist without ceasing to exist. That this is the key until the next key, when the building bricks of quarks are discovered. The scientists watch the particles cluster and the clusters disintegrate. In Stanford stadium the Brazilians sprint in threes and fours across the perfect grass, weightless, green and yellow as the humming-birds, before detonating apart, an atomburst of pain and laughter, to reform in the centre circle, squirting water into each others' mouths. Inside the darkness of the accelerator, the traffic of light roars on.

10

This might be San Carlos, it might be Redwood City. Or some relaxed, identical suburb. The road has a Spanish name that means Avenue of the Fleas, and the house numbering is into the twenty-five thousands. I am the only person on the streets and have been so for the last three hours. A rat runs up a palm trunk into the blond beehive of fronds. An electric mail cart trembles at the kerb.

I am the solitary pedestrian and the drivers let me know it. The men stare and smile, the women look and look away. Then an Olds slows down and the drawbridge of a garage descends to admit access, a triple garage with a red baize pool-table and assortment of powertools and jetskis. I glimpse a television, a closet-sized fridge. Garages here are good places. Out-patient departments for the long-term desperate. They smell of jasmine and fresh coffee, old barbecues, good times. People can live the most important parts of their lives in garages. They play music, modify a database. Whatever people do these days, they do it in garages. And such garages.

Standing quietly at their garage doors at midnight, the lemons pale in the driveway trees, the garage people listen to the engines of their automobiles ticking like crickets, the water settling in the rads. They smell the night, they smell the car upholstery, which is the lost, heartbreaking smell of our parents. Outside, a lemon rolls over the swimming-pool tarp. Two deer approach the electric fence. The garage people hardly breathe. They stand on the brink of understanding, here between the spreadsheets and the lubed and silver body of the vice, its jaws agape. This is the moment that imprints itself forever, like a football score, the shape of the Great Bear. Something is swarming about them, something invisible.

Then the garage people exhale. They sigh like their Oldsmobiles and the deer vanish into the darkness, faintly as a video rewinding. That shy rustle. Someone calls from above in the half-lit body of the house. The garage people check the locks, examine the stamen of mercury in the glass, and walk upstairs into oblivion.

11

"Yeah, I'm a hypocrite," says my companion, flicking a glance into the wing mirror, starting to overtake. "But that's good, knowing what you are. It's the first step, like an alcoholic standing up at AA and admitting it in public. I'm a hypocrite and I'm working on it. One day at a time."

He slots a tape into the stereo and a song called 'I hate my life and I want to die' comes on as the exit signs for Los Gatos's fifty two restaurants and nineteen nailshops flash past. That was the town boast. Nineteen nailshops. I thought it meant iron-mongers until I saw the Mexican girls painting each other carmine and silver. Manicure, pedicure are art forms here. So are aquarobics and tongue-piercing. But the real, the oldest art form is driving, and I can feel my friend's quiet exhilaration as he squeezes the gas and the Harley Davidson grows tiny behind us, the avocado trees blur into dusty guacamole.

"Like, it doesn't matter how many organic peaches I eat. If I drive then I'm a hypocrite. If I own three cars then I'm a hyp-ocrite. But I'm dealing with it, I'm coming to terms with it. So that's cool. And remember. It's hard in this country. Everybody wants to be Thelma and Louise, or Peter Fonda walking into that bar in Hicksville and all the girls watching him. We all want to be Easy Rider and it's easier in a BMW, know what I mean? So it's hard. But that's cool.'

This man is not only a hypocrite. He is a liar. Owning up to three cars is fine, but what he doesn't mention is the RV parked in a compound a mile from his house. RVs are Recreational Vehicles, the largest of which are bigger than circus caravans and better equipped than apartments at the Sheraton. RVs are the tourist equivalent of the Sherman tank, and allow whole families with pets and neighbours included to cross Utah without worrying about two-hundred mile stretches of 120 Celsius saltrock between motels, or running out of Evian in Nevada. Although we overtake RVs regularly, I don't mention them. After all, my friend is an environmentalist. A member of the Sierra Club. To introduce the subject of his personal RV would be like asking a scag addict about his sex drive. Definitely infra dig.

I understand what he means about driving. As long as we are driving we have not arrived. And if we have not arrived then anything is possible. Driving means we have departed, so something has been decided and we have acted on it. Which is satisfying. But even more satisfying is the fact that we have not arrived. I look at the driver's face as the driving music plays. Doctor Feelgood, Vivaldi, scored for the road. The satisfaction shows as a clarity, a smile in the eyes as he guns forty thousand dollars' worth of German technology through the billboards and prickly pear. If you want to surf, says a banner hung over a bridge, don't do it on the freeway. We cross into what I take to be the fast lane. There is an intermittent white diamond emblazoned there.

"Car pool carriageway," he explains. "At rush hour, only buses or cars with two or more people can use it. Or that's the theory."

Ahead, the road is out of focus, a photograph taken into the sun. Around us now are sand dunes with eagles over the wadis, a closed airforce base that has been returned to the apricot farmers. A blonde in a convertible overtakes on the right, coming out of nowhere into nowhere, impassive as royalty. Lee Brilleux's cancerous voice gives us a third rewind of 'Milk and Alcohol'.

"At least I'm not one of those holier-than-thou bastards who preach off of some Mount Saint Helens of moral high ground." My friend wears scuffed denim, snarls with BMW teeth. "One day at a time is cool. I'm a hypocrite and I'm dealing with it. Anyway. What about you airport hopping six thousand miles to tells us about air pollution. Man, we invented pollution. We perfected it. So shall I tell you what pollution really is?"

I don't answer. There is no stopping him. Not that I wish to. This is Highway One soliloquizing fuelled by speed and the idea of a continent rushing out to meet us. A racoon pelt like a black and white scarf is ironed into the macadam.

"Pollution is Elvis getting hungry and phoning up a delivery place for a snack. Peanut butter and jelly sandwiches if you must know. Real homey. So the restaurant delivered. Apparently Elvis had an account. Only the restaurant is in LA and hungry boy Elvis is in Memphis. Gross eh?"

"He could have died of hunger."

"Uh uh. Elvis died of America. Which is not the same thing. Not the same thing at all."

12

I try to decipher the graffito on the back of the seat. There is an S, in fact an S.A.T. Someone has sat here, somebody bored, looking out the windows at the avocado trees, the homeless woman in her festering armchair that is slowly turning to penicillin, her bags of aluminium cans, a cent every return, heaped about her at the rear of the supermercado.

That chair, occupied or not, is a feature at the railside. I have started to look for it, a landmark on this journey, along with the discreet neon in palatino font erected above a funeral parlour, stating 'we deliver'. But the black indelible holds the attention now. Saturn, satire, I'm almost there. Satin perhaps. But really it's obvious. The word is SATAN and I stare at it like something that shouldn't exist, a blemish I had never noticed before on my own skin.

Yet the Caltrain rarely threatens. It is difficult to imagine a gang of football fans running in the aisles, refusing to buy tickets, dousing each other from plastic flagons before collapsing into the burgundy cushions of first class. In the Caltrain everyone is first class. Even this week's six foot eight Apache who confronted us with the kind of paranoid cabin fever that only booze or angel dust can generate. I knew my companion was scared. She had started whispering in a different language. The Apache leaned across to us, a radiant demon.

"I've had e-fuckin-nuff."

This was, I considered, a reasonable statement, especially as we were passing an International House of Pancakes and moving towards a branch of Denny's, a restaurant chain recently found guilty of deliberately offering bad service to certain customers. Black customers. And for all I knew, Apache customers. But the large man didn't look as if the cause of his satiety was a forty minute delay for baby ribs. I held his gaze for three quarters of a second before looking back towards Satan. We then retreated to the corral of our newspapers.

Jackie O was being sanctified, Kurt Cobain beatified. Everywhere there were obituariess for the mute empress of American politics whose only interview about the death of her husband is sealed in a bank vault until 2050. Everywhere there were epitaphs for the little blond humpback who carried an electric guitar and a heroin needle, his pain gone double platinum, his body not found for three days. Ten million fans and nobody missed him. Cobain wrote a song called 'Rape Me'. I had played it once crossing the Golden Gate Bridge, turned fire-engine red in the morning light. An exonerating breeze came out of the Bay, blowing towards the island of Alcatraz, a holy site to the native people of the area, turned by the state into a dungeon of human guano. Down on the shore I could see children listening to the wind organs, their parents warming the day's first hickory chips.

The song wasn't some sexual whine. It was a raw complaint about fame, the microchip's ability to smog the planet with celebrity. Fame wasn't the balm people thought. It was a malarial spasm. Benzedrine from a dirty lab. Cobain took his revenge on fame by blowing off his face with a shotgun. And became more famous by doing so. But perhaps it was to be expected. Rape victims get moody and look at the lyrics printed with the CD artwork. Pathological, pleading and deep down lost. Jackie O couldn't give it up for a while. She married a man who upholstered the bar stools in his yacht's cocktail lounge with the foreskins of whales. But she held on, beat the sickness, started living. That's it. She beat the sickness. The fame virus. This global tinnitus. All those voices in my head that won't turn off. That get louder. Now, past the armchair and the mortuary the train runs on, and we ride with Satan south towards the citadel of fame.

Paul Bodin's Blues

I have a theory about computers. It is quite straightforward. They are going to kill us. Simple as that. I started to develop, or at least think about (develop is a portentous word) my theory on returning home after four months away.

There was a new room in my house where the attic used to be. Where there had been darkness and old clothes and rusted cisterns was now a brightly painted study. In the new space was a skylight that permitted a direct view upwards into the moist atmosphere of this seaside town, and at night the constellations were no longer obscured by the amber fug of the street sodium. I could see the grey tumour of stars in Taurus, the Little Dog that seemed to consist of only one hind leg, and sometimes Venus, low over the school field, loitering like a child unwilling to go home.

Under the skylight was a computer. It comprised a monitor and a slim box no bigger than an attache case or one of those designer atom bombs that arms salesmen are hawking round the Middle East. The computer was mute of course, and yet it whispered. It whispered "use me. Pick up *Macs for Dummies*, find a window and use me". So I did. By the end of the week I was playing chess against it. Some friends had installed computer chess for my daughter but now she could not get near it. There were nine levels of proficiency and I played on the first. Sometimes I won. Sometimes the computer did. I vowed to progress to stage two only when I had beaten the computer in three straight games.

In my brief time at home I never reached stage two. But I did make the computer think. You could tell when it was thinking because if I made a move that was unusual or unexpected, the computer's responses would slow and a face appear on the

135

screen. The face was of a bald, bespectacled man, a fist massaging his temple. At first he looked like Ezra Pound but then I saw him more clearly as Sigmund Freud. This was the enemy himself, the computer nerd revealed. Sometimes Freud would rub his head for ten minutes before answering my move. I would sit observing his concentration, hating his pale face and glasses, detesting his baldness and determination. He reminded me of someone from my past I thought I had escaped, someone from school or an interview panel. And then he would make his move and I would rub my fist into my temple and glare back into the monitor at the black and white constellations we had scattered between us.

My theory grew clearer a few days later. I was sitting in a darkened bar called Horizons at the airport. The bar was darkened to conceal the expressions of the drinkers, which were, in short order, smouldering, recriminatory. Before them, the last speckles of frost were vanishing from their phials of Labatt's Blue. Probably the most expensive lager in the world, an Orsonic voice breathed over my head. I shook myself and returned to the glossy leaves of *Time*, a kind of Book of Revelations for the leisure moment. Because there it was again. Evidence. The spooky proof of how computers are going to kill us. Of course there was other evidence all round me but this was different. My flight ticket has been processed and printed by computer. The banknotes in my pocket had been debited from my account at the Dominion by a computer. The Dominion was a modern bank. Every time I crossed the threshold, an electric beam read the account number on the cheque-book in my jacket and made a charge. How else could they pay for the air-conditioning, the trilingual cash dispensers, the plush red ropes, like those in a theatre foyer, that directed you to the correct queue. Even the till at Horizons was a computer in disguise, a diddle-proof casket of voices and lights masterminded by a microchip.

But *Time* was not interested in this mundane technology. *Time* told of computers of the near future, and because time has speeded up, like an exhausted runner going flat out in the final straight, the near future is now. Or already yesterday. *Time* told me that all I needed to do was wire a camera and microphone to my computer at home and anyone else on the Internet could watch and hear me as I busied myself in the new room under Taurus and the Little Dog. Did I want to wire up the gizmos? Not in a million years. But what if somebody else did?

There is nothing as delicious as paranoia. At the very least it makes life worth living. At best it is the source of my most significant dramas. There was, it appeared, a camera and mike already fitted to the computer in the University of Waterloo's Science Club. Big deal, most people would say. And yet, what happens now in the club is a television programme in its own right. Forget the Five Hundred Channel Universe. Uprate to five billion. In ten years time we will all be on the Internet. And the Internet will be American. It will speak American and think in American. And we will all have our own shows, our own soaps, celebrities at last, all gassed-up on the superhighway. Computers? They make the H-bomb look like the hulahoop. I know they're going to kill us. The only question is how.

My flight was late, the monitor announced. I had waited an hour, there was another hour to wait, and now, out of nowhere, another hour on top of that, a portion of time I didn't want, an alien hour. I imagined the Tristar grounded in an eastern city, the nitric choke in the aisles as the ground crew de-iced the undercarriage, men in earmuffs and tukes and quilted parkas joking around outside in the thirty below.

In the dark mirror my face was white and swollen like a bruise that didn't hurt. We had flown here across a frozen country. The lakes and rivers were spills of milk, the earth a riven expanse where nothing grew and nothing ever was. The captain said there was a settlement below, but I saw no trace in that desert, only a straight line that ran over valleys and hillsides, that did not diverge from streams or precipitous rock, but extended north to south, south to north, out of sight and reckoning. A line like a road that was not a road, illuminated with snow. It's a pipeline, somebody had muttered, but it didn't look like a pipeline to me. A UFO skid, said someone else. This is their territory. Land of the Big Sky. I gazed below at the plateaux and cirques, seeking intimations of colour, discovering only pumice and lightning and atolls of ice. The glaciers that had harrowed the country had shrunk northwards, the direction of their retreat gouged in the purple rock. Then the clouds came lower and a dirty veil was drawn across the landscape. Topography disappeared and all that remained in the universe was the wingtip light, an intermittent martian glow.

We had landed through a freezing fog on the city's floodlit snow, courtesy of the computers on board. The tundra of hours stretched ahead, but I thought about the microphones once more, the cameras and everything they might reveal. To whom, and why, were not important. And thinking about microphones, I was back again in Victoria Gardens, passing another miscalculated, apologetic hour. Victoria Gardens was one of my favourite places. I chose an iron seat near the gorsedd stones and watched the sun zig-zagging like a snipe through the leaves, and the leaves and the light and the yellow needles of the dandelions were a benediction that afternoon.

I was early for an appointment across the road in the library. An hour early. I could have stayed, but there was only milk-powder for the tea, like crematorium ash, and the room smelled damp. It was also full of computer screens with out-of-order notices cellotaped to the sides. So I went out and sat under a sycamore in Victoria Gardens. The town was warm and quiet. It was, strange to think, the town where I was born. Yet I had no particular affection for the place. It was only chance after all. The hospital ten miles up the valley had been full. But the gardens were different. Here people relaxed, put down shopping, stared in silence into themselves or shouted in the district's outrageous accent over the irises and hydrangeas towards the bus station.

The place names shattered on a destination board as a driver spun the handle. A crowd gathered as if watching a conjuror.

"What's it like when a stranger knows your name?"

He was a grey-haired man at the other end of the bench. There was a bag between his feet from which he had been scattering seed. The sparrows and pigeons still fussed around.

"You know me?"

"Saw you in that film."

"What you think of it?"

The man smiled and I could feel it coming, the faint praise, B minus in my old form-master's spidery script, the blue report book still at home, twenty-five years later.

"Good to see the Albania bit. Now there's a place I often thought about."

"Been there?"

"No, but I admired Hoxha. He held out as long as he could."

"He was a murderer."

"Name a leader who isn't. He was mad but he fought against a different kind of madness."

"What's your name?"

"Jones. Dewi to you."

"Well Albania's changing. It's hardly a democracy yet. But that's the way it's going."

"Democracy? What's that then?"

Every park has one, I supposed. A solitary mister. Maybe I was one myself.

"Well the best bits, which were the worst bits, if you follow, never made it into the film. Anyway, didn't we play Albania recently?"

"Qualifiers for the European Championship. Two nil to us at home."

"Thought I might go back out," I said. "The return's next November. Any excuse like."

"Well make it a sight-seeing trip as we're out of the cup already."

"Yeah. I been away. What are those weird teams we lost to?"

"Bulgaria. Nothing weird about Bulgaria. Before that it was Georgia. Before that, Moldova."

"Moldavia?"

"Moldova. It's behind Rumania. Can't say I heard of it until last year. Anyway, they tanned our arses and we're out of the jamboree before it's started."

Dewi threw some corn and I could see a greenfinch in with the gang of sparrows, an olive body and wings barred yellow. It was a bird from my childhood, a moderately unusual visitor to the back garden.

"And it's held in England, just to make it worse. Wall to wall telly and we're not there. Bulgaria might be but not Moldova. And Albania's got less chance than us."

"The old story," I laughed.

He looked at me then with a passion that surprised. As yet, the greenfinch hadn't picked up anything. Nervous feeders, I remembered. Back of the queue.

"You mean the World Cup? Jesus. I can still see it. What was that boy's name? What was his name now?"

Here we go, I thought. Welcome to the national nightmare. Much less than a year had passed but it felt like ten. Well, why not? Time was fast-forwarding naturally towards something increasingly predictable. I could still feel it, an almost sexual anticipation. Christ, it was better than sex. BBC television, as is its wont, tortured us with previews and prognostications, its vivid trailers better than any programme. We were playing Romania in the World Cup qualifying rounds. If we won, we would go to the Finals for the first time since 1958 and for the first time ever in the global media age. Even a draw might do it. In fact, a draw, said certain saloon bar mathematicians, would undoubtedly do it, if some other team in our qualifying group, I can't remember which, lost their last match. The World Cup Finals. In the USA. Media heaven. An audience of three billion. A draw would undoubtedly do it. Ryan Giggs in the Citrus

Bowl. Ian Rush battling heat exhaustion to tap one in at the Rose Bowl. Jacks and Ninian boys together sampling the sweet Dominican beer on the Lower East Side. And all those people in Paraguay and the United Arab Emirates nodding their heads and saying simply, "Ah yes, Wales," as some clever dick on the panel of experts pointed on an electronic map to the blue edge of Europe.

He had once played for Cardiff City. A good, steady full back who liked the overlap. Now the player placed the ball on the penalty spot and squinted up at the Romanian goal. The goalkeeper would try to cheat by moving before the ball was touched, but they all did that, even Big Nev down the other end. Especially Big Nev. I clutched my wife. She held on to our daughter, who seemed, in the fleeting look I was able to give her, insufficiently mesmerised by the tension. I took a short draught of something alcoholic and put it on the floor by the sofa. Okay, we weren't there. We were not actually at the National Stadium. We aren't those kind of fans. But who is these days? There are no action replays, no close ups. You don't see the goals from five different angles with instantaneous computer editing. You can't channel surf in the boring bits. Okay, we weren't there. But we were still there, if you know what I mean, and I know you must.

He placed the ball on the spot, squinted at the Romanian goal, walked back, turned, and seemed to jiggle. We had been having a bad time. The Romanians were, in football vocabulary, which has, it appears, subsumed the entire lexicon of witchcraft, spellbinding. They were magic. They were simply the better team. What's more, they were leading one nil. But we were coming back. Resurgent is the word that sports writers use. We were coming back heroically, cockier and confident, and the Romanians, who were sort of Latin, sort of surly Romany, sort of decadent Eastern European bloc kind of people, didn't like it. We were coming back, the Romanians were rattled, and then at last, clearly, indisputably and with flagrant home team luck, we had won a penalty. I could feel that resurgence like I can now

141

feel a computer chess match when Freud appears on the screen rubbing his temple. When he rubs it too much I know I've got him. And now we had them. We had them in check and almost checkmate. A draw would be enough, indisputably enough, but put this away and the floodgates, something else those sports writers always talked about, would open. Rushy at the Rose Bowl. Ryan like a scarlet swallow swooping over the astroturf. The choirs of Aberdare and Caernarfon bringing Chicago traffic to a halt, and some sirloin-jowled copper with a nightstick saying yes, his mother did come from Queensferry. Now push off.

Up he stepped towards the ball. In proper footballing parlance you take a penalty. A penalty is taken. Sports writers, however, have begun to embellish this simple act. Now a penalty can be hit, mishit, smashed, knocked, blasted, tucked or stroked. I love that word. Stroked. It suggests ease and confidence. It defines certainty, an assurance of what is right and what will always be right. Yes, it implies faith. A faith in the penalty taker's own skills and the correctness of his cause. And a faith in the outcome of the penalty, not merely the banal dividend of a goal, but in a result that brings justice, and with justice, order, into the world. For without justice there is no order. Especially on the football field. And especially when a penalty is taken. Or stroked.

The full back did not stroke the ball. Neither did he hit, mishit, smash, knock nor tuck it. The full back blasted the ball which assumed an upward, slightly right-sided trajectory. It was in the air, I calculated, for one fifth of a second. During that one fifth of a second our telephone rang, my daughter shut her eyes, my wife kicked over a purple can of Buckley's Best and I hatched a scheme to wangle an all expenses-paid trip to the States to cover our World Cup adventure as one of a new breed of culturally acute, artistically sensitive sports journalists. Rising quickly and slightly to the right the ball struck the Romanian crossbar with the Romanian goalkeeper, who had not moved first, beaten all ends up. ('All ends up' is another phrase used by sports writers.) Travelling at seventy-five miles per hour the ball struck the Romanian crossbar and rebounded into hell. Hell. Taking our former Cardiff City and now Swindon Town full back, penalty-taker and foolishly courageous man, into one of its warmer suburbs.

"Did we win?" my daughter screamed, running for the phone.

The beer bubbled into the carpet. The crowd in the capital started a futile chant and we the fans, the real fans, stared unseeing at an endless series of balls thudding over and over into the Romanian crossbar, the penalty taker standing petrified, yet hideously aware of what he had accomplished. At a stroke.

There were twenty minutes to go but everyone knew it was pointless. Sometimes you know and wish you didn't. But you know. Toshack was watching but couldn't help. Neither could big John Charles from his council house in Bradford. Neither could golden-handed Gary Sprake, nor Ron Davies of the corrugated forehead. Cliff Jones no longer scooted like phosphorus. Mike England had a grudge in his smile. The match ended with the Romanians playing football never seen before in Wales. Cruel, balletic, ingenious. The ball belonged to them and their unshaven captain, Hagi. This sadistic visionary smuggled it on instep and thigh into previously unexplored regions of the park. Then stood patiently, waiting to be challenged. The Welsh team could see the ball but never touched it. They must have thought it was radioactive. When the whistle blew, Terry Yorath the Welsh manager, a blond and doomed Apollo, came out and waved to the crowd and his executioners within it. To conclude the evening, two brothers from Wrexham released a marine distress flare. Horizontally. It flew shrieking and smoking across the pitch like something out of *The Exorcist* and struck a man from Merthyr in the chest, killing him.

The Romanians in their yellow shirts joyfully lapped the stadium and were given a ragged, shocked ovation. They were going to the World Cup Finals in the USA. Media heaven.

Rushy did an interview, knowing now he'd never feel the dust of Pasadena. The former Cardiff City and Swindon Town full back was reported to be as well as could be expected. That night, lights in the Welsh Football Association headquarters in Angel Street burned long and low. What a game.

Mind you, the blameful one who should never be blamed is still playing and scoring penalties by blasting, tucking or stroking. There are those who claim he is lucky. Look what happened, they murmur darkly, to that defender from Colombia, a country which went all the way to the World Cup Finals. In fact, Colombia were fancied, globally fancied, to do well. They were a team of pigeon-chested ball-jugglers, preening, temperamental, tropical. But sabotaged by over-confidence they were quickly brushed aside. In the one game they seemed to be winning, their full back, Andreas Escobar, scored an own goal and that was that. Back in Colombia two men approached Escobar in a restaurant. He was a disgrace. He had dragged the name of their country in the dirt. More to the point, he had cost them millions of dollars in drug money that was riding on Colombian cup fortune. An argument ensued and Andreas Escobar was shot dead. If there is a soccer afterlife, St Andreas is now showing off his considerable skills. But say what you like, Colombia is a country where they take their sports seriously. And then some. Colombia is a country, after all, that people have heard of.

"Paul Bodin," I replied.

"Yeah, Bodin. Poor sod. God help him now that history's got its hands on him."

"And what was worse, I was over there before all the big games."

In May to be precise. The Irish had been ubiquitous, the shops full of Italian and Brazilian but mainly Irish gear. Irish shirts, books, booze. The Irish bars had been going crazy, but then anywhere you go in the world there's an Irish bar going crazy. A not inconsiderable contribution to civilization. No matter if it's some dirty back street in Malaga or a low rental between the laundries and crackhouses on the Tenderloin, there will always be a counter with a plastic shamrock and special offer on Harp lager. Always was and always will be. And in media heaven the Irish were everywhere. Jack Charlton, Roddy Doyle and St. Patrick massed in defence, James Joyce was the roving striker, the terrifying Behan waiting to come on should the going get rough. But what's for us now? Back to the dustbowl of heritage. Back to the acid reign in Redwood City and the governance of droids. Back to political mime, the mad cow statistics and television's psychic opencasting.

"Not that the Irish team's Irish any more," said Dewi. "But look at us. If they're not from here they're not in my team. Simple as that. I got no time for mercenaries."

"What about the Scotts?"

"Good squad but they never made it either."

"No. The Scotts. As in Gibbs and Quinnell."

Dewi's mouth wrinkled. "Insane. Twenty years old and fretting about their pensions. Says it all."

"Bloody traitors," I added. But then I'm easily carried away.

"Watch it," shushed Dewi. He gestured at the sycamore leaves above us. There were now two greenfinches amongst the sparrows, one feeding, one waiting.

"What's up?"

"Trees have ears you might say. And voices."

"How d'you mean?"

"It's us talking about getting the unwholesome end of the pineapple again. Set me thinking of all this Normandy beaches bollocks on the telly. My question is, what about the Fourteenth forgotten fucking Army?"

"Burma?"

"Caught amoebic dysentry over there. I was living in an opium den."

"No wonder they're trying to forget you."

"That's what I mean about voices. The Japs hung microphones from the trees and made the prisoners talk into them. You could hear them in the dark, some poor bastards from Bedlinog or Swansea, telling you to give up or they'd catch it worse. Crying like babies. Calling for mam."

"But you can't talk like that now. Mr Sony wouldn't like it."

"Bugger Sony."

"You don't fancy the Albania trip then?"

"Too late for me. Anyway, give it five years and Thomsons will be flying sun specials there and western history will have Hoxha down as some kind of Hitler. The man we love to hate."

I looked at my watch. "Have to go."

"Where to?"

"Across the road. I got two hours teaching poetry."

"How the hell does anyone do that?"

"Trade secret."

"Two hours of bullshitting more like. You won't remember but I seen you years ago down here with John Tripp. In the Full Moon. Now there was a man of interesting politics. Jack Spratt I called him, but he'd never have had much truck with the likes of Vinnie Jones."

Beneath us the land was growing dark. The white craters of the lakes haemorrhaged into frozen earth. I could already pick out isolated stars and soon the constellations of the northern hemisphere were visible through the aeroplane perspex. Nothing moved below on that frugal ground. The people who had once discovered it were long dispersed in exile, their sciences extinct. In my lap I held *Time*. Another leisure moment, another revelation. The map of Europe and what for now is called Russia was spread out in yellow and green and grey. There, to begin with, was Albania. And there, after a period of searching, was Moldova, unheard of but triumphant. After a little investigation I discovered Georgia, scene of a five-nil thrashing.

There were other places too, other countries. Lots of them. Chechnya. Ingushetia. North Ossetia. Kabardin-Balkaria.

Adygheya. Further east was Mordova. Tatarstan. Bashkortostan. Komi. Nenets. In the south, Altay. Khakassia. Tyva. How did *Time* put it? "Of Russia's restive regions, among eighty-nine ethnic and religious units, many dream of autonomy."

"It's a hell of a World Cup," I thought, and went back to considering computers. In our chess games I was always white. I usually played a conventional king's side opening that created a Cassiopeia of pawns in my half of the board. And the little man who looked like Freud would stare out from the monitor, paused a moment but wracking his brains, trying to kill me.

One for Columbus

In the Armoury the usual things happen. Warehouses are gutted, earth-coloured bricks replace sixties macadam, a seventies mall and its glass caverns snow plaster in a pneumatic assault.

The bistros are opening with green cane and opera posters. The wine merchants wear mocassins. Everywhere the lights are going out on the empire of polyester as the ecru-punks arrive, the unbleached hordes bringing pesto sauce and micro-brewery porter to the post-industrial and now post-poverty market district.

The tribe that squatted in the derelict bakery must emigrate to the draughts of the subway, pushing their shopping trolleys into exile, huddled deep into sweltering summer overcoats. Black kids on mountain bikes patrol the newly busy streets, selling chemicals for a dollar, advising on prescriptions. This is work after all, and everyone has to have a deal.

The sidewalks are full of hustlers who understand that genius is not to create fashion but to anticipate it. Foreskin piercing, that's a fashion, like solar power or cars with fins. Today's fashions are Iroquois charcuteries and celibacy manuals, desk-topped tarot consultations from a girl in an alb heavy with surf-board wax. In the newspapers they have stopped trying to make sense of it and merely suggest that the galleries have emptied their lunacies on to the street. After all, if art can do it, why not life? I see an exit sign from the melanomic sunlight and find myself in the chilled, empty barn of the Happy Gathering.

At a counter of urns a tattooed youth is defrosting a refrigerator with a hammer. Small white splinters have lodged in his hair. His upper arms are pumped so big the deltas of veins show as ridges above the skin. Behind him a blackboard offers what must be fifty different varieties of coffee. There is no-one else in so I can take my time.

"What's Swiss?"

"Sort of strong with a chocolate flavour."

"Is it good?"

"Nah. Sickly. But people buy it."

"What about Recaff?"

The boy scratches himself under his tee shirt.

"You heard of Decaff?"

"Course."

"Well this is the opposite. Instead of taking the caffeine out they put more in. A bit like those Phillip Morris cigarettes with extra powerful nicotine which they don't tell you about on the packet. So you get hooked quicker."

"How about the Suicide Note?"

"That's a triple Recaff. Comes in a extra-large mug with a disclaimer from the management. Nah, only joshin'."

"I'll try one."

I thought this might impress, but the boy doesn't blink and turns to his pharmacy of tubes and jars. The splinters have become transparent in his fringe.

Normally the first thing to feel in an empty place like this is that something must be wrong. Herpes on the hand towels. A psycho manager. But I carry my bowl of myrrh to a corner seat and decide to stay. There is a stage at the far end with a tangle of microphone wires. Down here is a pool table with baize the colour of the Cardiff City shirt before the New Age sponsors got to it. Royal, real royal blue. An unarguable colour. Tracing my finger over the surface it feels as hot and soft as a font-anelle.

The next day I am playing on it, nudging the spots and the colours round with an immigrant's deference. The triangle was under a heap of free arts listings, the white in a jar above the counter, dirty as a pickled egg. At my table another Suicide Note is steaming gently into the Happy Gathering's perpetual twilight.

I like pool, despite being only a semi-literate baize scuffler and cue chalker, who took up the game three years ago. At the time I was experiencing pains in the chest and arm. What I diagnosed as imminent heart failure, the doctor described as stress. At last, I thought. A fashionable disease. He told me to direct energy differently and suggested a sport. I looked blank. Squash was the pastime of masochistic realtors. Golf a parade of unspeakable trousers. Football was definitely out. Few sights are more ludicrous than that of seven or eight men of undisclosed age (say forty) kicking a ball about on a muddy public field, with another figure, usually some Iberian-dark gym teacher in track-suit with whistle cord around his neck, offering dictatorial attention.

Cricket was another impossibility. The last time I played I found myself in the outfield, positioned under a skyer, preparing to take an heroic catch. The ball caught me on the bridge of the nose and the blood stained the grass like a trampled carnation. Sport was dorkish. Even the sight of a canvas bag with protruding racket-handle encouraged my spiteful fantasies. For years I had felt at war with jockstrap culture. Now my doctor was requesting surrender. The pains in the chest continued. The result was a magnificent compromise.

I took up snooker. Signing on at the local club afforded glimpses of rituals that were almost masonic in their seriousness. Heading down a corridor towards the main hall, I could hear the ivory chink of colours before anything became visible. I thought of Tony Hancock describing the rustle of ice in a glass, the foam of tonic over the vodka. The best sound in the world. Imagine, said Hancock, not drinking. Imagine waking up in the morning and knowing that was the best you were going to feel. All day. All night.

For me, the snooker balls made that perfect sound. And then I entered the hall. The room would be forever a June dusk whilst outside the November afternoon turned black. There was a blue shade, like an old-fashioned police light, behind the bar at the far end where the silhouette of a man dried glasses. Between us stood nine tables, four with matches in progress, brilliantly-lit meadows seen from the air, the five others a darker moorland oppressed by cloud shadow.

Instantly, everything about the hall was right. The barman in his sour pool of illumination, the colour of the Brains diamond: the thick velvet pelt of dust on the long shades above each table: the way the triangle fitted to the edge of the shade and was always replaced there: the ancient brass-featured scoring abacus. The ceiling was low and tarry with smoke. Everyone, it appeared, held a cigarette, but I never once saw ash dropped on the baize. Instead, the smokers immaculately cued it on to the peat-brown reef of the carpet.

Everything about the hall was right. Except one thing. The tables were too big. Contrary I might have been in suggesting snooker as an exercise sport, but considering table size and my level of proficiency, I estimated that in each match I walked at least three miles. A pensive, interrupted, direction-crazy three miles, but nevertheless a significant step. This was the slacker's sure-fire way to get fit.

The main problem, however, had been created by television. Snooker is perfect after-midnight viewing for an audience whose critical faculties have been sharpened by several shouts of the local superstrength followed by chips doused in a curry sauce that resembles the contents of a smoker's lung. The colours merge and scatter, the reds orbit the sward, the black remains on its spot like an eclipsed moon.

And the mathematics of it all are calculated by the players. Little boys in gunfighters' waistcoats. Grizzled olders pros with embarrassing perms. Top seeds haughty as school-prefects, ruffle-shirted cocoons of concentration staring down a barrel at the white. It was the players' fault. They made it look so easy. Steve Davies imprisoned an opponent between the cushion and the green. Hurricane Higgins poured a Diamond White into a pint of Guinness and watched mystified as the cue ball ricocheted out of a pocket and into the audience. It was the ideal television sport. The table looked about as big as a chess set. A forkful of takeaway oriental starch paused midway to my mouth. I felt my chest, massaged my arm. I could do that. I could play snooker. So I joined the club.

Poised for the first time over the baize, the table stretched away from me like the lawn of a small crematorium. The flock of reds, packed tight as an infantry square, appeared both unreachable and unbreakable. My handicap was the lack of a mis-spent youth. When I should have been hustling the miners eking out their compo in the Con Club, I was struggling with the Italian Wars. Instead of learning trick shots from reprobates in the Non-Pol, I measured Jurassic time. I looked back on a wasted life and winced. All those years in a straitjacket, seeking academic excellence, a career, safety, death. All that time listening to the wrong voices. In my hands the lance and its blue ferrule were implements of a culture I had no right to share. Between thumb and forefinger I balanced the cue, breathed in and stepped off the edge of the known world.

Considering my ineptitude, I wasn't half bad. I played with my father, his first game for thirty years. It lasted three hours and although the points awarded for foul shots were somewhat in excess of the scores made by skillfully sunk reds or flukey pinks, we both felt something had been achieved. Sport, after all, is up for grabs. The best soccer players are Saudis and Nigerians. Western Samoa is the new rugby hotbed and the proletarianisation of golf seems limitless. Near my home what was once a stretch of shearwater-haunted coastline is now arc-lit at night as youths with shaven skulls and up-all-night complexions, perfect techniques on the driving-range, the trampled dune before them suddenly white as a mushroom field under the sodium glare. Sport has exploded and everyone wants a piece of the shrapnel. Even pebble-lensed nerds and saloon-bar Platos are shouldering arms, working on the principle that if someone can go round the school-field in a *wheelchair*, then they can start lifting more than the TV zapper or twenty fluid ounces of personal disorganiser.

But snooker proved beyond me. I remained overawed by the atmosphere and relicry of its temple, the unselfconscious art of its devotees. My lack of talent meant I monopolised a table as the more proficient waited impatiently in the blue glow at the bar. Miscueing the white and missing by a yard meant I was starring in an exhibition of how not to play the game.

Finally, paranoid with the idea that players were visiting the club simply to watch me convert snooker into snakes-and-ladders, I relegated myself to the more comfortably sized pool tables found in local hotels. Here the instruments were smaller, the baize rougher, and luck a more potent ingredient in every game. The chink of ice in the tumbler was not quite as distinct but at least I was more comfortably sun-screened from shame. Exiled from the shadowy hall, I stayed nevertheless one of snooker's would-be recidivists.

"Got four quarters for a buck?"

I did but I wanted to keep them. Quarters were useful, comfortingly large coins that fed the phone, placated beggars and triggered the avalanche of balls from the locker in the pool table. I wanted to hold on to mine.

"No, but we can share a game. Playing alone's too easy."

The woman agreed and hung her motorcycle jacket on the cue stand. Short, rotund, with three silver studs in her left ear, she yet did not look the biker type. Poised over a Harley her legs would not have reached the ground. Short legs, I thought, are not much help to poolsters anywhere.

The three matches we contested could be described as determined, unironic, mediocre. We were largely equal in our inability to build a break, but both of us were better at the negative aspects of play. Unlike snooker, pool is not overly concerned with potting. It is instead all about prevention of an opponent building a score. Covering the pockets with your own colours, finding a position for the next shot, leaving the other player impossible angles are all part of a game that can swiftly become a mean-minded, futile skirmish. Each time, our tournament was settled on the black, and each time it was mishit into an unnominated pocket, cancelling whatever decent play had gone before.

My companion was called Andi. She liked pool she said because every single game that had ever been played in the history of the world was unique, and yet there was a clear set of rules that prevented it from becoming arbitary. As she said herself, slowly, there was a severe sense of structure that somehow didn't overwhelm the individual's freedom to make an almost infinite number of decisions.

"Yeah," I said. But I knew what she meant. I also wondered why she didn't apply the same aesthetic sensibility to short legs and leather trousers. Short legs are difficult enough, but watching Andi creak round the table in her shiny black pants, adorned with what looked like watch-chains and the tiny metal pulleys that hang out of cuckoo-clocks, I could only suppose that she liked making life difficult for herself. In the aromatic gloaming of the Happy Gathering there were about six other customers, but none appeared interested in pool. We decided against a decider.

"Got to get ready to come back," she said, putting on her jacket.

I asked what she meant and her answer was to nod towards the cafe's notice board, efflorescent with posters and events literature. She gestured at a sign that made a gentle proclamation.

"Tonight. Poetry Slam."

I wanted her to explain.

"Come tonight and find out. Happens up there."

She pointed to the stage and then was gone, leaving me to practice with the white and sip what was left of the cool acridity of the Note.

I returned about eight. The Armoury was almost deserted, the only traffic a few yellow cabs and the vans of the deli owners shutting up shop. I walked under the black, metallic statue of Columbus, gesturing now only to pigeons but which earlier had dominated a square filled with resting office-workers and bratwurst stalls. The monument was there to mark the quincentenary of America's discovery, a nice touch, but somewhat puzzling to the town's Iroquois inhabitants.

How could the continent, they reasoned, be discovered, when their ancestors were already living here? When they had created their own United Nations of tribes? When their art thrived and their ceremonies celebrated the landscape and the sky?

It was bad enough having Daniel Day-Lewis shaking his buckskin in a farrago of prejudice and sentiment about the last of the Mohicans, whoever they were, without the barbecues, the parties, the pizzas with maps of the New World laid out in white mozzarella. In a word, the Iroquois were miffed. Their influence on civilization had somehow been squeezed down to a dodgy haircut and perhaps a canoe made from birch bark, which was not exactly a lot of use when travelling on the subway.

Until Columbus, it appeared, America had been a people-free zone filled with spotted owls and ivory-billed woodpeckers. And then, as soon as the New World nonsense had died down, the World Cup arrived. The Iroquois felt the Ice Age of anonymity grow colder. A tribe of Bulgarians was discovered living in New Jersey. Warriors from Cameroon laid siege to California. The Swedes did well and the whole of Minnesota was revealed as genetically a suburb of Stockholm. So the Iroquois wrote letters to the newspapers. And shrugged.

For some, history was a no-win business. The world belonged to the colonials who made films, exterminated the spotted owls and woodpeckers before trying to save them, and published the 'good Indian' guides. Colonials were sad people but they won the National Lottery every week. Colonials had clear ideas of how other people should behave. Indians, for example, should be Indians. They should not wear garage-sale Levi 501s or drive secondhand Pontiacs. It made them look kind of poor. Even kind of threatening. The Iroquois shrugged. They understood the missionary energy of the colonials. They knew that the colonials did not recognise how deeply sad their colonial lives were. Or that they were following a phoney map, mozza or not. But what could the Iroquois do? There was no talking to the colonials. The colonials were not good listeners. So the Iroquois shrugged again. At least they were still there. "We are still here", they said to each other from their rutabaga fields, the restrooms of their drycleaning businesses. It was a long game, a very long game and would go to extra time.

I moved past the wine importers, then the gun shop, a fortress of steel and lasers. Earlier, this had boasted more customers than the grocery, large men cruising the racks of pistols and hunting rifles, the glass case of machine-gun bullets like a display of expensive ballpoints. There were derringers and buffalo-guns, sheath-knives and cartridges of mace disguised as aerosol hairspray. Guns are like orchids. No matter how common, they are always unexpected. But guns are also like books. Somehow unowned and destined to outlive the people who use them. I had watched the browsers spin the chambers, stroke the handles of horn, the polished snouts. The winery, the gym, the gun shop are all places of worship. The cameras in their ceilings measure our faith.

Nearly one hundred bodies were pressed into the Happy Gathering. Every table was occupied and people sat on the floor, the edges of the stage and across the pool table which was protected by a wooden board. Behind the coffee howitzers a tattooed team was administering shots of Guatemalan Reserve and Bayou Soup. This time I had to pay for entry and the man taking the money inquired whether I wanted a spot in the Slam. He wrote my name at the bottom of a list and scrawled a time next to it. Balancing a cup I squeezed into the crowd.

Poetry is a strange world. It makes professors of certain of its practitioners and beggars of others. Exquisite lyrics are conceived by nuclear-powered egoists. *Decameron*-length verse autobiographies are churned out by otherwise ironic and amusing drinking companions. It is an hallucinogen and a tranquilliser, a

DIY therapy kit, a source of suicidal frustration. Overall, it is a tiny, teeming universe, bizarre as a rainforest, unknown and uncared for by ninety-nine per cent of the population. Not that this matters to the poets. The poets are largely obsessives or lucked-in mediocrities, characterised by their own unique psychological scar tissue. Most published poets are tormented by what they see as the inability of their genius to metamorphose into fame, to leap the unbridgeable chasm between promise and achievement. For most of these writers the future offers only small press oblivion and then extinction of the confidence, as opposed to the desire, to write. Of the few published poets who have apparently hit paydirt, all other published poets are hilariously scathing. Poets who are paid to teach poetry are prostitutes and charlatans. After all, poetry cannot be taught any more than talent can be concocted in a test-tube. And poets who are paid to edit other poets are treacherous know-nothings who have taken the arts council's shilling and confused Olympus with a dunghill. The oversubsidized writings they publish are literature's equivalent of a Kraft dinner. Campus poets, of which the US boasts an army, magazine poets, selected poems poets, collected poems poets, poets with gold medals, Queen's medals, Pulitzer Prizes, Nobel Prizes, bursaries, travel grants, gratuities, departments, doctorates, professorships, groupies, harems, dark glasses, dreadlocks, talk-shows, record deals, world tours, hotel suites, statues, headed letter paper and editorial boards are scum. They are the problem. They are in the way. Troughing it at everyone else's expense, they refuse the others their rightful towel in the literary sunshine. The published poets hate these other published poets. They hate them almost as much as they hate the unpublished poets. Those scary beings. The unpublished poets, meanwhile, hate nothing but themselves. But that is why they are unpublished poets.

The Happy Gathering, happily, was not about publishing. Possession of a slim volume, emblazoned with what you said was your name, was meaningless. The Happy Gathering was about

157

performance. It was an arena for the spoken word and when the staff turned off the Paraguayan harpists and quieted the symphony of percolation, words were going to be spoken. Lots of them. Even now the microphone was being tested and providers of the forthcoming entertainment rehearsing at the tables.

By my side a woman unpacked a portfolio of immaculately printed verses, each sheet protected in a transparent plastic wallet. A cowboy in a stetson examined a scrap of paper before crumpling it back into his jeans. And then we had lift off. The MC, a pale man with baby's thin hair, welcomed us to the third heat of the New York State Poetry Slam, warned us laughingly about a few of the more notorious readers who had been discovered on the evening's agenda (they entered all the heats, poetry after all being New York rodeo), adjusted the microphone and introduced the judges.

This was unexpected. Beauty contests have judges. Ballroom dancers and gymnasts live and die for judges – teams of them, dealing in the decimal points of paranoia and favouritism. Poetry readings might attract the bored, the desperate, the ambitious and the absorbed, but I could never remember any being judged. At least, not by judges. I looked at our literary arbiters. First was a young man in a Che Guevara beret. Then an old man with a sheepish grin and goatee beard. He looked like Colonel Sanders. In fact, he was the dead spit of the Colonel. Third was a woman with hair so short and stiff it stood up like the spines of a sea-urchin. Okay. The Colonel I could take. He sat quietly, eyes twinkling, a kindly megalomaniac. Sea-urchin had an attitude. You could sense it immediately. Black beret wore a black beret and that was enough for me. Reach for the garlic. Get ready to hold up the crucifix. Black beret leaned over to speak to the Colonel who continued to gaze genially into the middle distance. It crossed my mind that perhaps old Sanders was deaf, which would be a nice touch. But there was something about him. I could feel myself warming. And then the Slam began.

Reading poetry aloud in public (or performing it, as opposed to giving a recitation) is a skill few people have ever sought to learn. Mouse training has its adherents. There are collectors and exchangers of phone cards. Synchronized swimming was briefly popular at public baths. Some of these pursuits require more talent than others. The performance of poetry, however, makes only two basic demands. One is the possession of an ego that can light up the national grid. The second is the existence of an original poem or two on which to base the performance. The former is by a considerable margin the more easily achieved.

The first poet on stage was equipped with neither essential. Her allotted five minutes began with a whispered introduction that haltingly evolved into a description of the first poem she might read. This, it seemed, would be a paen to a summer-house in the Adirondacks. The audience reaction was impressively negative. The hissing started after thirty seconds, driving the poet deeper into the thickets of circumlocution. After less than a minute I heard the first cries of "get off". The terrified reader backed away from the microphone into satisfying inaudibility. I looked around. Packed together at the tables, the crowd was having fun. There were no obvious bottle-throwers but heckling was clearly a part of the entertainment. Poetry as bloodsport. The woman was led from the stage, traumatised but at least able to walk upright. She was headed, I could imagine, straight back to her maplewood porch with its wind chimes and laptop.

Up stepped the cowboy. He was a Vietnam veteran and performed the usual veteran's material. Stoned in charge of a rocket launcher. The colours of napalm. Brothel fatigue. He read fast and with an anger that was carefully controlled, the energetic cliches daring the audience to react. The cowboy used the word 'fuck' seven times and all the other correct ingredients. Silent until the end, the crowd applauded hugely, eager to offer reward, and then cheered again as the judges held up their magi-rite scores. Che showed an 8.65, the Urchin 8.25 and Colonel Sanders 6.50. There was grumbling at the Colonel's parsimony, but his goatish smile did not waver as he displayed his white card and stared straight ahead.

A comedian with a loud voice followed, then a serious youth whose eyes never left the page, and whose tone was nasal and important. And then it was Andi's turn. Emphatic in her leather and chains, she clutched a computer print-out with a grey ribbon of text down the centre. It seemed to go on for yards and she held it carefully, like a treaty or a will, almost afraid of what it contained, reading from it in a child's accent of surprise, as if this was the first time she had ever encountered such words.

I wanted Andi to do well, and she sailed through, her piece the archetypal American poem, huge, baggy, packed with detail as if the writer had been afraid to cut anything out in case what was lost was the part that made the poem a poem. An American poem. We all know the sort. Art as the elevation of the polemic. Artists as disc jockeys of the hormonal universe. The saying of the right thing.

Andi's five minutes were up but she was still reading an American poem. In Andi's poem, irony had been turned out of its mansion and was pushing a shopping cart around Penn Station. What had started as a lyric had O.D.'d on political steroids. The baby-haired MC had to interrupt the narrative and she looked up, startled. Andi appeared set to go on all night, but the audience was generous and the sea-urchin awarded her a phenomenal 9.15, the highest score of the night. Black beret, who had been increasingly circumspect, offered 8.0. The Colonel, who was obviously a man who knew what he didn't like, and was not to be swayed from it, came up with a typical 6.25. Now Andi, we calculated, was tying with the vet, and the others nowhere. For a non-alcoholic venue, the noise was staggering. Baby hair came back to call the last contestant. It was me.

There must be another word for masochism. Something that means public self-laceration. No-one had specially invited me to read. No-one was paying me for the privilege. In fact, I had shelled out three dollars myself. I had also brought a book. Simply happened to have one about my person. That ego again.

It had done for me. As I pushed through the crowd the only images in my head were those from the home-video footage shown on national news of a man who had climbed into a lions' den at an English zoo. He thought he could talk to the creatures. He believed they would understand his mission. Two hours later he was liberated from the tranquillized pride, one arm reduced to stewing-steak and his schizophrenia intact. Perhaps a white light in his eyes.

There is an infantilism to those who seek out public arenas in order to share their writings. There is also an element of madness. I once saw a celebrated author carried dead drunk from a stage before he had uttered a word. Ever since I have revered this man as a true hero. Horrified at the ordeal ahead, he had done the decent thing and partaken, perhaps over-liberally, of the waters of oblivion. The audience, an unlovely beast, which had also dosed itself with the same refreshment, and was already prone on a field of yellow grass and splintered plastic vases, awarded this demise the loudest cheer of the day.

But I stepped into silence. The kind of silence that people thought I might fill. That I knew was my insanity. On the measuring scale of silences, starting at one and culminating at ten, which is utter and unbreakable silence, the silence of the Happy Gathering scored a creditable seven. Occasionally it is only silence that makes life liveable. But tonight silence was a disease I had to cure. Immediately.

Looking up, there was nothing. Only the hot wand of light that Baby-hair was directing knowingly into my eyes. The audience had vanished. The page before me glowed sickly as kryptonite. The words I would read were laid out in verses like a series of neat graves. I heard a voice like a call for help but I was rooted to the spot. Whoever it was would have to drown. Then the light was gone, the audience was stirring, and I was gazing straight into the eyes of Colonel Saunders who was smiling his secret smile and looking through me. Looking right through me. Then he held up a rectangle of card with three figures written on it.

In the Pagoda

They found the bodies in the sand near the well. They were curled like ammonites in rock and there were traces of pottery and other possessions also in the grave. It was a good place for a settlement. Ffynnon Pwll provided fresh water. The sea and its pools were less than half a mile away. Behind in the cwm was dense woodland, alder now with its riven trunks, perhaps alder then and skimpy birch. It was a famous discovery and today the bones are displayed behind glass, guarded by video.

But sand is an uneasy resting place. Rabbits burrow ten feet down and cast pollens and potsherds back into daylight to lie with the plastics. The medieval windmills and wartime concrete shooting ranges disturbed the neolithic landscape that sand had slowly anaesthetized. And sand itself has no constancy. Where it has ebbed for generations it will begin to build, its glacial tongues depositing the ocean's effluvia in breasts and tors. Then it retreats through a thaw of centuries, and what is left are the bronze slivers of sewage pipes or lizards like sprigs of iron. Sand archaeologists such as myself need a sense of humour. What resembles a human cranium might really be the hub of a smoke-alarm hurled from the sea.

And how easy it was to sweep the refuse away and see beyond even the terraces, the shops, the neon geometry of the fairground, the caravans with their tiny windmill generators. I squeezed my eyes shut and they weren't there. All that existed was the camp with the fire that never went out, mounds of mussel shells and crab husks. And people, as many people as might be found in The Sportsmen's on a Friday night listening to the bar band, people working, laughing, crouching at the freshwater pools where the plovers flocked, their thin dogs rolling in the shoreline marram, people in animal skins and crude cloth.

Then there was the stream, a richer colour in that plain. I traced it back to the cleft in the dune, to the spring that was hardly an utterance in any dry spell. The well and its people were as clear as this shoulder of the bay with its sprinkled lights, and beyond that the island, a horizon all its own, a shell-ground and crab-lair where the shearwaters dived, reachable only by the strongest swimmers. The island was a perplexing country that disappeared like the moon. Like the leaves. What it offered it took back. A country that concealed, then reinvented, itself. Unnameable in its circlet of foam.

Here in the pagoda I can see the hotel and try to interpret its deejayed sounds. It's a special night for Halloween, a Teenage Inferno, due to end in a few minutes. The witches will appear at 11pm this Halloween, this night before winter, with their Rocky Horror Show underwear and snakebite breath. And escorting them will be their princelings, their surfrats, their blockheads. I am waiting for my daughter and her friends, having walked from the house. Already there is a line of cars parked outside the dance suite, the drivers come to collect their off-spring. They cannot see me. I am fifty yards across the common. In the pagoda.

This is a place where visitors come. Lovers. A tiny Japanese temple, welcome and incongruous, next to the open air swimming-pool, that bathpit of green cement flushed by the moon. I love the pagoda, fear the pit, where waters taste dangerous. In high winds children cling to the pool's rails like birds impaled on thorns. Beyond it are the razored gutters of the rocks. Then the sand, then the sea.

The pagoda is the place to sit. I'm cold but not too cold. That humming is the ocean, but there is another sound, something closer. Perhaps an engine, a dynamo, a faint subterranean bass I might never notice on a fine day. It is the vibration of the pumping station. Beneath me the town's waste is moving in its channels. The visitors would not know that. Nor the lovers. The Inferno goes on. I can see the lights and imagine the witches dancing to some Bronx rap, the new Essex lyricism. I feel sad for the hotel, staring at its pale turrets and the upstairs windows, uniformly dark, while the secret river flows away from the pagoda.

The Welsh team used to stay at the hotel before every home international. Run around the local side's field and have a chat. That was training. No scrummaging machines, no cynicism. Butchery yes, but elegant butchery. Now the Welsh team publishes a magazine called Dragons. There is a Cotton Traders logo on each dragon breast. But it's five to eleven, and out come the first werewoves, the first witches. There was a shop on the Lower East Side in Manhattan where you could buy witches' stuff. Witches apparently have stuff. They need stuff. Those Americans are something else. Everything's a product, so package it. Even witchcraft. And once it's in the package it never comes out. Those Americans. They can take the trouble to hug you goodbye at railway stations, with the silver, double-decker Caltrain impatient as a stallion, and still turn life into something you might buy at the Seven-Eleven. Even witchcraft.

But perhaps feeling sad for the hotel is wrong. Perhaps the hotel doesn't want the rugby business any more. It has the Inferno business instead. Because look at the team. Look at the players. No necks. Shoulders thickened on the weights machine to an intimidatory yoke. Hair shaved to pig bristle. A shining black strap around the forehead so tight it makes the eyes bulge. Gumshield smiles. Red, white, black. Black smiles. The players are like the blockheads those American sleaze mags talk about. Yes, blockheads. A class of men created by pornography. Note that word. Created. Blockheads work themselves. They work out. They sweat. Blockheads drink in gangs at nightclubs. Shimmers Wine Bar down the road. The Dynasty on 42nd Street in New York. Want to see a blockhead? Go to Shimmers or the Dynasty. Blockheads sweat in gangs at night clubs. To express themselves blockheads put fists through plate glass. So blockheads often have bandaged hands. And blockheads eat pornography. They eat it. They have no imagination and pornography only exists where the imagination is not present. Where humour does not exist. Pornography is not funny. It cannot be. If pornography was funny it could not be pornography. Blockheads are not funny either. But they are not dangerous. On the weirdness scale they are not particularly weird. Four out of ten. But they have no imaginations. They work out. They pay their rent. They eat pornography. So what is blockhead pornography? Do I have to spell it out? Actually, if I was talking to a blockhead, that's what I'd have to do. Spell it out. No imagination, see, which sometimes, fleetingly, might be attractive. Tyrannized as the rest of us are by the imagination. But blockheads are not bad people. They never asked to be born. They never knew they were becoming blockheads when at twenty-five or fifteen or six they felt that numbness. That kind of subterranean shiver, like the echo of something passing through the ground beneath them. A secret river. Blockheads are not bad people. But my question is. Why do they have to play for Wales? With their black straps. Their black smiles. Their no necks. Am I on their side or are they on mine? With their pig hair. Where did they come from, so many and all at once? Who said they could play in my team? Who let them play? Look at them. There they are. Those blockheads. With their blockhead lives. Maybe they're aliens. Is there a Planet Blockhead? Yes there is. It is here. The blockheads are with us. At Shimmers Wine Bar down the road. In the shattered glass. Being led away from a broken mirror. Blockheads hate mirrors. No necks see. But what good is a neck anyway? Sweating. A surgical glove of perspiration. Tighter. But don't look too hard. The blockheads might speak and blockhead language is terrifying. There are no answers to it. So don't let them speak. Come away now.

Perhaps it wasn't so easy to sweep it from view, but I looked from the hotel to the condemned condominium at the end of the street to the blackness of the dunes behind. To me the dunes was always the place of cuckoos. I would go there in May or June and the cuckoos would be sitting on the wayfaring trees, crooning to each other with the sound that water makes in lime-stone. And then I would approach too closely and they would retreat, low to the buckthorn, two, sometimes three of them, like big, slate-coloured thrushes, loud in their mockery, an unearthly disdain.

The sound the grasses made near the well was like rain, but there would be no rain. The grasses that grew there were not meadow grasses. They had thicker stems that quickly lost their colour and rasped yellow as I passed. The grasses were six foot tall, each sheath and flower high as a car aerial. And as dry and sharp as paper. I stepped in and they covered me, a child again in a world of tropical strangeness, powerful and powerless at once, those childhood feelings of exultancy and guilt inextricably woven as the grasses, supporting each other, moving together in the imperceptible breeze.

I would edge down the dune to the cleft that concealed the spring. People of the area call it a well, but it has never been plumbed or explored. There is a cave made by willows and a wall of sand. In warm periods there is nothing but stones and an orifice between them. The soil might feel damp but there will be no water. Yet in winter after rain the well can be heard before it is glimpsed. As a turbulence somewhere beneath the feet. A coming together, a racing away. Once I stood there and found a brimming pit carbonated by the spring's maw. Bubbles rose like quicksilver from the earth. A torrent poured over beds of wild turnip and cress, and after a series of convolutions, disappeared under the burrows. But in July or August, especially after an old fashioned June, my bare shoulders would be darkened by sun-burn and would feel as if they had been rowelled with teazles. Blond grain would skewer the eyelets of my boots.

It is a curious place in daylight. But it is stranger to walk there beneath an August full moon, the marjoram broken underfoot and the corals disintegrating as you push through the shooting ranges where marksmen were trained, upwards to where the mullein rises to head height, and the path is only an idea of a path, a faint sketch of the imagination and memory. In daytime this part of the dune has a ferruginous sheen. Nothing grows on the eminence. Every beetle that crawls there is red and the shield bugs are emblems of fire. Broken tin flashes in the crevices. A sheet of corrugated iron is an eyot of rust. In the dark it is important to remember provisions. Stubby bottles of barley wine empty slowly and are recommended for an appreciation of the steelworks moon and its smoky continents. An accompaniment in the woods will be the sex-cries of a vixen, while below on the plain the teenage infernos will be burning amongst the driftwood once the anti-gravity rides and terror-tours of the funfair have shut at ten.

The witches are still coming out but I don't see mine. It's a pity about the hotel, where the music is stopped and the indigo light of the dance-floor has been swept away. Tommy Cooper stayed there once and twisted the coathangers into animal shapes. Pete Townshend also, because The Who were playing next door in the Pavilion. They must have had the same dressing-room, the one like a cupboard, with pink bulbs around the mirror. It's also a pity about music. The witches might think what they were listening to tonight was invented for their benefit. Which of course it was. The same three chords of ten thousand songs. This is the dance-hall they used to play those Amen Corner cuts, Andy Fairweather-Low's skinny Cardiff R&B, the only bluesman who sang through his nose.

That voice. It sounded as if it was coming from nextdoor's bathroom. And that smirk. Why not? Being the world's first double-barrelled blues singer was a considerable joke. Unless Blind Lemon Jefferson counts as a double-barrel. I'm not sure what has happened to Andy, though he was part of the Eric Clapton unplugged event. Not that he should be bothered. Robert Cristgau names two of his albums in the 'gone but not forgotten' section of his survey of the History of Rock. Those records are bracketed with James Brown's 'Sex Machine' and the Everley Brothers 'Roots'. Not bad for a skinny kid who looked like a trainspotter wandered on to the set of *Top of the Pops*. After that, it might be hard to care about anything.

But it's still a shame about the music. Take that Shimmers place, where the blockheads go. Up the same scruffy alley was once another little club. The Kee Club. You could hear Astronomy Domine played live through tiny amps set up in a vault of glazed brick. Marc Bolan and Steve Peregrine-Took jumped on stage wrapped in wizards' cloaks. (This was the brief period when J.R.R. Tolkien replaced Presley as the chief icon of pop.) The Kee Club is a warehouse now, and is almost erased from memory. Those who were present have apologised and forgotten. It was all a mistake. Anyway, most of those who spent their Fridays there have quit this town. They went to Bristol and Uttoxeter but it might as well have been Utica. Perhaps the Kee Club was the only real thing that happened to them, with the Groundhogs' leaden riffs and cheap acid. And now the survivors accompany the witches to their Cavaliers, the witches who smell of that nightclub smell, cooling sweat and excitement, the violet glow still in their eyes. Tonight might be the first night the survivors decide they do not understand their daughters.

I step out of the pagoda, colder than I thought. Behind me the tide has ebbed as far as it will go, a white horizon in the moonlight, the whisper of something domestic that usually hums unnoticed. And beyond that is the island, exposed at low tide, a dark atoll of wrack and pathogens. It is impossible to land there but one or two people claim to have stood on its outcrop, the edges of its pools sharp as gull beaks, and the whole emergent tier garlanded with indestructible ship's rope, historic jetsam. The Vikings gave it the name we use. Older descriptions have vanished. Twice every twenty-four hours this skerry appears and the sea is incomplete. Under a full moon I have watched waves grind sparks against its bones. And in the morning glimpsed it once more. Uninhabitable. And mocking in its uninhabitability.

Cautionary Tales

1. The Jacket

In the Exchange the first thing I see is the jacket. It is obviously old. Taking it off the rack, I can feel the welts in the sleeves, the cracks in the oak bark-coloured leather. It is small, too small for me, but I have not come here to dress myself. I desire another garment, satisfaction, delight, the sense of some inscrutable duty done. The jacket is for my daughter and now I need not look elsewhere in the store. Girls browse among the rails. They wear lumberjack shirts, long white petticoats, metal-tipped workboots. There are rings in their noses and ears. One, with her midriff bare, has a series of golden hoops pierced in her abdomen. Her belly is hard and shiny as a mirror. The store assistants are indistinguishable from the customers. Most have their hair shaved or beaded in the style of extinct local tribes, and some display tattoos through these pale, stubbled patches. Tattoos are the art form of this city. The skin is a canvas and its most famous illustrators are this year's heroes of the lifestyle magazines. The designs on the women between the clothes racks reveal their educated leisure. Dolphins, Buddhas, hummingbirds, Tibetan characters peep between their shreds of lace and denim. Ecological good taste is broadcast as poetry on the flesh. This is some place, this Exchange. Voyeurism burns like an incense spill as we imagine ourselves renewed by these dusty raiments, our loved ones fulfilled by our inspired choice of clothes. Each person in the store is twinned with someone they wish to be, someone who follows them through the aisles, laughing, insisting, looking back from the glass with cool or satirical eyes. My own twin pauses, seems to fade. I am still tattoo-surfing, acknowledging I represent an untattooed generation that never knew the army, the back street needleworker. Sometimes, just old enough for pubs, we'd meet some terrifying woman with *mild* and *bitter* on her suddenly naked dugs. And there would be soldiers and football supporters at the beach, daubed in woad and cartoon ink. But we stayed white as typing paper, our skin censorious.

The jacket has a petrol-blue lining that feels like silk. Surprisingly it is only slightly torn and almost unstained. The zips at the front are heavy brass triangles, good it seems for many thousands more tugs, moving up, down with an oiled precision. I see my daughter twist herself into the sleeves, her fingers discovering another continent's sweet tobacco dust in the pockets, the scars of Highway One in the creased elbows. She fastens it under her chin, the zip like a crucifix. This is Kurt Cobain's jacket. It also belonged to Marlon Brando and Walt Whitman. Thomas Jefferson wore it, and some befuddled grunt on R&R down an avenue of strip joints in Taipei. Now it will be waxed and paraded before another looking glass. It will stay over the back of a chair or within a wardrobe's scented shrubbery. Later, I will hear her talking to a friend on the telephone. She will say she can never wear that jacket out of the house. But she will never let anyone else put it on. It is too, it is too... The word never comes. It doesn't matter. I know exactly what she means.

2. Deliverance

First class? You must be joking. Think I've time to weigh those things? Or even look at the denominations of the stamps? Here's my system. Five minutes of first class, five minutes of second. Then repeat. Frank the stamps, put the packets in the basket, wheel the basket to the sacks, and sort. Salop; London Districts; Overseas; Local. Anyone can frank if the table isn't too crowded, and sometimes I ask for help. Don't ask what franking system the helpers use, I couldn't care less. Just move the stuff. But sorting is different, a real skill learned slowly and painfully. After a while I don't even look. Five minutes every afternoon to get my bearings and then I don't even look. There. Bristol and Avon, bullseye. I know it's in the sack, the canvas sack at the far corner of the honeycomb metal frame, one of the forty canvas sacks I'm filling for the 6.17pm to Paddington. Remember that parcel you wrapped so carefully with its beautiful Christmas paper and colourful Christmas stamps? I clubbed it with the date-stamp, dropped it in the basket and skimmed it like a hub-cap into the top left corner of the frame. Newcastle and the North East? That's where it's going. There's an art to packets, especially late in the shift, when the last collections are coming in and the sorting-office is piled higher than a superstore at Christmas and grown men and women are saying things which if remembered the next day would astound them. Stress? Don't talk to me about stress. You do afternoon packets and you'll understand everything about stress. The profanity of it. The liberation it brings. Hygiene for the soul.

Now Local is full so I unhook the sack and tie its neck in two movements, so swiftly, so nonchalantly, that if I could gaze down at myself from the ceiling of the sorting-office, I would not recognise that person. Neither the grace displayed, nor the concentration, which is beyond thought. I would not know myself. I imagine it sometimes. A figure, an angel perhaps, in a misty yellow radiance up at the ceiling, watching me as I take the sack from its frame, tie its neck with the neck cord and label, hook up a new sack and keep sorting, keep sorting, the mountain behind me growing bigger as the collections come in: a van load of headache tablets from Miles Laboratories, an orange esgair of jiffy bags packed by the local publisher. My packets, mine, in flight to the places in the world you have decided they belong.

There is only one duty better than packets. It is mornings on this delivery, with the dawn appearing like that angel on the ceiling and the litany in my head. Out here I am a magician. But invisible. You never notice me but I put the news into your hands, moving between these hedges with their rigging of maresmilk and the campion stems taller than schoolchildren, and the litany in my head and on my lips as a benediction for these places: The Enchanter's Rock; House in the Speckled Land; The Merchant's House; The Summer Dwelling of the Rock. In my hands, in my sack with its frayed strap and rainwater stains, is what you have been seeking. The squares of the coupons, the magisterial communications, the blue aerogrammes as thin as bank notes with their surprising stamps and senders' names and addresses. Here at Prospect House once a month, a blue aerogramme with its sender's name. I know that name. Every month I bring the news of someone I know to someone I do not know, the owner of Prospect House. That name. I watched its owner dress slowly in the robes of the country he was to visit. Long skirts, brown and grey, the colour of desert uplands, a device of animal skins on his head, and the red boards of a passport, his book of spells, prominent on the dresser. Every month his news arrives in an aerogramme, so delicate in my hand, and I slip it through the brass lips of the letter box engraved with the word 'welcome' in the door of Prospect House. I am a messenger and this is the service I perform. Until next week. When it is sorting again and I pull the wicker cart, piled high, towards the honeycomb, and send the packets skimming on their journeys towards you and away from you.

3. The Zone

One hundred people have used this room before me but it is impossible to imagine any of them. I find the remote and tune into local services. The announcements are in Cree but the writing is in English. These services are very local. Someone has lost their glasses on Main Street. There are job opportunities at the Thiessen Mine. The Cree announcer puts on a country and western song called 'Hello Vietnam', whilst across the road two ravens paddle in garbage pails and children come out of school. It must be 3 pm because the children always come out of school at 3 pm. But when I touch the zapper the 5 pm Detroit news hour comes on. This seems strange. The children are coming out of school, so it must be 3 pm. Yet here are the Detroit killings and burnings, the Easter wedding offers, the Association of Professional Psychics. This seems strange but I get used to it, because television is always ahead.

When I turn the television off there is still that noise. It is not the silence of the room or the breathing of the furnace that extends its silver limbs under every floor. It is not the humidifier. The refrigerator trembles but it is not the refrigerator. What I can hear is a monologue of the weather, the dry air inside, the dustbowl of outdoors that has somehow found its way within me. I touch the light switch and it crackles like a firework. The switches on the oven send shock waves through my hand. This is static electricity alive in the room, a garment around me. The air dries the skin, shrivels lips. Thimbles of white salve litter the glass shelves above the sink.

And the ringing continues when I go outside. There is a shell to my ear and I eavesdrop on an ocean. But the ocean is frozen. The ocean is a lake and as far as I can see there is ice over the ocean with one, two islands, two islands and their stands of tamarack. The aeroplanes are parked out on the ice. Across the road is an Arctic Cat dealership with some boys testing the machines. I turn right and the meltwater is running down English Street towards the lake. An old man in pigtails takes an Eldorado out of the Pizza Drive Inn. The shocks are gone and the clunker foams through the lagoon where the sidewalk should be. At the Watering Hole I order fries and gravy at the bar, then play the video lottery under antlers and the gleam of sturgeon. The province gets richer as the people feed their quarters, the size of sturgeon eyes, into the slots. At the machines the girls smear salve across their lips, each pencil a

173

bullet of ice, while over the lake the northern lights are the faintest green efflorescence, like a shadow of the Hollywood Video waterfront store.

But there can be no northern lights: it is hardly evening. Although I have seen the evening news the evening has yet to begin. Back at the lodge I watch a Cessna land on the lake and the pilot walk towards us over the ice. He comes into the lobby and says hi. On the wall above the television is a map that shows the twenty three thousand lakes in the province. Every one of them is frozen. I peer at where the map says I am standing. If I keep going north I will enter the blasting zone. This is drawn as a crater with lines radiating from it. The television in the lobby shows a picture of a suicide bomber. His mother urges others to follow his example. I thought if I came north the whispering would stop. I thought the weather in my head would change. But here on the edge of the muskeg, on the perimeter of the blasting area, the weather is the same.

Back in my room the 7 pm news is coming from Toledo. This feels strange for a while. Here it is 5 pm, but I have already seen the 5 pm news hour from Detroit. In Detroit it was 5 pm when the children were coming out of school across the road at 3 pm. But on television it is 7 pm because television is always ahead. Not that it matters. The news from Toledo is the same. Killings and burnings and Easter wedding offers. In the lobby I read the paper and the pilot says hi and walks out across the ice to the Cessna. The boys are going round on the Arctic Cat, bucking like rodeo riders. On the television in the lobby the Discovery channel shows a Stone Age tribe in Indonesia that was not thought to exist. This is embarrassing for the Indonesian government, which is image conscious. The Pacific Rim is not Stone Age. The Stone Age people were discovered by a satellite that was mapping the area for a mining company. There are diamonds in the Stone Age people's land, there are rare earths. The Stone Age people stroke the beards of the white men who had gone into the forest to where the satellite told them to dig.

It is difficult to know what to do with them now, the Stone Age men and women. The television says the programme was made five years ago.

I go outside and the meltwater is running down English Street, a thousand channels into the lake. I keep an eye out for the lost spectacles. The lake is thawing but it is difficult to tell. Next month, the month after, the lake will be an ocean. But now it is frozen and my tinnitus roars. Everyone I know here is unwell. The first person I met said, "hello, I have mono."

"Mono?" I asked.

"Oh you know, tired all the time. Exhausted really. Swollen glands, prone to influenza. There's always a lot of influenza about at this time of year."

"Ha," I said. "Thank goodness it's not stereo."

There was a silence.

"Mononucleosis," said the first person I met, "is not a joke."

But that was way back then. Now I pick up a box of soda crackers at the Co-operative and wait at the checkout. There is a magazine stand there which displays a famous magazine. Its cover shows the skulls of a race of horned demons that inhabited the earth before mankind appeared. I go out into the twilight. The ravens have vanished but the melt is running down English Street into the lake. An old man with pigtails in an Eldorado is foaming through the lagoons, water up to the fender. I could go to the Zoo but the Zoo is scary. You are looked at in the Zoo, you are listened to. All you do is sit there with the your bottle in front of you and people come up and stare at you. After a while you start to understand that's why it's called the Zoo. Instead I wait in line at Orange Julius then take my tray to the table in the mall and watch the children throw pennies in the fountain and fish them out and throw them in again. Then I go back to the room and the news is coming from Milwaukee.

In Milwaukee it is 9 pm. This is as it should be, although here the sky is not yet properly dark. Here it is 7 pm. But television is always ahead, so I watch the killings and the burnings and the

Easter wedding offers. In Milwaukee there is a frozen lake with girders of ice around its banks chaotic as the debris of fallen buildings. In Milwaukee the lake is an ocean like the ocean outside my window, white as the last embers of a bonfire, the islands of tamarack now a part of the darkness. The boys in the Arctic Cat are faint as a star out on the ice. Sometimes it appears as if they are coming towards me, and sometimes as if they are going away. When I turn the television off there is still that noise.

4. *A+*

"A commitment ring," she said, across me, above me, her fingers cold in the pale underpart of my arm, searching a vein.

"Never heard of it," said the nurse at the next bed, over her own prone donor. "Eternity yes. Course I've heard of eternity. But commitment? Typical though when you think about him. John that is. Sort of slimy."

I looked up through the glass panel in the roof. A gauze of cloud crossed a piercing sky. The great currents were wrestling overhead, the New Year breezes straight off the sea one hundred yards to the south, where the rock pools were gluey with ice.

John it seemed was a driver. In fact it was John who had manoeuvred the blood refrigeration lorry into the church driveway that morning. He had been seeing one of the nurses, on and off for a year. She talked to her colleagues about him and they in turn discussed his future. But slimy? That was a woman's word. I couldn't see it. Instead I imagined John in the blood wagon changing down on the corner at Tafarn y Jem, or braking on a hill in Aberystwyth, the windows misted up, headlights strafing his cab, a cargo of chilly plasma stacked behind. I pictured him clearly, a big man, trouser seat polished to a dark mirror, plotting his future as carefully as he chose his routes to the church halls and community centres. A big man, and sweaty whatever the weather, the royal blue uniform not hanging too well.

176

My nurse was still searching, and then a doctor arrived, checked my identity, and pushed in the needle like someone using a staple gun. Wait till tomorrow, I thought, when the brown stippling of the blood-bruise appeared, the small ache of a good conscience. I gripped the peg, started to clench and unclench, and a jet slowly left a double line of chalk across the pane. Out of sight at the bedside my blood was leaking into the plastic bag. Not that I could tell. There was no pain and no sound. Bog standard A Positive, as furtive as an after-hours pint.

Yet apparently they never took that much. It was always three quarters. Or half a litre now. I remember being strangely dispirited when I discovered that, as if my heroics were somehow less admirable, and I remained mired in the commonplace. The adverts didn't help, trying as they did to turn this, the gift of a man's heartsap, his own private source of the distillation of existence, into a mundane chore. Beside me lay an insurance agent. Coming up behind was a holiday shop manager. The advertising campaign had triumphed. But it was still a curious business when I thought about it, a useful reminder of the weirdness of the corporeal.

Not that it was easy to give blood these days. Reading the AIDS leaflets, signing the sexual disclaimers, trying to remember any history of high pressure and the dates of countries visited had all become an obstacle course before the first finger-pricked globule floated slowly down the test-tube. Look, I sometimes wanted to say. You've already destroyed the mystery of it all, the ritual bleeding and so forth, so why bother with all this? I got it, you pour it, just take it as it comes. Anyway soon we'll be making a genetic purée that everyone can use, so we won't be needing these sessions any more.

But perhaps I was confusing donating blood with something else. Making wine for instance. I thought of my rank of demi-johns of elderberry and its petroleum sheen, the stinging rinse of the metabisulphite that was supposed to sterilize the equipment, the siphon-tube inserted in the empty bottlenecks of Strathglen and lava-red Bardolino, my lips dry from sucking, and then the gravity-defying ascent of the shining elder oil, the pistoning of corks.

The trick was to drink the elixir as soon as possible. To be avoided was the conservationist's instinct to build a wall of black glass and anticipate flavour as the bottles gathered dust. That was to accept the mistaken belief that maturity improved the raw spirit. Any dealing with drink, my wine making had taught me, required a touch of contemptuousness. 'Plenty more where that came from' was the only philosophy necessary. Diffidence antici-pated disaster. Like giving blood. After all, I was a twenty-four pint man now, the doctor had told me, one hell of a boy.

"But the daft bugger," hissed my nurse. "Would I get a ring like that from our Dil? In a pig's eye. Where would he put it? Through my nose?"

I lay on the recovery bed and thought again of earnest John, built like a darts player, and the considerate bilingualism of his blood wagon, warning the public as it reversed. I pictured him in the corner of a hotel bar opening a tiny satin-filled box and offering not marriage, not eternity, but commitment, a young woman peering over her bottle of Strongbow Ice and regarding the future he held between his fingers. And here he was today in another church hall, still awaiting an answer. Wasn't it always the same? You found your voice, chose the words, and then had them torn into the confetti of the absurd. Well this one's for you John, I thought, and lifted my restorative tea. Empty bottles, son, empty bottles. See you in six months.

5. *London*

Pushing trolleys as far as the turnstile we found the airport train empty. Slowly relaxing, my companion regarded the allotments, semis and tiny cars that constituted his first views of England. Quickly Middlesex was left behind and a yellowbrick city lay all around, its streets of big-chimneyed Fullers pubs and samosa kiosks, its air greasy with reuse.

Very soon the carriage was filled and the train burrowing underground and the floor spaces blocked by backpacks and Aryan youths as tall as goalkeepers and a family of Croatians with birthday balloons and Irish children team-begging for their parents at the last station. Our breath mingled, our perspiration cohabited. Every time the train stopped nobody got off but many people squeezed in, so that it was difficult to disembark with the cases and to ride the three escalators to the Northern Line north-bound platform. And then we were rising in a reeking lift and making our second mistake.

Our mistake was not to hail a taxi but believe we could walk with the luggage.

It was a record-breaking August, the sunniest for three hundred years, the third hottest. Or so September would tell us. And although my companion had come prepared for everything, he claimed he was travelling light and that his partner had made him leave the biggest suitcase behind.

After we had paused for the fifth time within a hundred yards, and caught our breath on a hill in Highgate, I asked him what was in the second biggest suitcase.

"Books, of course."

It felt like books. Their melancholy deadweight. Books to sell, books to give away, books to exchange for other books.

And a tweed overcoat. And because the tweed overcoat was very warm, a light mackintosh. And walking boots. And a smart jacket, just in case. So smart trousers, too. And because of the smart jacket, another slightly less than smart jacket. And because of the slightly less than smart jacket, a knockabout, scuffed and comfortable jacket. And because of the smart trousers, some slightly less than smart trousers. And because of the slightly less than smart trousers, some knocked about, stained and comfortable trousers. And because of the walking boots, a pair of decent shoes. And because of the decent shoes a pair of slightly less than decent shoes. And because of the slightly less than decent shoes, a pair of knocked about, scuffed and comfortable shoes.

And the usual sundries. Which included: an electric iron with adapted plug; a hair dryer, ditto, with disperser; an electric tongs; a laptop computer; a Walkman and tapebox; a camcorder and tape box; a camera with lens box.

"What's in the carpet bag," I asked.

There were presents in the carpet bag.

"And the haversack?"

There were shirts in the haversack, a pristine block of underwear wrapped, I imagined, as carefully as a stash of opium.

And the big, scuffed, stained, comfortable-looking leather holdall with the mapleleaf sticker and crocodile mouth zip?

There were maps in the holdall, and guides to Thames-side walks in London, to blue plaque London, to rural London, guides to Cambridge and Stratford, guides to Wordsworth country, Brontë country, Hardy country, guides to secret England, to unknown Scotland, to mysterious Ireland, to undiscovered Wales.

And in the plastic bag?

There was a litre of Jamesons in the plastic bag, a litre of Johnnie Walker Red Label with a Johnnie Walker Red Label tumbler attached, a sceptre of perfume, a cushion of tobacco, a broadsword of Toblerone.

We stood on the pavement in Highgate and leaned against a wall by the Dick Whittington. There was a memorial nearby to Whittington's Cat.

"So what's in the bag you left behind?"

My companion concentrated, his face pink behind a cellophane of sweat. All traces of that morning's thunderstorm had vanished. The London sky was the colour of sour milk.

"All the stuff I didn't need, I suppose."

6. *Finding a Voice*

I

Everything was packed into two bags. Hopefully the car would arrive before my room-mate returned. Now there was nothing to do but wait for midday.

Monday morning and the hall felt deserted. This early in term fewer students than usual were cutting lectures. But try as I might, I could not remember where I was supposed to be. Monday morning was a blank on my timetable, that oblong of coloured squares. And here I was, slipping through one of the cracks between the days, or tumbling off the end.

I looked around. A long time seemed to have passed but my watch said seconds. There were the two bags full of the things I had brought with me. Almost nothing to show for the time spent here, nothing but the seven hundred-page Coleridge in its blue boards, each leaf trimmed in gold, so that the book appeared bevelled, like a mirror. It lay on my coat over one of the cases.

I had discovered it in the upstairs room of a second hand bookshop. It was part of the Frederick Warne and Company Landsdowne Poets Series, Notes, Life etc, printed by Clay and Taylor of Bungay, a serious undertaking, triumphantly achieved. The faint inscription in ink like dried blood told that an E. Coome had presented the volume to Miss M. M**** in May, 1880. But all I remember thinking at the time was that here was a real book, one that had lasted for a hundred years.

At the counter I opened the flyleaf so that the assistant could read the pencilled price. I handed over the twenty five pence, trembling not at securing such a ridiculous bargain, but because there was the possibility that I would have to speak. To say something. Something like Thank You. Or Ta Very Much. Or Diolch Yn Fawr. Or Goodbye. Something complicated like that.

Speech had become a problem recently. Or at least more of a problem. Words sprouted gorse leaves and spindle fruit, pricking and purging. At the clinic I could talk through a straw and converse by means of a small pebble in my mouth, but such remedies hardly sufficed for encounters in the great indoors. In the bookshop, for instance, with the girl of my age behind the counter, descending the ladder from the top shelf, pale-hair flourishing in an elastic-banded ponytail, her bony-arsed jeans washed down to the denim's white root. When she turned and smiled I could not look at her, but thrust the page forward with my money on top.

Or that earlier time in the second year form-room, Guto gruff as a hooded crow, hating the fact that he had to speak English to us and could not merely alternate between Latin and Welsh. Guto who swung boys round by the hair, his gown floating about him like a tutu of charred paper. Guto, who one day discovering me in less than fluent form, stood me up to recite the phonetic alphabet, as if he was seeking a new career as speech therapist, swinging me this way, that way by the vowels.

And yet, I could lie to myself, things were usually all right. The problem was seasonal, intermittent, a curious verbal malaria. Textbooks told of lobes of the brain, as if the condition was a product of malfunctioning technology, of psychological damage, of laziness. I wasn't sure about any of them. But I did suspect it might be getting worse.

I picked up the book again. There were parts that looked unpromising. 'The Death of Wallenstein', for instance. But Coleridge, I had come to understand, sometimes offered rubies in the dust. Choosing a passage at random I discovered *See! I confide in you. And be your hearts my stronghold!* And there was always the 'Rime' and the wretched 'Work Without Hope' and above all on page 189 a nocturnal meditation of quiet cadences that had shocked and then stilled me as I read it there in the bookshop, a candle flame of blank verse burning close to extinction, the girl on her ladder shifting stock. Then tyres sounded outside on the gravel, a greeting note was banged on the horn. There still seemed to be no-one else in the building, and my room-mate was staying clear, making a day of it in the town.

The silence was like the silence at the end of a poem. Now there was nothing else to do but swing the bags and go.

II

This was it. This was the finish. And here I was in the familiar anonymity of a hotel room, a wet evening outside, television in the corner, switched on with the sound off, tea-bags, thimbles of UHT and an opened bottle of untouched red wine on the bedside table. The unimaginable last place was, after all, entirely predictable, down to the cigarette burn in the sink enamel, the guide to nearby lakes and mountains.

There were forty minutes to go. I calculated it would take ten to walk to where I had to be. So half an hour to prepare, the final half an hour. But all the time in the world.

Of course, it could have been done on the train, in the waiting rooms, last night, last week. But there is an art to procrastination. It is gambling for the faint hearted, a risk taken for the law-abiding. This was as close as I would come to driving without headlights, playing chicken on the railtrack.

The wine's first taste was huge. It shrivelled my mouth. The Granada news shuffled stills of missing children. This rain would keep the people away, but I had to prepare. I had come a very long way to do this, and now there was panic in my stomach and in my throat, the places where it always lodged, cold as a jewel, much more precious.

Because this was what I had come for: the fear; its shivering blackness. I sat naked under the reading lamp and memorised the feeling, as the pages opened and closed on Lorca and Ceiriog and Shakespeare and Idris Davies and Wordsworth and all the others whose work I would recite tonight. And then it had vanished as it always vanished, a diamond dissolving as the words flooded everything, the words on pages 189 to 191 of the second book I would take through the rain with me, the words that Coleridge had written two hundred years previously, five hundred and seventy-one of them in seventy-five lines of blank verse, words he had kept hidden in a drawer because he was not sure of them, but words which certain people glimpsed, and copied down, words that astounded those people and made them happy or unhappy, words which constituted the finest thing Coleridge would ever write, although he lived another forty years and wrote many other words of criticism and philosophy and despair, many words that made him famous, although perhaps not famous in the way that we understand fame.

I thought of the words that are read every day. More than the cells in my body, simple, dangerous, each with its photosphere that decays immediately and is forgotten. But not the five hundred and seventy-one words between pages 189 and 191 of the second book on my beside table. These possessed a luminosity that was irreducible, and in half an hour's time I would walk on to a stage in a public place and speak what Coleridge had consigned to a drawer and apologetic pamphlet two hundred years previously, the words which the Landsdowne Poets Series had offered to me, which I would read to an audience of bookshop assistants and school teachers, a spotlight on the one hundred and twenty-five year old volume in my hands, on the gold fringe of its pages.

In my throat the panic had returned. There was a jewel in my guts. But it was always going to come to this, the mathematics of fate had ensured it. I sat naked in the room's aurora. The page felt flimsy and when the light shone through it the paper glowed like peach skin. Twenty-five years previously I had bought this book for twenty five pence. Now twenty-five years of preparation were about to find completion on a stage in an unfamiliar town. Coleridge and Ceiriog and Shakespeare had written these words but now they belonged to me. I glanced up and the missing children were still gazing through the Granada rain. It was almost time to go.

Hoodoo Motel

"Cutting the big trees? S'nothing compared with it. Ozone destruction? Doesn't even get on the diamond. I tell you it's one of the worst environmental problems we ever faced."

"I thought we were leaving."

"Just let me do this. I got clinkers here. And I don't mean coke."

I had assumed we were ready but there is still a rubble of personal effects strewn across one of the beds. Mars Barlow has his right cheek pushed up against the mirror. His left forefinger is forcing back the tip of his nose. He has tried a tweezers but that was too painful. The silver cigar-butt slicer proved impossible. Now he is experimenting with a pair of nail scissors.

"Male nostril hair, man. It's a plague."

"You got the map?"

"What's that rap about hairy men? Esau and the goatskin forearms? Got nothing on me. I got hair sprouting from every Horovitz."

"I'll put your stuff away. Still want that *Sun?*"

"Jeezus. What you call that bit between the nostrils?"

"I'd say it was thirty minutes max."

"Like that part of a woman. Bout an inch, a half inch? What you call that?"

"But we still need the map."

"Don't forget the Heidegger. Maybe it's in the can."

We had taken the Jeep as far as we dared along the track. A sign had said no access, all vehicles forbidden, but it was early, there was no-one about, and I wanted to discover what was behind the hill behind the hill.

Getting out, I realised how cold it remained at 9 am and how the earth crumbled under my feet. The tyres had torn two deep creases into it. Grey earth, like a badly-mixed cement. I had the sheepskin on, a comforting overcoat that smelt of smoke and dogs and French fries, and the pair of Dakotas that might be acid- and electric shock-resistant, but which I knew let in the rain like sponges.

I locked my door and started to walk down the valley. Immediately the crushed sage infiltrated the air. The first crocuses were visible in the dew. These were blue and hairy as blotters, properly called pasque flowers, the blossom of resurrection. I lay stiffly on the soil and pushed the blue lens of the camera within six inches of the first blue petals. The sage was a powerful kitchen smell and dew darkened the sheepskin. The camera protested because the film was finished.

"Don't die on me yet, man," wheezed Mars, lumbering up behind, cramming the bag that had held an egg McMuffin and carton of orange juice into his leather jacket. "And if you're listening for buffalo it's like a hundred years too late."

He looked round suspiciously at the valley. There was a path that followed a stream, not well marked, but at least providing a sense of direction. On either side the curious hills now glinted brighter as the sun rose. They were pitted like pumice, ridged and ribbed by the corrosive wind. A hawk hung over one of the round summits. A small flock of birds passed in a whisper over-head.

"So this is it?"

"Sure is," said Mars. "Seen enough?"

"Start walking."

"Like where? We're here. Go ten miles and it'll be the same. This is as bad as the badlands get."

"Not bad enough though. This is moderately bad. I want very bad."

"Yeah, well you want bad so bad they'll be finding your bones in six months time and putting you with the rest of the relics."

"Come to that ridge. It's only a mile and we can look over."

"And see another ridge. Only this time with a line of fucking vultures on it."

"Wagons ho." I set off down the track and Mars follows. After all, it is now a clear Easter morning and the light shimmers. There is sage in my hair, earth like coffee creamer under my nails.

The previous day we had driven into the province and in the evening asked at a gas-station for the nearest cheap rooms. A girl with the face of a dead rock star over her breasts said go straight on for a mile, then turn right into Thirty Third for the Hoodoo Motel. Can't miss. Forty bucks for a double.

We had found it with little effort, a low, one storey affair with twenty rooms. There was a Plymouth parked in front of 9. The door to the suite was open and a child stared at us from the shadow inside. The television was on, flickering without sound. By eight this morning, a Sunday, we had checked out. I remembered waking up and wondering where I was. There was an empty twenty of Jack Daniels next to the kettle.

"Better than an inhaler," the asthmatic Mars had claimed. "Jacky Dee has that powerful fume, all I do is uncork and breathe in. You can feel the vapour on your eyelashes. Bit like gasoline. Sometimes I rub it over my chest. Christ, you can even drink the stuff."

On the floor was the opened white square of a takeaway pizza box, revealing a last congealed slice. I had gone to the bathroom and found it was flooded. Mars was already up and absent, presumably outside checking the Jeep. I looked at his bed. Even the standard issue polythene sheet was rucked to one end. The blankets lay in a crumpled moraine over the carpet.

"Can't stand it tight," I remembered him saying, as he untucked the sheets. "Sleep is bad enough. Okay, we have to sleep but we don't have to enjoy it. And if sleep wasn't bad enough, what about the torment of dreams, the wooze, that taste of death in your mouth and the cornflakes in your eyes? And if even that wasn't bad enough, people want you to sleep in a bed like a straitjacket, held down so tight you can't turn over. Do you know what hell is, man? Hell's a made-up bed. Give me the floor any day."

And he had proceeded to re-design our lodging to his specifications. On the table beside his eroded Lazyboy were a map of the province, three dirty glasses, one dirty coffee cup, one full bottle of Great Western Gold malt beer (alcohol content 7%), one empty bottle of the same, a pizza crust, an O Henry wrapper, an empty packet of nachos, a half empty jar of medium hot salsa, a packet of gum, a packet of throat pastilles, a plastic inhaler, three brown plastic tubs of different shaped tablets, a plastic tub of codliver oil capsules, a tube of haemorrhoid cream, half a cigar, a silver cigar trimmer that Mars calls The Axe, a Walkman, two bronze Walkman batteries, an earthquaked highrise of tape cartridges, two quarters and seven cents, the brochures for the dinosaur museum, two postcards from the dinosaur museum, a leader article cut from the local *Sun* and a paperback entitled *The Roswell Incident* that I had glanced at the evening before.

Mars had said everything in the book was true. It described the crash-landing in New Mexico fifty years previously of a space-craft, and the autopsies carried out by US government surgeons on the four aliens found at the site of the crash. There were details of the alien writings discovered on pieces of wreckage, and the whole history of the subsequent cover-up.

"They're out there, man," Mars had said. "Sure as bears love honey and I ain't getting poontang. You know, with all these stories of abduction and close encounters and shit, you'd expect books like this would be better known. Instead, all you need say is you have an open mind on the subject, and it's serious dweebsville. Christ, you'd think more people would try to get out of this country. Sometimes I go down Eighth at night, just on to the prairie and look up at those burning stars and all I want to do is rush around shouting, 'take me, you bastards, take me'."

For some reason, habit most likely, I turned on the television. And that is what I remember most clearly about the Hoodoo Motel – the television, a big cable job, and that programme on channel 37, the programme about miracles.

There was a preacher in an expensive suit. Before him sat a vast congregation. The cameras panned over row upon row of middle aged and elderly people, black, white, Asiatic, all well dressed. The preacher was screaming at them. More particularly, he was screaming at one elderly man who was squinting back, eyes squeezed up. Then the preacher touched the man on the shoulders and held him in a short embrace. "Now He has come into you," he was screaming. "Now He has made you well. Can you hear me? Now He has come into you. Can you hear me?" The man nodded. Nervously at first, then vigorously.

"So take them off," shouted the preacher. "Take them off." The elderly man took off the two hearing aids he had been wearing.

"Can you hear me?" shouted the preacher again. The man nodded.

"Then get up and rejoice. Run around the aisles like the others did. Run around now and rejoice."

And the elderly man rose from his seat, looked about him, and started to move down the long aisle, past the rows of people. He moved carefully at first, but then his pace increased and he was running and waving and the people were waving back at him and shouting and clapping.

"Can you hear me?" called the preacher, and the man shouted back that he could hear him, and he was still running and still waving, and then he was hollering something that was difficult to catch and then he was back at his seat, and the preacher was beaming into the camera and exclaiming that the deaf might hear and the halt might walk only with faith. It was faith that healed. Faith in Him. The deaf man's children, on their knees, wept around their father.

Then the preacher stood before a large black woman with

callipers on her legs. He started shouting at her.

A message had appeared on the bottom of the screen. There was a telephone number. If I rang the number I could order a keyring with a tiny vessel of anointing oil attached. Getting out of bed I drew the drapes an inch. Outside was the grey soil of the badlands. Our neon motel sign glinted in the ravine. Below it the neon temperature gauge announced 0.

I looked at the zero, transfixed. Nothing. The figure was a wreath, a wreath wire. Across Thirty Third stood a green plastic dinosaur, life-size I imagined, and an advert for the Flintstones village somewhere out of town, not far it said, with parking, shopping and good eating in the canyon.

When we had checked in, the man behind the desk at the Hoodoo Motel office had not moved from his chair. He slid about on its castors, first to the honeycomb of boxes where the room keys were kept, with packets of mail for longer term residents, then back to the desk, then to the magic eye that read credit cards, and once more to face us at the desk. Behind him on the wall was a poster of a car with giant wheels, the chassis of this red sedan a tiny cockpit attached to corrugated aeroplane tyres. The vehicle had left a trail of crushed wreckage behind, and was poised to destroy another automobile stalled in its way. The faces of a terrified family were visible behind the windscreen. I received a dagger-like key from the man in the sliding chair. There were spots on his nails like drops of sour milk.

The preacher had progressed to a woman with breast cancer. After he berated her she ran around the aisles, waving her arms, mouth out of control, a woman who clearly never ran, who had forgotten how to run. She ran because she felt the cancer die within her. It had left her like a breath, she said. It was a miracle in a programme of miracles. The television light anointed the darkened room.

"Gotta get some carbo," announced Mars, crashing the door against the stop. "Time to go." He looked around approvingly at the debris. "We really trashed this place. Remember Keith

Moon in Flint, Michigan? The police actually drove him to the airport. Boy, they said, those cops said, boy, you been bad. And don't you ever even dream of coming back to Flint, Michigan again. Anyone seen that Heidegger I was reading?"

"What's the rush?"

"Nothing much. Only if I don't get some food in my craw I'm liable to pass straight out."

And so I had dressed and paid at the office. When I came back to the room, Mars was sitting on his bed looking at the TV.

"You missed it?"

"What?"

"Rwanda. Like all twenty seconds of it."

"So?"

"So even the Oilers transfer plans get whole minutes, and that's hundreds of miles away. But Rwandans, they got no happy plastic, and boy in this world, if you got no credit cards you don't get on the news. Genocide? People round here think it's something to keep the weeds down. Come on, let's get to the drive-in."

And Mars had moved as far as the mirror, looked into it, sneezed, pressed his right cheek against the glass, and begun to examine the lianas that were torturing him.

Above, the hawk is still a witness to our progress. It is warmer now so I unbutton the sheepskin. Mars is twenty yards behind, sucking his inhaler. He might have known where the badlands were, but already we are further in than he has ever been before. Mars has never been so bad. The stream runs beside us, red with ferrous salts. To the right are the abandoned workings of a mine, and a hundred yards away a bleached tipi erected amongst bushes. I strain to see the Jeep but, satisfyingly, it is already too distant. Novices of the badlands, we are surrounded by desert. About us the hills are small bone-coloured tors, worn by winds and glaciers into perplexing shapes. I point at a phallic eruption of stone, the height of a man, crowned with a flat rock. Mars

191

glances over and waves.

"Yeah. That's a hoodoo. And when you've seen one fucking hoodoo you've seen them all. Satisfied?"

"Let's find some bigger ones."

"Could be miles. I'll run out of gas."

"And fossils. We want some fossils."

"We did the fossils yesterday. Like the biggest dinosaur museum on the planet."

"I want wild fossils."

"Jeez." Mars sits down on a rock and opens an O Henry chocolate-covered peanut bar, the size of a building brick. "It's time for a vug."

"Time for your sugar trance more like."

"Vug off."

There will be no shifting him for twenty minutes now. I walk to the wall of the low cliff and examine the exposed strata. Vug is Mars's new word, a real word, and one he discovered yesterday. He says it is his duty to rescue it from obscurity. And to be fair, Mars's dinosaur museum had been worth the trip. We had stood in temples of Silurian and Ordovician time gazing at a hierarchy of bones. Above us loomed the resurrected creatures, a cladding of armour around mote-busy daylight. The Albertosaurus with its stone-crushing jaws and thalidomide arms left its footprints in a riverbed. A posse of razor lizards ran squealing across a video screen. The museum had been built in the badlands because the badlands was a rich seam of dinosaur remains. The badlands had been a dinosaur death camp. Whole tribes had died very quickly here; whole species. No-one knew why. Perhaps it had been a flood, an asteroid-hit causing a nuclear winter, a dissatisfied Creator pressing the delete button. Whatever, the badlands was a place of extinctions, and the museum was dedicated to the memory of the extinct and the theories of their demise. Crocodile bodies and shark eyes rose from a green hologrammed swamp. Empty heads as large as Cadillacs swung suspended on steel wires. There were nests of dinosaur eggs, rusty as Brazilian geodes, restored from thousands of tailings. Against one wall was a cross section of a badlands hillside, the fossils packed in levels like clothes in a suitcase. Some seemed real creatures, composed of substances that might be touched or felt. Others were only impressions of what had vanished from the rock, like the outlines on buildings in Nagasaki of vaporized people. Mars and I had split up in a tropical swamp. I met him an hour later on a higher floor gesturing with his inhaler at a glass case.

"'I love it, man."

"The air-conditioning? It's another ice age in here."

"Read this. Read and discover vugs."

"Vugs?"

"Kind of spaces in rock that fill with crystal or dolomite or whatever that shit is, and then go back to being like, just spaces. Kinda holes."

"So?"

"Don't say 'so'. It's adolescent. So vugs. Now there's a vug in this rock here, just a space, like a hole in cheese. But man, what about the vugs in our brains, our imaginations? It's like the word that says it all. So we lead vuggish lives. So we are afflicted with vuggery. So we vug out. It's brilliant, man. Vugging ace."

"Vugs aren't fossils then?"

"You not understanding vugs is because of the vugs in your intelligence. A vug is something that should be there but isn't. Or. Or a vug is there, but kind of different to what it should be. Comprendez? Okay, well it isn't really those things, but vug is a word that has to be liberated from vug-infested science. And I found it, so keep your mitts off."

"A vug means something exact. And you've changed that already. Congratulations."

"It's a metaphorical metamorphosis, man. A vug is a state of mind. And the time of the vug is now."

In his extra-terrestrial script Mars wrote down the geological definition of vug in a vug of the museum programme. And now he sits on his rock surrounded by fossils, chomping an O Henry, the atoms of corals and dinosaur eggs a white cement on his boots. The red-tailed hawk floats like a piece of burning paper away down the valley.

A few yards further on I find myself stroking the side of the cliff as if it was a friendly animal. The fossils in the soft stone are ideas of themselves, meek and persistent. There are animals in the rock. There are insects that are the rock. I think of crematorium ash blowing back on to the sleeves of the living. In yesterday's *Sun* had been a story about an operation on a seventy year-old woman. She had complained of pains in her side, and x-rays had discovered a shadow within her abdomen. Fifty years earlier the woman had conceived, yet outside her womb. The foetus had grown nine inches tall and weighed perhaps as much as our volume of Jack. It nestled in her side like a rib. But there could be no birth. There was nowhere for the baby to go. So slowly the creature within her became calcium. A mannikin of lime. And now fifty years later there it was on the page, the stone child, like one of the acid-eaten gargoyles on a Polish cathedral. A tiny hoodoo, born in the badlands.

"Who lives in that tipi?"

Mars stands up reluctantly. There is a grey horseshoe of dust on his backside. Forefinger and thumb explore the stubble in his nostrils. "Hippies maybe. Some old Blackfoot. Dinosaur hunters."

"Not these survivalist types."

"Christ, no way. They pack more iron than the paratroopers. So they need basements and such. Magazines, nuclear bunkers. And you mean the militias. They're kinda like tribes, with slightly different philosophies. But basically they believe the same things."

I remembered the other story that Mars had ripped out of the *Sun*. There was a town not far away that served as the militias' capital. Or that was how the newspaper described it. Banks of computers; a vineyard of E-mail; millions of high velocity rounds. It appeared the people in the militias didn't like modern society. It was corrupt, brutalising, deeply conspiratorial. Mars was a one-man militia who had armed himself with an iridium-tipped fountain pen instead of Gulf War-surplus bullets, each with its fragmentation pattern and glans of uranium. He talked frequently about the militias, and when he did he lowered his voice to its confessional register. His eyes narrowed pasque-blue.

"Okay, some of them are major assholes. New Age Nazis, the Klan gone eco-freak. And plenty of psycho-loners along for the ride. And for some it's a Jesse James scene, a Clint thing. But I tell you man, they got a point. After all, paranoia is the first human instinct. It's just self-preservation."

There is a skull buried in the earth near our path. Dislodged, we kick it around for a while. Probably a sheep.

"See what bonds them is fear. Fear of microchip implants in every new baby. Christ, in every citizen. Just so the powers-that-be will know where you are. Kind of like Social Security numbers, only more so. Fear of the gene-labs. Fear of the global money-houses. Fear of some airplane crawling with weird viruses landing at Boise, Idaho. You see, these people honour their prophets. They believe in them." Mars pauses, spits, and holds up five fingers. "Like off the top of my head. Think about H.G. Wells. Swedenborg. The Book of Revelations. That guy who wrote *Neuromancer. Jurassic* fucking *Park*."

"They're alienated."

"Well aren't you? Seems to me that a cabin in the woods with an M16 behind the door and a book on the rocking-chair with the old Sioux names for healing herbs is not such a bad way to live. Guns are nothing. It's the guys with plutonium in their attache-cases that scare me."

We are at the foot of a hill of yellow scree. I am regretting the sheepskin and Mars's face is red and damp. He mops himself with a spotted bandana, wincing at the landscape as if it was an unflattering photograph of himself.

"Anyway. Here's one survivalist who won't survive much

longer. Any Seven-Elevens out here? Any of those DIY colonic-irrigation latte bars?"

The pasque flowers are fully opened now and it is difficult not to tread on them. A sixty-four ounce Super Big Gulp lies half-covered by the badlands ash. I climb higher and Mars is a long way behind, struggling with halfmast jeans, his mutinous breath. He is walking like a man who has never walked, but has suddenly discovered how. From here he is both comically determined and furious with faith. I look over the ridge and discover what is behind the hill behind the hill. That is where we are headed, down there, down the dusty slope with its prairie crocuses already blowsy, already on the turn, down over an attenuated outcrop of rock and its silver fringes of sage, down to the fence and through the gate in the fence and into the car park and through the car park to the Flintstones village where the inflatable Freds and off-the-shoulder sabre-tooth tigerskin Wilmas wait in line at the dino-diner and a green plastic Albertosaur surveys its canyon empire, open to families, spiky with hoodoos.

Half way up the hillside, Mars stops in his miraculous ascent and mimes a question.

"How bad does it have to get?" I hear him wheeze. "How bad?"

But it is impossible to answer a demand like that. At least, not if you don't know how bad it was supposed to be in the first place.

Ryan's Republika

It is now close to midday when the bus is due to leave. But I cannot move. The rain is molten outside the overhang that protects me, protects the students, the clerks, the police, who all stare into the continuous explosion of traffic. So I sit on the marble sill, collar up, listening to the stories of gamblers and genealogists, the soundtrack of Sunni prayers broadcast to the throng. I hear this as a lament, but I have infidel ears.

The building that shields us was once an office of state. Today it is a theatre and a series of agencies selling slots and video poker. Across the square is a hero, a warrior on a warhorse. Further away, aerials bristle on apartments, a grey cyrillic. And the beggars lie under their polythene as the torrents run beneath and around them, dying beside us. They do not require my tablets of soap from SupaDrug, my wafers of JuicyFruit. What they need is not going to arrive. The hero on the horse is imprisoned in metal. The crag he bestrides is unscalable. So we give the beggars room to die, awarding them the opportunities of daylight. No one has appeared but the candyman, and he must make his retreat soon, to the waiting bus.

A pity really. The previous day I had come out of the drug store with bursting pockets, and walked past the market research woman. "Excuse me, sir. Could you tell me what you've bought?"

"Sweets. Chewing gum."

She ticked boxes on her chart. "For yourself, sir?"

"No."

"Might I ask who the products are for, sir?"

"The beggars."

"The beggars." She searched but there wasn't a box. "There are beggars at Stansted airport?"

197

"Not that I've seen. These are for another country."

"Of course, sir." She looked relieved. "And do you think you received value for money with these purchases?"

I answered and the woman filled in the spaces and now I pull my coat over my thighs and make a dash for it, half a kilo of Glacier Mints bouncing against my heart.

Like many thousands of people I used to be a football fan. That is, the only type of football fan that counts. The type that attends matches. My excuse is that I was very young. So young in fact, that my father would always have to take me the twenty-two miles up a Roman road for Cardiff City home matches. Not that I need to apologise. The memories are emblematic. However we gained access to the ground, there was always a shock of green. The pitch was huge, an immaculate sward, boundaried in white, perfectly edged against a track of red cinder, the nets glinting like chainlink. The Captain Morgan sign, spelled out in the biggest letters in Wales across the corrugations of the stand roof, was not an advertisement but the emblazonment of identity. This was Ninian Park. This was special. In ten minutes Ronnie Bird would put one of his thirty-yard piledrivers over the bar; Greg Farrell start a mesmeric sortie into the enemy half before losing control in the penalty area; Bob Wilson pull his cap over his eyes, squint into the sun and send the ball into orbit. And Brian Harris, and Peter King; and Don Murray, forehead red as a house-brick, the centre-halves' centre-half; and Jimmy Scoular, the manager on the bench, a grizzled mannikin of pig-iron; all of them would be our public property.

Scoular was a particular hero. He once offered to fight Brian Clough for City honour after Derby put five past the Bluebirds. There he sat, broken-jawed in the dug-out, knuckling his eyes, exhorting in Lallans the limp figure of seventeen-year-old John Toshack, who always looked weak for his size. Jimmy Scoular, a paid off gladiator, squaring up to destiny. Today I sometimes see pictures of Scoular team reunions. Without the boss, of course. Mostly now the lads keep pubs or trophy shops. Some have retired to crown green bowls. Occasionally I wonder about Greg Farrell. He always reminded me of Terry Collier from *The Likely Lads*. Came to no good, but got there with sullen humour and a natural braggadocio. As fitting an epitaph as any. Because when he wanted, Farrell could play, leaving full-backs scything air, holding on to the ball beyond all hope of progress, as if he was still a boy on some car-free, redbrick English street, shouting to confused mates to take it from him. And Scoular too will not disappear. At least in memory. A Scottish bantam, whisky-voiced and hard-mouthed, working out the goal averages and groaning, because third place was pretty good but really no good at all. Scoular the nearly man. A man who would die for you if you said the right things, vanishing into the tunnel to clap every one of his players on the back, whether they had died for him or not. And then the crush of thousands out through the gates into the fume and velvet of a capital night, faggots and peas in waxen cones, and the Man on the Bob Bank whose page appeared in the *Pink Echo*, perhaps my first literary existentialist, cynical, affronted, but there on the terraces until it killed him, simply because there was nowhere better to go, no place worthier of his time, not the Vetch, not the Arms Park, not home.

Two hours before kick off at 2 pm there is no suggestion in the city that an international soccer match is imminent. The rain's assault continues so I retreat from the traffic up the steps and bubbling green carpet of the Dajti. The bus will wait. In the bar there are deals being done over Turkish coffee. The toilet smells of paranoia. Maybe the cellars were once torture chambers. But, reward for my insubordination, here are the officials of the Albanian team, waving papers, and with them a few of the players in crimson tracksuits, talking, laughing, unpressurised. Albania are out of the European Championships. The only team with a worse record in their group is the team in the hotel two hundred yards away, the team that flew into this country the previous day, and which will make straight for the airport after it has showered and changed. Wales did not want to come to Albania but the fixture was decided two years previously. So, responding to rumours about the country, the management has brought its own provisions and chef. Crates of bottled water were wheeled through customs and stacked in a blue pyramid on the Stansted tarmac. Boxes of food and blankets were forklifted to our aeroplane. They have proved unnecessary. The Welsh are booked into a hotel that is three months old and cleaner than anything at home. The expected beggars at the doors have been replaced by taxi drivers whose Mercedes diesel chokes the driveway. The plumbing works, the restaurant is pristine. Last night a Maitre D with a Mercedes smile gripped my arm as we came down from our rooms. The waiters were lined up like pallbearers. They were decent rooms but there was mayhem outside. In the decent rooms the sapphire light of the adult channel suggested a thunderstorm. The pictures on the screens disintegrated and reformed like a culture observed with a microscope. There was a child on the screen. Soldiers arrived. Then the clamour outside seemed to shake the windows. Everything was drowned but the horns and voices. The child came apart like velcro and the first thunder threw itself against the glass.

There are no keys to the rooms, but microchipped cards changed every day. Unless they are playing for Wales, or amongst the party of American forestry workers, there is no chance of encountering anyone unsavoury. This US presence is not surprising. Nor is the story of what has happened to Albania's trees. The chainsaw of poverty has done for them, so that the rivers are haemorrhages of topsoil, the hillsides a naked phthalo green running to khaki and grey. But the tree scientists are happy. They have downed six bottles of wine with lunch and in this little-league country discovered generations of work. Only the noise unsettles. It seeps into the mirrored vestibule where the *International Herald Tribune* is displayed, into the prismed lifts. Even the double glazing cannot keep out the bacteria of noise.

Something is in the air and it is not football. A tray of cappucinos appears, foaming like meadowsweet. But the Welsh committee men in their blazers and crested ties laugh it away. The committee men sip a different welcome and grin at everything. The Faroe Islands, downtown Tblisi, all pay homage to these gentlemen. "There was a fellow in Torshavn," says one, "who was mowing his lawn. On the roof." The committee men wheeze like new shoes, so good is the joke. Then they laugh at the one about harpoons. The players file in, smelling of shampoo, Umbro on their chests. "Whales, geddit," the blazers hiss. They rise slowly, put on overcoats, but rock in mohair at the absurdity of it all, all of it, the madnesses lining up like weatherfronts from Iceland to the new republics of oilwells and curfews. "You need to be a geography professor these days," says one dignitary. "I pack Diareeze. Cherry flavour."

So I listen and look and decide what is happening is hysteria, which is all that can happen when impossibilities begin to occur. Because the impossibilities are occurring now.

Outside in Skanderbeg Square the traffic is reassuringly psychotic. This, after all, is how we measure progress. By vehicle density, in quality of chrome. The lights, and I note that there are now traffic lights in Tirana, are red and the green pedestrian sign vivid through the squall. Yet the traffic does not stop, merely casts its spindrift over the pavements, over Catholic and Muslim alike, under a vault of black umbrellas.

Earlier, in the lobby, I had watched the Welsh team return from their only training session, soaked and steaming in Umbro blue. In Umbro black. Neville Southall proved intimidatingly large to Albanians, Eric Young a colossus. "African," a taxi driver whispered to me, a fellow member of the titches' brotherhood. "No Africans in Albania."

"He's Welsh," I say as Young glides past. "He's an Umbro man."

And then there is Ryan Giggs, dripping before us on the hotel carpet, slipping his boots off before going up in the lift. Here is the boy-saint, his hair in thorns. But not as good as he used to be, is the clamorous whisper. A burnt-out case, suggests the front page of a football glossy I saw at the airport, the type of specialist publication that reveals how many times a player might touch the ball in a game, how often enter the opponents' half or make diverting runs. The type of information that is the antithesis of knowledge. But Giggsy doesn't care. He is Mercury who must find a new way through the thickets. No one understands how swiftly he might travel if he really tried, how he could soar above the chasms that are dug for him. Whilst the writers in our party occupy the restaurant, discussing midfield balance and centre backs pushing up, whilst they confront an international break-fast, Ryan Giggs travels skywards in a silver elevator, boots in his hand, the Illyrian rain in his hair.

What is unusual about the Welsh party is the absence of Alun Evans, ex-secretary, ex-chief executive, ex-public figurehead. For years Evans was the official voice of Welsh soccer, the vital link between the anonymous cardinals of the game, and the public who dreamed of success in the World Cup and all the media bullion it would ensure. A notoriously bad-tempered figure, given to spiteful remarks in sarcastic speeches, he nevertheless created for himself the role – and performed it impeccably – of making Wales appear a real, not-to-be-underestimated profes-sional outfit. Without Evans no-one here is looking over their shoulders. There is a guarded lightness about proceedings, a possibility of high spirits in the camp. A little I consider, like Albania without Enver Hoxha, who had sealed his country's borders and imprisoned its population within his own delusions for forty years. After Hoxha, what passes for democracy in Albania is inevitably bewildered. The dictator's grave was smashed by people celebrating his demise, but the real vendettas are reserved for the informants and secret police who created a culture of betrayal.

The Albanians are small and muscular and resemble Dean

Saunders. In the first minute they hit a post, in the third score
a penalty. Eric Young is thirty-five now, playing perhaps his last
international. A terrier goes past him and all he can offer is the
professional's foul. The Albanian careens in a mist of spray and
Eric removes his headband and bows low to hear the judgement
of the referee. Before he has even touched the ball there is a
possibility that he will be sent off. But it proves a merciful uni-
verse. Big Nev, perhaps the only man I have ever seen who can
look menacing in a pink and yellow designer top, appears to be
able to touch both goalposts at once. Yet he goes the wrong way
and the red flags with a blaze of eagles soar above the brollies
opposite.

A bad start, but at least I am watching the game. Thirty
minutes previously I had wandered out of the ground, thinking
to take in another Turkish at the Dajti, and then found my
return barred by army, police and an ancient ticket-tearer, who
gestured that I could now enter only the unsheltered half of the
field. My responses, in careful order were, incomprehension,
rage and the grief of bereavement. What saved me was the
English language. The director of Albanian television outside
broadcasts happened to be passing, heard my complaint, and
ushered me to the wooden confessional where technicians were
repairing a camera. To pay for my keep I held the screwdrivers,
passed round the JuicyFruit.

Across the pitch the Welsh fans are confined to a corral, their
heraldry tied to the bars of the prison. There are twenty of them,
led by someone dressed as Father Christmas. We love you
Wales, O yes we do, is what they sing, a robust chorus, not with-
out melancholy. I hear it as a lament, but then I have not come
footsore on the pilgrim's way from Durazzo, wondering at the
reapers in the fields, the spilt bile of Chinese foundries. The
dragon flags on the wire are embroidered with tribal names:
Caernarfon Borough, Newport AFC. They have been packed
like clean linen. During this half there is one fight, watched with
amused tolerance by the machine-gun-carrying security forces.

Then, after forty minutes, Giggs collects on the left and crosses to Pembridge who heads the equaliser. Below us the scribes at their schooldesks scribble furiously. One-all and all to play for.

Our manager is an Englishman, greying, dapper. He prowls the touchline shouting "cornerflags", and sends on a young player with a golden perm. The manager is a lucky man. He has a job in international football, a contract, and nothing much to live up to. The previous boss had been unpopular with the players. He drew diagrams on pieces of paper and sat hunched and remote on the journeys home from the steppes. Five-nil in Georgia is as close to disaster as it gets, and it's a long aeroplane ride to suffer the migraine of defeat. But before he had intervened there had been chaos. This involved the mystery of the forty-day reign of John Toshack, a Heathrow press conference at which sinister dealings were intimated, and the Ninian exile's subsequent second abandonment of British soccer. Toshack, a month previously, had returned to Cardiff as a Basque-speaking miracle-working Welsh team manager. No greater transformation had ever been seen in football than the metamorphosis of the stooping City centre forward into the confident generalissimo who in stadium after Iberian stadium brushed rose petals from his shoulders and made ecstatic the Sunday nights of the faithful.

And then, after his first Welsh match, a heavy home loss, the players bemused by an intricate continental defensive system that went against their kick-it-and-see instincts, Toshack had delivered his cryptic VIP lounge accusations and retreated to where he was venerated. It was as if the Messiah had been turned away by Customs at Cardiff Airport. But at least it is good copy for the back pages. His tantalising absence will excite Welsh soccer, and the peevish inquests into its condition, for the next generation. While there is a king over the water there will be hope. And at the bottom of Group Seven in the European Championship, with Welsh caps offered to any Third Division clogger as long as he can tie his own laces and has a granny who comes from Presteigne, hope is the only denomination left in the currency.

There are three reasons why I remember John Toshack. The first is for shrugging off the scorn of the Bob Bank and grandstand alike, where risk-taking is confined to whether or not to order a Clark's pie with the halftime tea. The second is for publishing one of the worst books of verse ever to appear in the UK, the glorious *Gosh it's Tosh*, a rarity now and worth a few quid. The third is for severely upsetting an army of Leeds United supporters, during their visit to Swansea City whilst Toshack was manager there. At this time the Swans were at the top of the First Division, and regularly skinned Man U and Liverpool alive. I drove my brother-in-law to the Vetch, past naked men camped under the cross of St George, a posse of union jackals distributing their armoury. We stood in the Leeds end and listened to the riot plans. Make a disturbance, entice the police into the crowd, isolate and then kill them. Swansea were five-one up and I was sick with feigning sickness as the net bulged below me yet again. But this was theatre with compulsory audience participation. "Yor goona get yoor fookin ed kicked in," is what we sang, as the Jacks played like they had never done before and have never done since. I learned about Chapeltown on that day, and what happened there. I learned about the Yorkshire Ripper, the British National Party, about why Toxteth and Brixton and St Paul's were burning, about a different kind of nationalism. But most of all I learned about crowds. Then out we squeezed of the ramshackle Vetch, past the prison and the locked doors of The Glamorgan into the slap of a breeze off the seafront, still trying to work out how many of us there had been pretending, and whether pretending was worse than whatever it was we had been pretending to do.

In the first minute of the second half Albania hit the post. Then Southall runs twenty yards beyond his penalty area to tackle a raider who has slipped Young's leash. At the other end, Giggs positions himself expertly in front of goal, but shoots wide when it might have been easier to score. He stands frozen, like someone who realises they have locked themselves out. And one-all is how it stays for the rest of the game, with bottle-green Wales threatening at the end, but proving too light, too reluctant to advance from a midfield as crowded as Skanderbeg Square. At the whistle, the director orders me to the bar down the corridor and lines up the cognac: "Five years ago I would have gone to prison for talking to you."

We sit under a *Forza Juve* banner, and I describe my bewilderment at a Tirana that is strafed with neon. He nods enthusiastically. The entrepreneurial culture is beginning to ferment. "Capitalism? Cannot stop it. The grass must always grow."

The bar starts to fill, and the Welsh come in, good politicians to a man. They talk dirty, act hard, but understand the process of backing down with dignity. They even wrap themselves in the flag, one example of which is held up for inspection, like some fragment of a shroud. This group is particularly well travelled. They can talk of air pollution in Georgia, brewing in Moldova, Gypsy music in Bucharest. Their lives are time-tabled by the fixture lists, their bedrooms are pennant-bright shrines. Here is the joker dressed as Claus, a pair of hard nuts who position themselves on either side of the group, and a professorial type with impressive goatee who hoards the bardic lore.

Their stories, if they told them, might concern the bestiaries of Amsterdam, subterranean Hamburg. Yet usually they have no time for totty, or are secretly appalled at the idea. Instead, these men drink Amstel, cherish souvenirs such as Big Eric's headband, and laugh down the gun barrels of another set of riot police. Next month Wales will discover who they play in World Cup. And the fans here, wet and hungover, without a vehicle for the blacknesses of the Durazzo road, are already saving for further expeditions to the arse-end of Europe. *Forza Uells*, they say, shuffling out after handshakes and backslaps all round, gunslingers, professor, Santa in his scarlet coat, leaving the dragon pinned to a wall dark with totalitarian smoke.

Author Note

Robert Minhinnick lives on the Welsh coast with his wife and daughter.

Badlands is his second collection of essays; the first, *Watching the Fire-Eater*, was Arts Council of Wales Book of the Year in 1993. Minhinnick is also the author of six collections of poetry, most recently *Hey Fatman* (1994), and editor of *Green Agenda: Essays on the Environment of Wales*. He has written for television, and has been a columnist in the *Western Mail* and *Planet*.